Acknowledgments

Many thanks go to my wonderfully supportive editor, Raphael Kadushin, and the University of Wisconsin Press. I am grateful to the early readers of this novel, particularly Claire Van Ens, Lee Potts, Christie Logan, Julie Williams, and Laura Furman. Much appreciation goes to Wellspring House in western Massachusetts, where I found inspiring companions and a quiet place to write in June of 2003. I appreciate the support of my irreverent book group—Les Grandes Dames (Lynda, Jean, Leslie, Mary S., Mary L., Biruta, Helen) and Stan. Lastly, deep thanks to my partner, Lynda Miller, who cast her clear and occasionally wicked eye over many drafts of this manuscript, and provided her usual insight and support to the ongoing project of living.

Death of a Department Chair

Death of a Department Chair

Terrace Books, a division of the University of Wisconsin Press,
takes its name from the Memorial Union Terrace, located at
the University of Wisconsin–Madison. Since its inception in 1907,
the Wisconsin Union has provided a venue for students, faculty, staff,
and alumni to debate art, music, politics, and the issues of the day.
It is a place where theater, music, drama, dance, outdoor activities, and
major speakers are made available to the campus and the community.
To learn more about the Union, visit www.union.wisc.edu.

Death of a Department Chair

A Novel

Lynn C. Miller

TERRACE BOOKS

A TRADE IMPRINT OF THE UNIVERSITY OF WISCONSIN PRESS

This book is a work of fiction. Although some of its buildings
share a resemblance to those of a famous research university,
Austin University does not exist. All characters, colleges,
departments, and events in *Death of a Department Chair*
are entirely creations of the author's imagination.

Terrace Books
A trade imprint of the University of Wisconsin Press
1930 Monroe Street
Madison, Wisconsin 53711

www.wisc.edu/wisconsinpress/

3 Henrietta Street
London WC2E 8LU, England

1   3   5   4   2

Printed in the United States of America

Library of Congress Cataloging-in-Publication Data
Miller, Lynn, 1951–
Death of a department chair: a novel / Lynn C. Miller.
p.   cm.
ISBN 0-299-21974-7 (pbk.: alk. paper)
1. Women college teachers—Fiction.   2. Texas—Fiction.   I. Title.
PS3613.I544D34   2006
813'.6—dc22   2006008064

IN MEMORY OF

Alice Adams

FOR HER WIT, STYLE, AND PLAIN GOOD SENSE

Editor's Note

When my friends first asked me to chronicle the misfortunes of last autumn, I refused. For who wishes to revisit the end of her world? The moment when the tenor of life forever changes its pitch is not one to sing about. But I found I could not forget, either—those events still haunt me, still hover in the atmosphere as the last breath of winter lingers in the March air. In time, the need to speak up won out.

My tenure at Austin University, a public school of extravagant ambition, had seemed secure. When I stumbled over the odd snag in my route—as we all do from time to time—I trusted the path would endure even if my own step upon it might not. But in the silencing of one human heart, all broke apart—the road ahead, my reputation, the stability of institutional life itself.

On a sunny, unremarkable Monday morning last October, Isabel Vittorio, chair of my department, a woman gifted with focus, intelligence—and, some said, an outsized sense of self-worth—was found slumped over her desk in her office on the seventh floor of

Helmsley Hall. Her face was swollen, her neck bruised, and her collarbone broken. Certainly she was dead, and had been for some time—perhaps for as long as two days, since she was discovered on a Monday. Her murder—for all signs pointed to that fact—seemed shocking even though we live in a country, and a state, noted for violence. After all, this is a college campus, where the tiniest happenings are scrutinized, measured, and catalogued with paranoic zeal. In such a place, a misplaced poster can assume the magnitude of a public indiscretion. Therefore, the sight of a slain middle-aged professor with her clothes ripped from her less-than-perfect body is shocking indeed.

The puzzling detail of her state of undress derailed the investigation for some time, leading the police to ferret out the victim's sexual history to the exclusion of other pertinent clues. Again, this is a college campus. If one chooses to focus on the sexual, the odor of indiscretion and intrigue pervades one's every breath. Have you ever witnessed a Texas gulley-washer? No? Well, trust me when I say that a dry creek bed can transform in seconds into a torrent barreling down on the unwary with the force of a derailed locomotive. A similar power is unleashed when someone whispers "sex" in the hallowed halls of academe.

How do I know that the police were misled in their search for the perpetrator of the crime? That they were as bewildered by the false scents of scandal as a birddog snuffling through a warehouse of feather beds? I know because I, Miriam Held, a faculty member in the Department of Literature and Rhetoric at Austin University, was with Isabel Vittorio in the last hour of her life. Unfortunately, I had also had a romantic liaison with the victim twelve years before. Worse, one of my oldest friends was being held political hostage by Isabel right before the murder. As if all of this were not damning enough, only six months earlier Isabel had prevailed against me in a bitter battle for the chairmanship of our department. I was perceived, to quote the inelegant language of one of my colleagues, to be "picking at my scabs and biding my time" until I could retaliate. And so, not just one motive appeared to implicate me in

Isabel's demise, but several. I feared for a time that even my life partner, Vivian Garnet, and my dearest friends sometimes doubted my innocence.

I don't want to mislead anyone: naturally my tenure at this tolerable (though not always tolerant) institution has been marked—a resolute course is not always a smooth one. The star of my career has flared and faded in reaction to the priorities and fashions of campus politics. Just as public interest lurches capriciously from one headline to the next, the judgment of one's colleagues seems arbitrary. Only the punctuation that accompanies these shifts—cries of despair one moment, rants of joy at another—is predictable.

I am a person of quiet habits, a woman with an intellectual bent who thrills to the chase of an errant reference much as the avid mountain climber eyes the north face of the Eiger. I am neither flamboyant nor reclusive, neither distracted by appearances nor careless of my own. A colleague in anger once called me a bourgeois lesbian. I was flattered at the reference—I like people and things of durable quality; I expect my household to run smoothly and well. I cannot begin to express the indignity I suffered as a suspect in the murder of my colleague and former lover, my past sifted through by careless hands, my private life exposed to public ridicule. Prior to Isabel's death, I characterized myself as a woman of thought, not action.

All that changed last fall. Galvanized to save my life and reputation, I unraveled the complex tangle of lies and trickery surrounding Isabel's murder. It's not true what they say about academics, that we're all brain and no brawn, in love with the idea of life rather than the messy details of living it. In graduate school I learned persistence and discrimination: I was driven to pursue excellence; I developed passion and stamina. These are qualities useful in many professions. In fact, I hazard a guess that the police academy prizes these very skills.

The following documents record the fruits of my research. I have arranged accounts from interviews and hearsay in narrative form, as I feared raw transcripts and unedited notes would poorly depict the complications of the people and events involved. To enhance a sense of objectivity in my history, I have adopted the time-honored convention of serving as Editor of this volume. Rather than relate my story in the manner of the late John Watson's "reminiscences" of Sherlock Holmes, however, I, like the Editor in Choderlos de Laclos's novel, *Les Liaisons Dangereuses,* reveal my own voice only in the occasional note and in the frame of the story. I toyed with the idea of borrowing the title as well (*Dangerous Liaisons* aptly describing many of Isabel Vittorio's associations), but I feared that some readers might waste valuable energy attempting to forge connections between the two works.

Forgive me if I have at times embellished accounts, but, as in any investigation, gaps and inexplicable behavior baffle even the most meticulous researcher. I have therefore taken some poetic license in my reconstruction. Please read and ponder those entries that interest you, scan or discard those that appear irrelevant.

Lastly, please pardon the placement of my own person squarely in the middle of this account. Circumstances dictated such a narcissistic focus, which I nonetheless find embarrassing. Given the broadness of the police inquiry and the wide consequences of Isabel's death, I fear this self-preoccupation to be almost a transgression of academic etiquette. As the reader may suspect, however, I am preceded in such a breach by a long line of distinguished colleagues. To say nothing of an entire canon of dead, white writers of a largely masculine persuasion. However, that is indeed another story. Accept that I offer my observations humbly in the hope that they may aid you in comprehending what remains for many unspeakable and sordid, and, more disturbing, what constitutes for others simply another example of the decay of civilized life.

RESPECTFULLY SUBMITTED,

MIRIAM HELD

August 1, 2003

1

Begin at the beginning, we are often told. But life loops back upon itself, twists and turns like a seedling avoiding stones and competing roots. How then to begin? "Simply but well," my first grade teacher, Miss Dodd, was fond of saying. "I'm trying," I always replied.

the editor

*T*he sassy cartoon on the newspaper's op-ed page spewed its contents into Miriam Held's eyes, which, as if allergic to its message, immediately began to itch and water. Flanked by the distinctive tower of Austin University, its sides overlaid with greenbacks rather than granite, a bloated, jagged-toothed rabbit raised a carrot labeled "Held's Folly" and trumpeted: "Not so fast, Doc!"

Miriam thumped her teacup on the table with the authority of a gavel silencing an unruly courtroom crowd. The cup teetered on the chipped ceramic of the surface. Miriam swept it aside. "Enough," she sputtered.

Fiona Hardison, who taught film and literature in Miriam's department, looked up from her own paper. The two friends had a standing breakfast date every Monday at eight a.m. with the vain hope of a moment of calm before the week accelerated out of control. "Something exciting? Usually when you read that rag you're nodding off by page two."

Miriam folded the *Austin Journal Observer* carefully and slid it into the stout leather handbag at her feet. Her lips thinned in a disparaging smirk. "Ha. You remind me of Vivian, witty early in the day."

Vivian was Miriam's partner of ten years. "Oh dear," Fiona said. "We've been working together too long. Soon I'll be so overly famil-iar I'll trigger associations with your mother. Or a favorite aunt."

Miriam smiled at her colleague—blond, with a smile both imp-ish and childlike, and at least a dozen years younger than herself. "I don't think so. My mother had brunette hair and stood a foot shorter than you. Not to mention she was forty years of age when she had me. Barely younger than you are now. To me she was always old."

Fiona pursed her lips, thinking of time's refractions. She relied on Miriam's maturity and wisdom so much that it was difficult to con-jure up her mentor as a small child who viewed her mother's middle-age at such remove. She lifted one shoulder. "As a mutual acquaint-ance of ours might say, associations are visceral, not physical."

Miriam retrieved her cup and lifted it into the air as a waitress drifted in their direction. "And what does that really mean? Daphne can be so obtuse," she complained. Daphne, a dabbler in the psychic arts with uncommon good sense, often displayed the irritating habit of perceiving the heart of a problem before her friends knew they had one.

"So what is it?" Fiona gestured to the paper and flicked an errant strand of streaky ash-blond hair from her forehead.

The older woman grimaced, the skin pleating around her pecan-colored eyes. "The *Observer* is accusing me of trying to profit from our efforts to increase the ranks of minorities and women. It's an outrage—it's okay to recruit one 'star' academic who happens to be white and male and entrenched and pay him three hundred thou-sand dollars. But it's seen as the height of greed and entitlement to try to raise pay—by awarding research fellowships on top of salaries—to attract a diverse faculty. We're talking about only ten thousand addi-tional dollars for a faculty member's first year!"

Fiona shook her head, the political labyrinth of salary equity and promotion at Austin U. an ongoing mystery to her even though she was a tenured faculty member. "This is news?" she asked. "Miriam, get a grip. The big surprise here is that anyone is even paying attention to what's going on with programs for women or minorities." She flipped to the op-ed page of her own newspaper. "I wonder how this guy even knows about your efforts."

Miriam's small face slackened in puzzlement. "But this is a public university. In a state with a huge minority population—soon to be the majority. Don't you think the people of Texas want their flagship university to reflect the population—and the concerns—of their state?"

Fiona nodded. "I'm sure the people of this state care very much about what is taught to their children. And who teaches them. And how they teach. But I doubt they care about our bureaucracy, which, let's face it, is just plain incomprehensible. Even to most of us who work in it."

---

editor's note:
I must remind the reader that the U.S. Supreme Court ruling restoring race as a factor in college and university admissions occurred only in June of 2003, after these events took place.

Miriam sighed and looked at her watch. "Where could Bettina be? Didn't she say she'd join us?"

Bettina Graf, the third member of their informal breakfast club, ran chronically late. Fiona laughed. "What did you call Bettina once? Oh yes, an 'omnivore.' She has so many interests, is intertwined in so many people's lives—and intrigues—that it's a miracle she can grace us with her presence at all. Do you think that's the secret of her popularity?"

"Ha," Miriam said grumpily. "She's too charming for her own good. But of course I adore her, so how can I complain?"

"True." Fiona reflected on Bettina's winning combination of physical attractiveness, affectionate nature, and wit, all of which together countered an occasional lapse into self-indulgence. "I keep meaning to ask her for her recipe." The door of the café opened, and

Fiona saw a flash of autumn colors before she felt the jolt of a fierce hug and a kiss by her ear. "Bettina?"

Bettina, her wavy auburn hair streaming over the shoulders of a forest green jacket, tossed her backpack under the table, scraped a chair across the bare floor, and sat. Her cheeks, aflame, spoke of a brisk hike in high winds. Fiona fancied that the sharp tang of pine needles wafted toward her as Bettina leaned toward them. "Thank God you're still here. Have you heard?"

Miriam sighed heavily. "The newspaper. The cartoon—yes, we were just talking about it. It's giving me heartb—"

"This is much worse," Bettina broke in.

Miriam's face began to fold into offended lines. Bettina touched her friend's forearm with a plump hand. "Darling, listen. This morning, at seven-ten, a custodian cleaning the floors on the seventh floor of Helmsley Hall walked into the department office and . . ." Bettina paused a moment, took a deep breath, and continued, ". . . and found Isabel draped over her desk . . ."

"Yes?" Fiona managed. "And?"

Bettina nodded. "And dead. Her neck broken."

"What?" Fiona's lips opened and then closed. Miriam's mouth, fishlike, gaped mutely.

Miriam finally blurted "Ohmigod . . . it's not possible . . . ," as Fiona gulped air, her skin pale and clammy.

Isabel Vittorio, chair of the Department of Literature and Rhetoric at Austin University for the past six months, had—during her brief tenure as head—been described as narcissistic, charismatic, brilliant, and opportunistic. Hearing this litany of attributes at a faculty party some months ago, Bettina had leaned into Fiona and purred into her ear: "No wonder she's so successful."

Miriam's normally alto voice cracked, "But Isabel was so powerful. So unassailable."

"Exactly," Bettina herded the various condiment containers on the table together as if to marshal her thoughts. "It doesn't seem possible that anyone who could attack others so cleverly, and watch her own back so assiduously, could ever be caught unaware long enough to be . . . well, done in like any ordinary mortal."

"Good Lord, you mean she was m-m-murdered?" Fiona's words tumbled together so quickly that her consonants went wobbly by the end of the sentence.

"Surely not—perhaps she fell," Miriam added hopefully.

Bettina propped an elbow on the table, rested her chin in one palm, and spoke to her friends with the exaggerated calm of a preschool teacher: "Look, you two, when people fall—for instance, they teeter off a stool when reaching for a book, or they trip over a door frame and collapse—they are found in a heap somewhere. In disarray. They don't end up neatly arranged on their desktops as Isabel did. For heaven's sakes, of course she was murdered!" She tugged at her long curly hair as if patience had suddenly deserted her: "How else can we account for her neck being broken while she was seated?"

Fiona struggled in a mental time-warp as her mind looped and stalled endlessly over the fact of Vittorio's demise. After a few moments, she felt positively giddy. "She's dead? Are you sure?"

"Am I sure?" Bettina's green eyes, a high-kilowatt beam, swept over the desolate shores of their faces. "Dennis said he saw them zip up a black body bag and—"

"Dennis!" Fiona's fear snagged at the back of her throat. The possible implications of what had happened began to solidify in her brain. She experienced a dismaying sensation not unlike walking on a fog-shrouded street she thought was deserted only to find her way blocked by a menacing figure emerging from the murk. No one was safe now. "Dennis . . ." she repeated the name. "What was he doing in our building? I hope he isn't a suspect!"

"Fiona," Bettina's voice dropped to a soothing level. "Dennis is a professor at the university. Yes, he teaches in another department on the other side of campus, but he has a right to be in our building. Plus, he was just picking up Darryl for their weekly racquetball game."

"Oh," Fiona breathed. "Thank goodness." Her dear friend Dennis, a warm and impulsive man, had a habit of landing in the middle of troublesome situations.

Bettina reached down to retrieve her purple backpack. "I've got to run. Just thought you two should know the latest news."

"News!" Miriam gripped her empty mug as if it were a life preserver. "This isn't news. What you're telling us is preposterous. It's a debacle, a, nightmare, a devastation, a, a . . ."

"Miriam," Fiona put an arm around her friend's shoulder. "Calm down. Maybe it's not as it seems. We'll find out."

Bettina rolled her eyes. "Oh, I think it's as it seems, all right. And we know the where and roughly the when. The question is why, and who."

Miriam groaned. "What a hideous way to begin the week."

Fiona stared at her two friends, her forehead puckering, her mouth trembling. She drew a ragged breath. "This is terrible. Do you realize that no one at this table has said 'Poor Isabel' or 'How horrible' or anything even remotely sympathetic to our dead colleague? How can we be this callous?"

No one spoke for a moment. "I'm afraid that Isabel wasn't someone who was exactly loved," Bettina said lamely.

"There's a big gap between 'loved' and 'despised,'" Fiona answered.

Miriam licked her lips and dabbed at her forehead with a wadded-up napkin. "Yes, there is. I don't think there are too many people who will mourn Professor Vittorio's passing."

Bettina raised one hand, and bent back successive fingers as she spoke. "You recall how Isabel refused to support Jane Sebourg's tenure, that she scheduled faculty meetings the day before Christmas two years running, that she threatened Darryl Hansen with a sexual harassment charge, that . . ."

Fiona broke in. "Oh, stop. Those things seemed important at the time but this is murder we're talking about! The things you're bringing up, in light of life or death, have no consequence at all."

Miriam and Bettina exchanged a sharp glance. Miriam looked away, her face carefully neutral, but Bettina, her eyes brimming with mischief, blurted out: "Well, you're the expert. You did write a book about this very thing, didn't you? *The Age of Inconsequence.* How could I have forgotten? Let me see, how did one review begin? 'In the world of high-octane academia, a world of few resources and grandiose expectations . . .' You know, this event could make that book seem even more topical—Ivory Power strikes again."

The year before, Fiona's book had caused a minor sensation around campus. Fiona, however, was sensitive on the subject of the work's notoriety, particularly a fable within the book called "Ivory Power," which satirized campus politics. Her face flushed a mottled pink. "Be serious! The very fact that practically every one of the thirty people in our department has a grudge against Isabel makes every one of us a suspect."

"Ah, so it's not your bleeding heart that's bothering you, it's your precious—and exposed—neck?" Bettina said, craning her own neck at a sharp angle.

"Oh, you're hopeless. I can't think why you're being so horrid about this. I've known you too long to believe you can be this un-feeling." Fiona began to pack away her papers and pen. "I'm going to leave, and when I see you next I hope the Bettina I know and love will be back."

Bettina finally absorbed the obvious fact that her friends had not had as much time to adjust to the news as she had. She felt plenty unnerved herself, and uneasily shadowed by guilt. Only that morning, as she contemplated an upcoming meeting with her chair, Bettina had complained to her husband, Marvin. "I suppose Queen Isabella will ream me out this morning—again—about my tardy report on graduate admissions. Sometimes I just wish that woman would drop dead. Fat chance. Why do the people you like the least seem to live the longest?"

Now, in the café, Bettina marshaled her will and relegated her quivering conscience to the background for now. She firmly took both of Fiona's hands in hers and tried for a reassuring tone. "Fiona. Of course I'm horrified at Isabel's death. I'm probably somewhat in shock. Forgive my poor attempts at humor. But, listen—Isabel as a human being was a misery, you know that as well as I do. And a major pain in the ass. God knows I didn't want her dead. But I did want her out of our department. And I think many people shared my views. That's the reality. And that gives every one of us a motive. Now, what the hell are we going to do about it?"

Miriam hefted her compact, round body out of her chair and snared her coat from the chair back with the snap of a wrist. Fiona detected a pinkish tinge in the whites of Miriam's eyes and a slight tremble in her fingers as she buttoned her coat. But Miriam's voice was steady as she said: "I don't know about the two of you, but I'm going to go to Helmsley Hall to see how people are doing. Someone might need to talk." She turned and stretched every inch of her five-foot-two frame to its full potential. "This is a dreadful business. We should all be ashamed of ourselves." She raised her hands in the air and slowly dropped them. And with that ambiguous flourish, she left. Her step brisk, Miriam negotiated nimbly between two tables of drowsy undergraduates.

The sight of the strained set of her mentor's shoulders tugged at Fiona. Miriam was so proud, yet so vulnerable. Fiona turned a sad smile on Bettina. "She's very upset. But she doesn't want us to think so. That worries me."

"Hmm?" Bettina ceased kneading her forehead with her fingers and leaned back in her chair. Suddenly parched, she finished Fiona's tea. "Your tea's cold, by the way."

"I'm talking about Miriam. Don't you think she seems awfully businesslike, given the circumstances?" Fiona's gray eyes, earnest and anxious, searched Bettina's face.

"What's that flavor . . ." Bettina stalled, running her tongue slowly over her bottom lip. "Vanilla? Or nutmeg?"

"Bettina, don't wander off on me. Please." Fiona begged. "I need some help with this. Why is she acting like it's her duty to counsel everyone else? What about her feelings?"

Fiona's distress triggered an upsurge in Bettina's own anxiety, which instinctively she sought to conceal. She hadn't processed the morning sufficiently herself to reassure anyone else. Yet by force of habit—her two children frequently demanded comfort at the precise moments she felt least able to provide it—she felt she must try. She sighed and shrugged her shoulders to relieve tension before focusing on Fiona. "Oh, all right. Is Miriam struggling for some control in a situation where she has none? Yes. But who wouldn't. Next question?"

Fiona shook her head. "You're certainly cool about this. I wonder why."

A pair of green eyes peered out from narrowed lids. "I'm trying to put this on hold until I figure out what it means."

"A good gig if you can get it." Fiona couldn't keep the disapproving tone from her voice.

Expecting a rapid-fire remark back, Fiona was surprised to note her friend's response. Bettina slumped in her chair as if her skeleton had given up the fight against gravity. She peered around the barely-occupied room with a paranoid air. "I'm not cool. I think I'm in deep trouble."

Puzzled, Fiona just stared. "You mean—" she finally ventured.

Bettina's hand gripped Fiona's arm with surprising force. "I mean I think I might be the last person who saw Isabel alive."

2

If things appear too complicated, they probably are. That's why people read murder mysteries, for their delicious layers of detail. It's like a chocolate cake: the denser the texture, the more satisfying the morsel.

Daphne Arbor, overheard at Isabel's funeral

"Paranoid" was one description of Miriam's state of mind two hours later as she closed the door of her office on the seventh floor of Helmsley Hall and locked it. Her heart jittered and jumped like a gerbil on a wheel. Isabel, murdered. A nervy cocktail of shock and dread coursed through her system. None of them would be safe now. No detail—no ill-timed outbursts, no unpleasant encounters, no public disagreements, no questionable liaisons—would be too petty or too sordid for the press to exploit. And the case had the greatest potential for exploitation possible: more than dollars loosely frittered, far greater than diabolic revenge plots, and exceeding the scope of a juicy grievance, absolutely nothing provoked the public and the legislature more than sexual scandal. A small moan escaped Miriam's lips—for nothing produced more outrage than a middle-aged woman who flaunted her sexuality. And, God forbid, Miriam thought, even the most restrained description of Isabel Vittorio's habits could only be termed randy.

For the only time in her life, Miriam wished that she practiced the Catholic faith if only for the comfort of crossing herself as she thought of her own history with Isabel. Twelve years ago, before Vivian—*before sanity,* a voice sneered in her ear—she and Isabel had had an affair. If a three-month intimate encounter with Isabel could be labeled something as possibly intriguing or satisfying as the word "affair" suggested. Miriam's brain quickly catalogued more apt descriptions: a collision, a pile-up on a crowded expressway, a hit-and-run accident . . .

Miriam's eyes fluttered shut as she groped for the safety of her desk. As her body slid onto the lenient padding of her chair, her cheek sought the cool surface of the desktop. She didn't have to close her eyes to recall her first sight of Isabel Vittorio. It all seemed so long ago, so innocent, so inconsequential. Her mind veered to the randomness of life, how a single chance meeting sparked such interest in one path that it was impossible to even notice the existence of other possible trails, let alone follow one. Afterwards, once happenstance hardened into history, it all appeared so inevitable.

Her initial encounter with Isabel resulted from a delayed flight in the Austin airport. Miriam had raised her head to check the flight posting when she observed a woman across the aisle reading a magazine. Or rather, the woman devoured it, her fingers skipping through the periodical's pages with the barest touch. Miriam was to learn that Isabel consumed rather than experienced life. The fate of the magazine, ending up in a crumpled and exhausted heap on the table next to her, illustrated her appetites. But her style of reading was not what arrested Miriam's attention. Isabel was almost forty then, yet she still appeared girlish: a mass of brunette hair flamed around her angular face, a piquant sprinkle of freckles dusted her nose, a pair of thick fashionable frames softened her piercing hazel eyes. Slender, wearing a tight black sweater that emphasized her high, firm breasts, she possessed an irresistible combination of impatience, intelligence, and girlishness. To Miriam's startled eyes she projected an appeal like that of an American Vita Sackville West—smart, handsome, and aristocratic. She didn't know then if Isabel had either brains or breeding. No matter. She was smitten at once.

At the time, single and restless, Miriam had been teaching in

Austin for five years and found the city both provincial and uninspired. She'd arrived too late for the city's glory days in the sixties and seventies, a time, apparently, of rowdy blues and easy sex. Left behind was a small city struggling in the shadow of Houston and Dallas, economically swamped by the crash of big oil, beginning to be discovered by technology companies in need of plentiful water and even more plentiful Ph.D.s. The university cranked out a steady surplus of the latter who lacked the will or energy to leave Austin.

Austin U. was her third teaching position and a more prestigious one than her last job at a small college in California. After six plus years of living in the moderate clime of Los Angeles, a city blessed with sea and shore and canyon views, Miriam's spirits deflated under the barrage of heat, humidity, and scrubby terrain of central Texas. Heterosexuality seemed as rooted in the landscape as native live oak; she found herself the subject of uneasy whispers in the hallways. Her colleagues tended to view her as an intellectual Californian, that is to say, smart but quirky and bohemian. Indifferent to football or country music, Miriam feared that the majority of her undergraduate students, whose most urgent worry seemed to be getting to the Texas–Oklahoma game early enough to locate the best tailgate parties, must think her a freak. A familiar mantra of the time was that she didn't understand Texas and Texas didn't understand her. She scoured the *Chronicle of Higher Education* with near-sighted diligence, hoping for the rescue of another job.

That afternoon in the airport, when equipment failure sidelined the flight to Chicago, she and Isabel had a drink at the airport bar. The drink turned into two and then three. They didn't leave the city that night, but ended up back at Miriam's bungalow in central Austin.

Miriam's initial fleeting thought that Isabel resembled Vita Sackville West wasn't completely off the mark. One of the things Virginia Woolf's lover had been famous for had been her seductiveness, and Isabel was sexy. Her long arms and long legs embraced Miriam with enthusiasm and finesse. For Miriam, Austin had been reclaimed. It was a city of possibility after all . . .

18

Miriam massaged her throbbing head with both hands. But having fallen for Isabel only to be dropped like a slightly used bar of hotel soap wasn't the worst of it. That was, after all, long ago. And since her lasting involvement with Vivian, far removed from her daily life. Her hand hovered above the bottom right drawer of the desk. Trembling, she pulled the handle and slid the drawer open. Inside rested a notebook with a hawk's face on the cover, its gaze keen

19

and dismissive. Miriam hefted the notebook onto the desk, wincing as if its binding burned her skin.

It seemed impossible that only the week before she had begun a new project with such hope and naïve joy. Miriam had always wanted to write a novel, specifically a mystery. One afternoon, as her imagination roamed during a droningly dull faculty meeting, she had excused herself early, locked herself in her office, and scrawled happily:

Death of a Department Chair

By Friday noon of the week before Christmas break, Maxine Durrell had launched several salvos of verbiage at her coworkers: she had blithely delivered bad news to an assistant professor up for promotion, disregarded her dean's advice by voting against the Provost's new measure to encourage minority hires, browbeaten the executive committee to approve her recommendation to raise her personal secretary's salary in spite of budget deficits, hung up the phone twice on her vice-chair, and presided over a faculty retreat where she excoriated her department for grade inflation, poor attendance at graduation, and a lack of community spirit. She played racquetball with a colleague half her age and won—her opponent was a new faculty member trying to ingratiate himself with his chair.

At four in the afternoon she sent a last barrage of emails demanding that all the year's committee reports be turned in before the Christmas holidays. She turned off her computer at four forty-five and emptied her voice mail. By five o'clock she sat slumped at her desk, her neck encircled by baling wire. Her body cooled slowly. Finally, she had nothing more to say.

Miriam, with a furtive look around the office—how she wished she had closed the blinds to her seventh-floor window!—slipped the notebook back into her desk drawer. She should destroy these scribblings. What if the police were to find it? Of course, she told herself, it's only fiction. But those words sounded worn and lame even to herself. Life imitates art—hadn't she heard that before? Miriam felt a sense of guilt, as if by writing the words of her story she had triggered the events leading to Isabel's death. What would her friend Daphne tell her? Probably that by rendering violent death on paper, she had released the possibility of its occurrence into the universe. Miriam buttoned her worn tweed blazer and peered out into the hall. In the corridor, students walked quietly, whispering, perhaps in respect for the recently departed, or possibly out of fear. Some faculty had cancelled classes, as Miriam had advised hours earlier, but others stoically insisted on holding them. The very air felt both tense and dispirited. Miriam ducked her head and made for the back stairs. She must see Daphne right away.

She parked her Subaru outside Daphne's small house on West Lynn, a street that angled sharply uphill from a major crosstown boulevard. The house, beige and squarish, was as nondescript as Daphne was flamboyant. Miriam's short legs carried her quickly to the door, and, as she raised her hand to knock, the door cracked open.

The tanned and creased face of her friend appeared. "Ah, Miriam. You're early."

"What?" Miriam's mind went blank. "For what?"

"Aren't we doing the flea market circuit today?" Daphne swept a long, fringed scarf, patterned with swirls of purple and green, around her broad shoulders. Statuesque, with wild silver curls framing her exquisitely-lined face, Daphne resembled a Grecian goddess, albeit one with a sense of humor.

"Flea market?" Miriam erupted into an odd, barking laugh. The idea of shopping urged her toward hysteria. "My God, you haven't heard? Isabel's been murdered."

Daphne inclined her head judiciously toward her friend. She had heard a report of the murder within an hour of its discovery. Her very person naturally attracted news, both fantastic and mundane. "It's very shocking. And so, for you, going out to Dell's Discount

Acres seems a little like fiddling while Rome burns?" When her words didn't even elicit an answering smile, Daphne's tone turned brisk. "Well, then. Come inside."

Daphne steered Miriam through a small entry, past a grandfather clock chiming the quarter hour, and into a spacious room, its wood floors anchored by two green couches in the shape of an L. She gently eased Miriam onto one sofa, plumping a large pillow behind her back. "Tell me all about it."

Miriam turned a white, stricken face toward her friend. She didn't look directly into her eyes. "Can bad thoughts kill?" she asked, her voice reedy and weak.

Daphne frowned at Miriam's childlike tone, evidence that Miriam's customary assurance had completely fled. She placed a large, firm hand on top of Miriam's small ones. "My dear. Hideous events occur. I know you didn't care overly for Isabel Vittorio. And that perhaps you didn't always wish her well. Maybe you occasionally thought hurtful thoughts about her. But that doesn't mean you had anything whatsoever to do with her death."

Miriam's round face rotated from side to side slowly as she refused to accept Daphne's consoling words. "It's not that simple. I comforted myself . . . I *entertained* myself with the idea of her murder." And she explained about the beginning of her novel and her eagerness over writing it.

"So." Daphne sat back and shut her eyes. "This was poor timing, I suppose, in your eyes. But nothing more." A few moments passed. "Miriam?"

"Yes?" Miriam found herself jarred, as she always was, by Daphne's gaze, one eye piercingly blue and the other a tawny cat's eye.

"Are you listening to me?"

"I can't think. I need help. Do you have any whiskey?"

Daphne left the room and returned with a tumbler of single malt and a pack of tarot cards. "Here. Drink this and shuffle these."

Miriam seized the glass with a glimmer of hope in her eyes. "Thank you." She took a sip. "Oh, Glenmorangie. You remembered."

Daphne didn't bother to mention that her friend consumed regular shots of single malt in her company nearly every week during their frequent talks and outings, so of course it wasn't any effort to remember her favorite drink. Miriam was simply not herself.

Miriam sat up straighter, her face less pale. "I don't think I want you to do a reading now. I don't want to know what the cards have to say. It might be too frightening."

"I'm not doing a reading. Merely a meditation. To calm you. Shuffle and choose just one card."

As Miriam continued to look dubious and resistant, Daphne reassured her: "I promise. Just one card to focus our conversation."

In haste, Miriam sloshed the cards on the table, stirred them with her palms, and pulled out a card. She held it stiffly away from her body and between two fingernails, as if it were a slice of charred toast that might offend her nostrils or blacken her hands.

"For heaven's sake, put it down where I can see it," Daphne said, her gravelly voice a pleasant growl.

Miriam put the card face down, forcing her friend to reach across and flip it over herself. The card, bright and bold, displayed a conductor, wand in hand, but a conductor of illusion, not music.

"The Magician," Daphne announced with approval. She sniffed the air as if the turning of the card released a pleasing scent. "Perfect."

"Ohhh," Miriam groaned and kneaded her short hair roughly. "I can't possibly listen to any of this. Isabel's been murdered. Somehow, I am responsible. Who cares whether the card is perfect? I'm in perfect hell."

"Shhh," Daphne pursed her lips and emitted a cluck of reassurance, soothing her friend as if she were a fretful child. "This card is you. A great communicator. One who channels energies: from the unconscious to the conscious, from the spirit to the material plane. You are a wonderful counselor, a magical transmitter of energy, a—"

"Please," Miriam protested. "You sound like you're describing Jesus Christ. It's ridiculous." Miriam, proudly but not devoutly Jewish, shook her head in refusal.

"Miriam!" Daphne swept the card from the table. "Stop feeling so sorry for yourself. You *are* a gifted communicator with a powerful mind. I'm trying to tell you something: one, that you can think and intuit your way to a different understanding of this situation, if you will but *try* . . ." On this last, Daphne's hoarse voice dropped a note giving its timbre the consistency of ground steel. "Two, you have the power to enlist others in your mission and to draw upon resources both inner and outer. In other words, use your strengths and stop acting like a victim in a B minus thriller."

Miriam looked up, her brown eyes glazing over. "That's it. This feels like a trashy movie. Bette Davis, á la Baby Jane, is Isabel, a diminished femme fatale made pitiful by her fate, and I'll be seen as Joan Crawford, face distorted by wrinkles and vitriol. They'll see me as fueled by jealousy, scorned, derided. . . ."

"Don't flatter yourself." Daphne shook out her scarf and smoothed its mauve fringe. "Come, let's go to lunch."

3

The story of each life begs to be told. Not by one person, but by many. If we don't tell our stories, if others don't talk about us, can we even claim to have existed? Life as theatre isn't just a metaphor: the stage can be seen as the playing field of a life, a life as a complex system of interlocking stages. Go ahead, tread those boards, strut your stuff, write your own script.

Dennis Reagan, introductory course in playwriting

*F*iona left Bettina in the coffee shop and made her way to her ten a.m. class in a confounded state. She planned to spend the time providing a forum for those who needed to discuss the tragedy. Yet her steps dragged as she neared Helmsley Hall; after what had happened, she felt an aversion to the building itself. Isabel, dead. No, Isabel, *murdered.* The word alone had the power to alter the shape of the universe. Isabel, a senior professor with an international reputation, a woman who'd come to Austin U. celebrated and empowered the year after Fiona had received tenure, had seemed invincible. Arrested by her thoughts, Fiona stopped on the sidewalk in front of the building in the shade of a red oak—the October sun still hinted of an incandescent summer—and tugged at a long silver earring. Isabel had been a study in paradoxes: invincible but unlikable, daunting but heartless, esteemed but not trustworthy.

She remembered only too well Isabel's interview in the Department of Literature and Rhetoric. At the time, Fiona had been the youngest of three tenured women in the department, something she had not found terribly significant before. But sitting in the conference room that day, watching Isabel, sharp-eyed and sharp-tongued, as she worked the room during her job talk, Fiona couldn't help noticing that Isabel never allowed her gaze to rest on her. She looked at Bettina and Miriam, and at other faculty members—Sigmund Froelich, the chair at that time; Richard Lester, a noted Americanist; even assistant professors like Craig Burnett and Carlos Lambros, young men who had virtually no standing at all—but not at her. Fiona found Isabel's imperious manner off-putting and her research only marginally interesting.

But Isabel had been hired, had in a sense been pushed down the throats of the faculty by the dean at the time, who found Isabel's international reputation and tough-minded style irresistible. The rumor was that Isabel was the dean's pick to be chair after Sigmund stepped down.

What had remained most vivid in Fiona's memory was that after Isabel's hire (the candidate had returned for two more interviews and continued to ignore Fiona), she had been grading in her office when Isabel, without knocking, slid inside the room in a reptilian way and coiled her long legs in the chair across from Fiona's desk.

"Fiona!" she had said, a hearty gleam in her eye.

"Yes?" Fiona remembered holding her pen in the air, poised, her only protection from this intruder perhaps?

"You know, we must have lunch."

Fiona noticed that this was not an invitation or a request, but a proclamation. Startled and annoyed by the sudden promotion from pariah to lunch partner in Isabel's regard, Fiona said nothing.

Isabel had the grace to cough. "Well, when I was here before, I thought you were an assistant professor."

Fiona waited for a further explanation; what was the woman's point? "No, I was tenured last year."

"Exactly! I found out that you have tenure, that you are . . ." She paused and arched an eyebrow. Isabel's thin, sharp features gave her a judgmental air. The hawklike eyes surveyed Fiona impatiently. Fiona imagined that Isabel's students dreaded that look, the accusatory "surely you understand" look that labeled the merest hesitation as stupidity. Fiona finally got it: Isabel's ellipsis after "you are . . ." could be filled in with ". . . a permanent member of the faculty," a.k.a., "a real person." Had Fiona not had tenure, Isabel could have devoted her energies to getting rid of her if she wished, or simply disregarded her as impermanent and inconsequential, *ergo* not worth bothering with.

A disconcerting wave of shame coursed through Fiona. Anger constricted her throat. She wanted to tell the woman to leave, to take her careerist self to another office where her strategies might be thought efficacious, but to her everlasting regret, as she sat there, shocked, a sickly smile erupted on her face. She had never met anyone quite like Isabel before. Could anyone be this obvious? So breezy about rendering someone invisible, so capricious in reversing her attitude and dubbing her—if only mildly—consequential a moment later? Was she for real?

Reassured by Fiona's face, taking the smile for friendship rather than the grimace of chagrin it actually was, Isabel stood and waved. "I'll call you," she said. "We'll have lunch."

Fiona watched her depart, stunned. The idea that this woman actually studied rhetorical strategies and yet behaved so cluelessly toward others was another of the ironies of academic life.

Yet, it was not until Isabel had betrayed her in a faculty meeting, publicly, that Fiona had completely hardened against her. She had reminded Bettina of this incident an hour before in the café.

"Do you remember when Collin Freed was first hired?"

"Of course," Bettina looked startled for a moment. "But why?"

"I was on that search committee with Isabel. She chaired it. She called me into her office and told me we desperately needed to hire a woman in American or British Studies because the faculty in both divisions was preponderantly male and the female graduate students were unhappy. I was uneasy about this—after all, Carlos Lambros does a lot of feminist research, and since when was Isabel worried about gender balance in the department—and I hadn't forgotten her little trick of ignoring me when she first arrived. And I thought, why tell me? Why not talk to some of the senior professors who would be less committed to hiring a woman? But I said, trying to be a good team player, well, fine, if we got the right applicants, with the right qualifications, well, you know the drill."

"Hmm," Bettina signaled to the waitperson for coffee. "I think I'm going to need a stimulant to get through this story. Keep going."

"So, we screened, oh, it must have been a hundred candidates for that job. Some really good people, many of them white men of course, but not all. There was an outstanding woman, an African American specializing in black feminist theory. She was smashing."

"Of course. Paula Fabian. Something strange is that—"

"Hold that thought. Let me finish. So two of the applicants come for the interview. The students go wild about Fabian, most of the faculty, too. The other person was Collin. He had the support of Sigmund and Richard Lester, naturally, but I thought a majority of the faculty would vote for Paula."

"Ugh, I remember that meeting."

"Actually, I think you were down with a cold. If you had been there, there might have been some hope."

"Oh, God, you're right. It was right before Christmas; I had a hideous sinus infection. I just heard about the meeting and it sounded so pernicious and I was so sick it all just blurred together in my memory." Bettina gave Fiona her full attention now, her broad face calm and generous.

For a moment Fiona felt flattered as she always did when her friend turned her green eyes upon her in that utterly focused way unique to Bettina, that "there is nothing I'd rather do than listen to you" look. It was very gratifying even though Fiona knew she wasn't its only recipient. She thought again how lucky Bettina's children, Carl and Clare, were to have such an empathetic presence in their household.

"Go on," Bettina prompted patiently.

"Well, the faculty, it turned out, was bitterly divided. Lester and Sigmund had done their homework well: they had lined up the votes of everyone who was ambivalent. And you know Paula's work, don't you?"

28

"Indeed. No holds barred on race issues, very political. Smart woman—we could use her around here. Which reminds me . . ."

"Please, let me finish. It's too sickening—I want to get it over with." Fiona brushed her ash-blond hair out of her eyes. Even though the event had happened five years ago, thinking about it still jumbled her insides as thoroughly as when an undertow sucks in and then disgorges a swimmer. She drew her thin frame erect. "So we hear impassioned speeches from both sides—Carlos was very strong on Paula. I'm thinking one more positive voice will put us over the top. So I look at Isabel and tell the faculty that the graduate students are strongly for Fabian and that the women—and minority students in general—have been feeling disenfranchised, that we need diversity on the faculty and in the classroom. At that point, Isabel gives me a kind of fishlike stare, very cold, stands up and begins to contradict what I just said about the students."

"She stood?" Bettina's face lit up at the appearance of a steaming mug of coffee, which she accepted gratefully from the server.

"That *was* odd," Fiona nodded, "I hadn't thought of that before. Her standing alone should have warned me."

Bettina laughed. "Yes, our colleagues' thoughts are so fulsome, their heads so heavy with theoretical conjecture, that it's all they can do to slump in their chairs, one elbow on the table, holding up those ponderous brains. God forbid they should discover a body attached to their precious cerebral cortex."

Fiona giggled. "Remember how Trollope wrote about men standing up on their hind legs in heated debate: he couldn't have imagined that the twenty-first-century variety would evolve into such spineless wonders."

"Spineless maybe, but prickly definitely," Bettina said primly, a merry look in her eyes.

Fiona rolled her eyes happily. Then she remembered what she was recalling and her face tensed once again. "So Isabel stood, looked around, particularly at me, and announced that she had polled each of the graduate students in American and British studies and they were perfectly happy with the mix of faculty we had at present, and that the women—*particularly*—had no complaints. They were, she couldn't resist pointing out, happy to have her, Isabel, as an advocate since some of her discourse analysis on nineteenth-century public communication overlapped their own research into the period. She then went on to support Collin Freed. You should have seen the tiny signal of approval that flew through the air from Richard Lester and Sigmund Froelich to Isabel Vittorio. The three of them lit up as if they were wired. Somehow, after that, the vote came in a tie and Sigmund, as chair, cast the deciding vote."

"She set you up," Bettina said with awe. "And beautifully. She got you to raise the race and gender issues, so that no one could say they weren't considered, but then she shot you down, neatly."

"One bullet," Fiona said morosely. She felt the humiliation of her defeat, still. It lingered, a bitter aftertaste that no amount of subsequent success could flush from her throat.

"The bitch," Bettina said. "But you have to admit, one clever bitch."

"Shhh. Remember what's happened to her," Fiona looked around nervously.

"Never speak ill of the dead?" Bettina smiled grimly. "My dear, you haven't heard the beginning of the dreck that's going to be dredged up around Isabel's death. Professor Vittorio aroused people's ire and passions—look at you, cool Scandinavian that you are, practically drooling in your rage."

"Oh, please." Fiona said, annoyed, and then she smiled. "Only the Hardison side is Scandinavian, don't forget my mother's side of the family: Scotch-Irish, heavy drinkers, romantics all."

Bettina's thin auburn eyebrows rose. "That could make you the number one suspect. Let me pull out my scorecard. Let's see, Miss Scarlet was in the ballroom with the knife after all . . ."

"Bettina, what were you trying to say a bit ago, when I was telling you about Isabel's betrayal?"

"God," Bettina brought her coffee cup to the table with a dull thunk. "Paula Fabian. Dennis is on a search committee with Isabel, and he said Paula is a finalist for the joint position between Drama and Lit. and Rhetoric. And get this: Isabel had been pulling strings for Paula this time, lining up the committee. Until, he said, last Friday."

"What happened then?"

"She reversed course and viciously attacked her. Dennis said he had a real knock-down, drag-out harangue with her."

"In the committee meeting?"

"No. Unfortunately, they were alone. In her office. On Friday afternoon."

The two women stared at each other a moment. Fiona looked away first. "Poor Dennis. He must be in a state."

"My dear, it's even worse than you think." Bettina glanced behind her and leaned in closer, her shoulders hunched over the table. "I think Isabel has been having an affair with the other candidate for the position, Hannah Weinstein."

"But Hannah teaches in Maryland."

"So they've been commuting."

Fiona made a face. "It's just so improbable. Hannah is Jewish. I mean, you know Isabel's views about . . . well, she's such a—"

"An anti-Semite as well as a racist? Go on, you can say it. It's not news. Isabel Vittorio has blocked every initiative we've had to increase minority faculty. And she's been completely unsupportive of perfectly legitimate complaints from our students about racist remarks in certain people's classes. You remember the grievance against Lester last year? So, tell me about it!"

Fiona felt as if she approached a calm, waveless sea only to have the water suddenly churn furiously and eject a slime-covered sea creature. Her world seemed far less safe and simple than it had a day ago. She grasped Bettina's hand. "What did you mean when you said you might be the last person to see Isabel?"

"Of course I don't know—the police have told us . . . me . . . nothing. But I was in the office over the weekend. I talked to Isabel Saturday around noon. I told her I would do everything in my power to see that she would not remain as chair."

Fiona's head felt like it was being pulled in three different directions. "But why?" She snatched at a conversational thread. "Because of Paula Fabian?"

"No, I hadn't talked to Dennis yet. I didn't know about that." Bettina's green eyes were hooded and sad. "Because of Miriam."

Fiona put out a hand, palm up, in mute appeal. "What?" she managed.

"You know Miriam's reputation: as the fairest, the most decent, the least self-aggrandizing endowed professor at Austin University?"

"Well, yes, of course."

"Isabel wants . . . wanted . . . to destroy her."

"She can't . . . couldn't. Miriam's impeccable."

"Miriam's not only Jewish, she's a lesbian. This is Texas—we still have a sodomy law on the books, remember?"

Fiona fairly sputtered. "But Isabel's a lesbian too. What can she possibly say?"

"Look, Fiona, you're terribly generous, you think the best of people. It's hard for you to imagine the lengths people will go when they feel the least threatened. It turns out that Isabel and Miriam had an affair when Isabel first came here. I don't know what Isabel knows—or knew—about Miriam but she told me she was determined to destroy Miriam's influence."

"It's the minority recruitment initiative," Fiona said. "That's Miriam's baby. She's determined to increase minority hires to at least 25 percent of the total. Somehow Paula plays into this too, doesn't she?"

"Of course," Bettina snapped. "I just don't know how it all fits together. It makes no sense for Isabel to resist Paula, not if she values her political life. Paula Fabian is a catch for any department. And the stakes are high: the reputation of the university as an exemplar of research and a force for social change." Bettina's brow crinkled. "There's something we don't know about Isabel's relationship with Paula. Regardless, Paula is too big for her to tackle. But Miriam is another matter. She's been here long enough for people to take her for granted. Isabel felt she could afford to have it out for Miriam."

"But Miriam's deeply respected. And, I think, loved by many. She has a fine mind, her books on Gertrude Stein rank right up there with the finest modernist scholars . . ."

Bettina dismissed such reasonable talk with a toss of her head. "I'm aware of her record. I know what people should think of Miriam. But that's not the issue—we don't live in a rational world. Here's the point, Fiona: I've worked with Miriam for eighteen years. She and Vivian babysat Carl and Clare. Marvin adores her." Marvin, a former academic who brooked fools not at all, was Bettina's husband of twenty-five years. "I would do anything for her, anything."

Bettina's marked shift in attitude—from an overly casual acceptance of Isabel's death to ferocious protectiveness about Miriam—alarmed Fiona. Yet Bettina's passion at the moment was unmistakable. Long strands of auburn hair curled wildly in a halo about her head, her face flushed a peachy-pink, her generous bust rose before her like a shield. Bettina looked like nothing so much as a blazing Minerva strapping on battle armor.

Fiona spoke softly, "Sweetie, you don't have to convince me that Miriam's wonderful." The set of her friend's face alarmed her further. Fiona laughed shakily. "You're almost acting as if Isabel intended to murder Miriam or something—" Fiona broke off. "Lord, is that what you think? Bettina, I feel frightened."

Bettina continued as if she hadn't heard Fiona, a gleam of saliva on her lower lip. "When she told me she was targeting Miriam, I let her have it and I told her that her days as chair were numbered."

The blood drained from Fiona's face. "But who could have guessed how few were left?"

Bettina stared across the room, a glitter of metallic gold flashing in the iris of her eyes like a misplaced mosaic tile. "One, maybe two. However brief her time left on this earth was, the end didn't come soon enough as far as I'm concerned."

4

Diversity is a word carelessly flung about by people who have never held a standard in their lives. As if skin color, sexual orientation, and gender categories were markers more significant than raw intelligence. There is no universal! they cry. If they'd only admit it, they'd claim the universal position in a heartbeat. They don't despise us successful white heterosexual men so much as envy us every day of their lives.

Richard Lester, at lunch in the faculty club with Sigmund Froelich and Collin Freed

A day after the discovery of Isabel's body, Dennis lay in bed with Carter, his longtime partner. He opened one eye cautiously, hoping it wasn't anytime near morning. A shaft of light streaked across the bed; somewhere outside the window a lone cardinal loudly defended its turf. Dennis blinked and opened both eyes to half-mast. Carter, blue eyes shockingly alert, stared at him, a dimple creasing one side of his lean face. "It's true," Carter said, kissing his neck. "It's too early to get up. And you're already late."

"And you're a sadist," Dennis moaned, hugging his pillow tighter.

Carter threw his long legs over the side of the mattress. "As Blake would say, in your dreams." He reached over and lightly slapped Dennis's blanketed rump. "Honey, it is time to get up. But if you don't want to, don't." A stream of water hit the tiles in the adjoining room as the shower splashed on and Dennis heard Carter's muffled voice: "I don't have a choice. Today's advisory board."

The phone rang next to the bed. With a grumpy sigh, Dennis cocked the receiver in the direction of his ear. "What?" He drew in a

34

sharp breath. "You think I—? . . . WHAT?" His hand shook as he placed the phone back into its stand.

Carter's head and shoulders, towel-covered, appeared in the doorway. "Who was that?"

"Bettina."

"Yes?" Carter prompted.

"The investigation into Isabel Vittorio's death—everyone who was in Helmsley Hall for the past five days is engaging counsel."

The towel fell away from Carter's finely molded neck. "Good Lord."

"She was murdered," Dennis said flatly. "Can you imagine?"

Carter, of course, had heard that fact before, the news having gushed through campus and community like a flash flood. But in deference to his spouse's seeming inability to digest this happening, he considered the announcement afresh. A faint smile shadowed Carter's face and then disappeared. "Well, yes, I suppose I can. I'm sorry. I just know how difficult she was."

"She was difficult. She was also a terrific advocate for faculty when the stakes were high. I don't think I would have been promoted without her. But, God, she was tough." Dennis chewed a finger and then jammed it under his armpit. "I'm frankly scared to death."

"Why?" Carter quickly came back to the bed and sat down.

"I was in the building when they removed the body."

Carter waited. "So?" he finally asked.

"I don't know. Even though it was apparently many hours after the . . . the deed itself . . . it worries me that I was anywhere near the vicinity. After all, I don't work in that building."

Carter's face creased in a puzzled frown. "Well, no, but it doesn't mean anything really, that you were passing by at that time. Hundreds of people were I imagine."

"Carter." Dennis' voice dropped to a hollow bass note. "I have to tell you something. I had an appointment with Isabel at four o'clock on the Friday before she died."

"Ah. So now I see."

"No, I don't think you do. I met her in her office. We had a disagreement. A loud one. Anyone could have heard us yelling at each other."

"But why would you fight? She's not your chair. She has no power over you."

"Not directly. I was on a search committee: for a joint appointment. Fifty percent Literature and Rhetoric, the other fifty with us in Drama. The committee wanted a very accomplished woman, African American, from Georgetown. We'd voted—it was one vote short of unanimous, actually. At least it was until Isabel decided that she didn't want her. She did originally, then reversed her position."

Carter tiredly rubbed the back of his neck. "I suppose Professor Vittorio had someone else in mind?"

Dennis' face flushed. "Damn straight. Someone she's probably having an affair with, if I know her tactics. A rhetorician from Maryland with absolutely no credentials that would help us at all. Isabel insists that she's written one play for children, unpublished—as if that solved the problem."

Carter looked at his watch. "Pity. Only nine a.m. You already look like you could use a drink." He smiled. "Sweetheart, other members of the committee will vouch for this dispute."

"Yes, but they weren't in her office on Friday afternoon. I was, as the chair of the committee."

"Tell me what happened."

Dennis blinked quickly. He remembered dimly his good humor last Friday afternoon. The day had been sunny and dry. He'd just played two sets of tennis with his good friend Darryl Hansen, the Dean of Liberal Studies. A match he'd won, not that it mattered. But he recalled floating rather than walking into Isabel's office on the seventh floor of Helmsley Hall. The administrative assistant, Anna, waved him in.

"Shut the door," Isabel had said in lieu of hello. She turned away from her file cabinet long enough to award him a chilly nod.

"Fine, thank you. And you?" he'd answered pleasantly.

Isabel's face looked harried, with deep grooves down the sides of her nose. *She's losing her looks* flashed through his brain. Isabel ten years ago had had an athletic figure and a handsome, strong-featured face, her whole appeal what Carter called coltish. Her skin looked pale now, deeply lined, with harsh shadows under her hazel eyes. She now looked formidable and somewhat grim, every inch Queen Bella with not even an echo of the coltish Isabel about her. For an instant, Dennis felt a pang of pity and wondered about the experience life had served up to so alter the woman in front of him.

Dennis sat down and looked around the office. Isabel's desk, normally swept of piles, was covered with stacks of folders and memos; a litter of pens, eyeglasses, and a yogurt container rested on top of the clutter. "Busy time of year," he said.

"God, yes." She sat down with a deep sigh. She looked at him and uncharacteristically smiled broadly at Dennis. "How's your gorgeous boyfriend?" she asked.

Dennis shifted in his chair. "Carter's good, very good."

"I heard he just got promoted to head of the literary archives at the Research Center."

Ah, he thought, that was it. Austin University's literary archives were world-renowned. Surely, Isabel was filing Carter away in her "potentially influential" file. "Yeah, he's thrilled. Nothing he likes more than digging through boxes of uncatalogued correspondence."

"Surely he lets the minions do that? Well, he's a very capable man," she said, her eyes hooding to half-mast as she licked her lips. "And fabulous looking."

"Can't say I disagree with you." Dennis's tone was mild but her referring to Carter like a side of beef annoyed him. My, the woman was hungry. He'd heard that Isabel was ambisexual: women of all persuasions, gay men, straight men, and God only knew what else were all prey to her. He assumed this was just campus garbage-talk, an attempt to diminish a woman so daunting she shriveled the balls of most men she met. Still, thank goodness he was with someone who was too sensible to mess around with the Voracious Vittorio, as Bettina called her. He crossed his legs uncomfortably. He wondered how determined Isabel might be if thwarted.

"So," he said. "I think we've paid our dues on this search. Paula Fabian is the committee's choice. Let's pass it by the EC and be done."

Isabel cocked her head to one side, like a robin considering a particularly juicy grub. "Yes, obvious. But I'm beginning to think we've overlooked Weinstein's potential."

Dennis groaned. "We spent one whole meeting considering just that."

"I'd like to reopen the decision: have one more meeting of the committee at least." She paged though her diary. "Wednesday okay with you?"

Dennis automatically lifted the stylus of his electronic diary before he stopped. "Wait a minute. The committee decided: four to one."

"I know," she attempted to smile sympathetically but her eyes were cold. "Only Mary Morton voted for Hannah. But I think she might have a point."

Dennis returned her look. "Isabel, even if you change your vote, it's three to two. I chair the committee. I'm reporting to my faculty on Monday. I have to say no."

"I don't accept that," she said stubbornly.

Dennis, normally a patient man, considered the raw-boned set of her shoulders, the strained face, the testy eyes, and felt heat flare from his chest to his neck. "It's over," he said tensely. "Let it go, just for once." He thought fleetingly of Daphne and how much good one meditation session with her would do the hyperstressed woman in front of him.

"Don't tell me what to let go of and what not to, my dear Dennis. Don't forget that I have been your ally and a valuable one. You owe me this."

Dennis flinched at her reference to helping him with his promotion five years ago. "My God, but you're a hard woman," he said with a bitter half-laugh. "And I thought you wrote that recommendation because you liked my work." He slapped his face in an exaggerated way and assumed a stereotypic lisp: "Silly girl. What were you thinking of?"

"Very funny," Isabel said stonily. "Act out all you want. I want the search reopened."

Dennis stood to his full six feet. He jabbed a finger down on the mess on her desk. The glasses slid off a pile of papers, skidded off the desk, and crashed into a lamp. He summoned his twenty years of actor training and at the top of lungs yelled "NO!" as if scaring off a snarly dog.

"I'm warning you," she said, her voice harsh and heated. "Just be a good boy and do what I'm asking you."

"Just be a bitch," he rejoined. "And see where it gets you." And he stormed out of the office.

"Christ," he said now to Carter. "I can't believe I rose to the bait. And stooped to her level." He smiled wryly. "At least I didn't call her a stupid cunt."

"Learn to tell the truth," Carter said. They both laughed. "But, seriously."

"You said it right the first time," Dennis said, leaning over and planting a firm kiss on Carter's mouth. "She is a stupid cunt. And I don't even like using that word—women don't deserve it."

Carter kissed him back. "Who said anything about women? We're talking about Isabel."

"Ohhh, bad boy," Dennis chuckled.

Carter pulled the covers off Dennis's body. "Try me."

Miriam pulled wearily into her driveway in Hemphill Park, a neighborhood dotted with trees and porches, and blessed with a high ratio of dogs per person. The day had been a nightmare, as she suspected every day would be until Isabel's killer was found. Dean Hansen had appointed her interim chair, something that seemed to happen to her every few years when a crisis arose. She thought bitterly how when she had wanted the chairpersonship six months ago, Isabel had managed to snare the position. Her insides felt hollow yet sore, and she genuinely wished Isabel were alive and still inhabiting the large office in the southeast corner of the seventh floor. She had spent the day fielding calls—from enterprising reporters, panicked parents, anxious colleagues.

She walked in the door and was greeted by Poirot, a sparky Jack Russell terrier. "Hello, my sweet pie," she said, fondling the dog's silky ears. "Vivian?" she called. When there was no answer, she went into her own study, Poirot padding behind her, and put her briefcase on the table next to the computer. Vivian, a freelance editor, worked at home, but Miriam remembered that today she had a late afternoon massage appointment.

Deciding to wait until Vivian's return to make a drink, Miriam opened her briefcase. In the pocket in the back was the notebook she had taken from her office. Her hands gravitated toward the shiny cover as if lured by a rare jewel that begged to be touched: she opened it to see the title on the first page: "Death of a Department Chair."

She shut the notebook, heart tittering. Then she slowly opened it again and stared at it. Miriam knew she was an analytical person, a natural investigator of human motives and political trends. Perhaps she should continue her story: maybe by writing this fiction, some detail would emerge from her subconscious that could help illuminate the tragedy. Taking action always made her feel better in any case. She picked up a pen; she sometimes found writing in longhand soothing. It reminded her of her apprentice scholarship as a young woman at the University of Chicago in the days before word processing.

---

editor's note:

Some readers may find my desire to continue writing this fictional account macabre. Others may deem it reckless, a dangerous tactic for a suspect to take: after all, haven't many famous murderers chronicled their own deeds, the narrator of Crime and Punishment *just one haunting example? I assure you I had no idea at the time that I was a suspect. In hindsight my actions were pathetically naïve and foolhardy.*

She situated her sturdy body firmly in a worn black leather chair by the window, her short legs propped on a matching footstool. Poirot grunted as he turned around twice on his dog bed in the corner and then settled in. After a moment's thought, Miriam decided if Isabel were to have the name Maxine in her account, she would refer to herself as Gertrude. An aficionado of the expatriate writer Gertrude Stein, Miriam had long been intrigued by Stein's one attempt at a mystery, *Blood on the Dining Room Floor,* which Stein wrote to make sense of some peculiar circumstances one summer at the rural residence she and her companion Alice B. Toklas had acquired in Belley, France. Miriam began to write, her gray hair wisping across her forehead as her wrist moved across the page:

After shock, the first emotion Maxine's colleagues felt was relief. It was as if a haranguing voice over one's shoulder, questioning every move, every thought, were suddenly silenced. Most academics suffer ongoing doubts from their inner critic as it is, so to add to that an external voice even more severe and unforgiving, as Maxine's was, was almost intolerable.

Maxine had a series of visitors the last day of her life, some of them unobserved, which would delay the police investigation a very long time. The chair's assistant, Flora, testified that she had entered Maxine's office at 2:30 while Maxine was teaching her senior seminar. At that time, the small table and two chairs that Maxine used for conferences sat squarely in the middle of the office. At five, when Flora discovered the body as she was leaving for the day, she noticed that one of the chairs had been moved—it now stood under the window. The window was open and the screen missing.

On the chair under the window lay a beautiful silk scarf in muted greens and blues, one that Flora had not seen before and certainly not that day. Flora told the police that the scarf was similar to one she had seen on Gertrude Pell, one of Maxine's colleagues. The two women had been feuding for months and their animosity was, in Flora's opinion, destroying the department. When questioned about this, Gertrude insisted that the "unpleasantness" between her and Maxine was 1) business as usual in academe, and 2) merely symptoms of long-buried faculty acrimonies and departmental dysfunction, which had finally erupted into public view.

"Miriam, where are you?" Vivian's voice, lutelike, called from the back entryway. Miriam closed the notebook, tucked it into the bottom right desk drawer, and padded on bare feet from her study into the kitchen where Vivian leafed through the day's mail.

Vivian hugged Miriam, and looked at her with concern. "How are you holding up, dear?"

"Barely." Miriam collapsed into a chair at the table. "How about a drink?"

"Excellent. It's lovely out—I think a night for the porch. A martini, perhaps?" At Miriam's assent, she busied herself with vodka, ice cubes, jalapeño-stuffed olives, a few shakes of vermouth. She slid two glasses into the freezer, "So, anything new today in the case?"

"Case, ha. How would I know? I was interviewed briefly by a young sergeant, Crane is her name. Very perfunctory. She asked me where I was on Saturday and Sunday. Fortunately, you and I were at the art fair most of the weekend and then we were with Bettina and Marvin Saturday night. I really couldn't be very helpful."

"Miriam." Vivian parked her long, angular frame at another chair. "It's not going to be this easy."

Miriam's throat constricted. "What do you mean?"

"I just talked to Hannah." Hannah Weinstein was a good friend, and former lover, from Miriam's days at the University of Portland, where she had taught almost twenty years before. Hannah now taught at the University of Maryland. Vivian paused, drew a slim hand through her salt-and-pepper hair, which neatly waved back from her forehead, and continued: "I'm afraid she was involved with Isabel."

"Oh, dear," Miriam said. "So the rumors that Isabel was trying to get Hannah hired over the objections of the search committee are true. Why didn't Hannah tell us?"

"She said she was afraid to—she thought you might be furious with her."

"Oh, for heaven's sake. Hannah and I were together twenty years ago!"

"Yes, but she knew about the affair you had with Isabel, and she thought it might just be too awkward."

"Too incestuous you mean? It is a typical case of lesbian embeddedness, I suppose. Oh, that's a nice pun isn't it?" Miriam's nut-brown eyes sparkled. "Well, I don't applaud her taste although I have no right to beef, having succumbed to the same siren song. In hindsight, a case of mistaken identity to say the least. But, also, Isabel has changed . . ."

Vivian smiled indulgently. "Don't we always say that when we are no longer involved with someone? That back then, when they were with us, they were kinder, better people, more hopeful, less cynical . . ."

"I can't say that was ever true of Isabel," Miriam retorted darkly. "She wasn't kind—exciting, yes—but not particularly kind. I should have had my head examined. Actually, I'm surprised that Hannah isn't annoyed with *me*—that I had the bad grace to fall for someone so unscrupulous after her. I would have been offended myself."

"Precisely—she thinks you might be offended now."

"For heaven's sakes! I'm happy, have been for too many years to even think of such foolishness. She knows I am very married, Vivian, and glad to be so."

Vivian leaned in and touched Miriam's arm with affection. "Happiness aside, something's off about this. I think Hannah was here this past weekend, that's what I think. She saw Isabel and now Isabel is dead, and she is terrified for all kinds of reasons."

"Sergeant Crane will have to know this, I suppose," Miriam

43

brooded. "Actually, the best thing is for Hannah to call Crane herself and explain she was here, and . . ."

Vivian's look was severe. "Exactly."

Miriam searched Vivian's face. "But by doing so she would put herself in danger?"

"God, yes!"

"But she has no motive: Isabel was supporting her hire, there was no conflict."

"But there is a conflict of interest," Vivian said shrewdly, crossing her arms across her chest. "The committee has voted to hire another candidate."

"I see what you mean," Miriam spoke slowly. "But, still, it isn't as if Hannah had a grudge against Isabel, if you see what I mean, and that is what the police would be looking for. Other people do— Dennis, for instance, and Bettina, who despises her and makes no attempt to hide her feelings." Her face blanched, "And me, I suppose. I lost the chair position to her in that fiasco of an election six months ago."

Miriam ran her finger along a crevice in the oak finish of the table. If only she could wipe worry from her thoughts as easily as a cloth flicked crumbs from a tabletop. "I wish I had never met Isabel Vittorio."

"You're not the only one, obviously. Come, sweetie, let's take our drinks to the porch."

As Miriam rose to follow Vivian, her thoughts tumbled back to the end of her relationship with Isabel, over a decade ago. The end of their time together had been abrupt. After several months of almost daily contact, Isabel became increasingly preoccupied and erratic about returning calls and keeping dates. Then came an evening when Isabel extended her customary two bourbons to three and then four. After a dinner punctuated by long periods of silence, they sat outside on the patio in the backyard of the tiny house Miriam lived in at the time. Light from inside the house cast shadows across Isabel's brooding face. When Miriam had suggested she go to bed, Isabel turned petulant.

"Not yet." Isabel raised her glass to her lips. "I'm not done drinking."

Miriam made the mistake of replying: "You should be. You'll be sick as a dog tomorrow if you don't stop now."

"It's not your problem." When Miriam didn't reply, a crafty look crept into Isabel's face. "So I'll be sick. And then what? You'll leave me because you think I'm a drunk? Is that it? I didn't know you were such a prude. Miss Prim, Mir-i-am," she chanted and laughed.

"I don't think you're a drunk," Miriam said, exasperated. Although, the truth was, she disliked surly drinkers and this evening prompted the thought that Isabel appeared to be one of those. "I didn't say anything about leaving."

"To leave or not to leave. The big question in any relationship, no?" Isabel said almost dreamily, staring at the sky.

Miriam had noticed that Isabel's moods could change unpredictably, but she'd never seen her behave so erratically before. "Isabel, let's not fight."

"Go ahead, leave," Isabel said, as she sloshed more bourbon into her glass. Her voice, rough and pointed, came at Miriam sharply in the dark like the skid of a tire on gravel. "I won't notice. Someone left me once. Someone I loved. Everybody else since then—like you—has been just passing through."

Miriam felt like she'd been slapped. "Just passing through? Isabel, no . . . that's not true. I care for you, I—"

"Stop." Isabel's eyes, red-rimmed now, Miriam supposed from the alcohol, glared at her. "For God's sake, don't tell me you 'care' for me, or, horror of horrors, that you love me." She dropped her glass and slumped forward, covering her face with her hands. In an instant, her anger turned into tears. "That's what people tell you when they're getting ready to take off."

Although Miriam tried, Isabel refused both comfort and conversation. After a tense half hour, she left Miriam's house, insisting, against Miriam's objections, on driving herself home in spite of her unsteady condition.

She and Isabel never spent any time alone together again after

45

that night. Years later, when she heard that Isabel's mother had died of leukemia when Isabel was only twelve, Miriam seized on this story as a partial explanation for Isabel's sudden, and complete, rejection of her.

Miriam was told Isabel's family history by an unlikely source, her colleague Sigmund Froelich. He took Miriam to lunch one day, trying to calm her agitation after an unruly faculty meeting, one in which Isabel had been unusually combative.

Sig, his feelings usually hidden behind a mask of pompous remove, was in the mood to be confidential. Obviously very fond of Isabel, he attempted to explain, or at least excuse, her behavior. "She doesn't let herself get too close. I don't think she ever got over the death of her mother," he said in a hushed voice. "She was a great beauty. And a superb horsewoman. She taught Isabel to ride when very young—little Belle was only five." He spoke this pet name for his friend, which Miriam had not heard anyone use before, with a proprietary air.

Miriam, distracted from her irritation over Isabel's recalcitrance at the meeting earlier, wished she had known this younger, more vulnerable Isabel. She regretted that she had never even seen Isabel on horseback. She could see it: that lean, proud figure joined with the power of a grand beast. That was where Isabel had belonged, with a creature as graceful and fluid as she.

"Isabel revered the very ground her mother walked on," Sig continued. "And looked up to her. I think she's always wanted to be like her and has felt that she's never measured up." He looked at Miriam with sad eyes. "A loss like that. Well, you just never get over it." He launched into a long discourse about the emotional toll exacted on children who lose a parent at a young age, especially a same-sex parent.

As Sig warmed to his theme, Miriam was swamped by the complex memories she had of her own father, who had died when she was in the fifth grade. Even after more than four decades, she missed Paul Held, not just for his quiet and warm presence, but for his utter sureness about who he was. But she didn't think that loss had made her suspicious of other people's overtures. Rather, it had made her seek intimacy. Perhaps from unworthy people, she thought bitterly, still smarting from Isabel's rejection of her.

During the lunch with Sig that day, Miriam puzzled over Isabel's secrecy about this devastating event in her life. Isabel had said nothing about her closeness to her mother on the occasions when Miriam had mentioned how much she missed her father. Miriam also remembered thinking that it was just like Isabel to harbor such a romantic portrait of her mother. In her experience, the greatest cynics always had someone in their past whom they'd elevated to the highest pedestal of their affections or trust. Of course, that someone had let them down, hard. So hard they could justify having no faith in anyone else ever again.

Isabel had lived a life of absolutes. One in which there were no second chances given, and forgiveness a virtue without value. Miriam reflected how such emotional fundamentalism was an indulgence few people could afford. Hurrying gratefully after Vivian, Miriam thought, *fortunately.*

Fiona arrived home at six that afternoon, fed a tuna Pounce to her calico cat, Dynamo, who sprang outside moments later, outraged at having been locked inside on such a sunny October day. When Fiona checked her phone messages, Darryl Hansen was on the machine:

"Fiona. How about dinner tonight? It's been too long."

Fiona pondered the message. She and Darryl had been involved for six months last year until they'd hit a rocky patch they hadn't been able to resolve. In the intervening months, even though she missed him, she had been holding firm at not resuming their connection. But these were not the times for isolation. Feeling frightened by the ominous events of the week, she longed to talk with someone she knew well: "Oh, hell, why not," she thought and returned the call.

They arranged to meet at a small café on South Congress in two hours. Meanwhile, Fiona checked her home email account. Among the usual spam and listserv updates was a note from Paula Fabian:

47

Fiona—

am coming in this weekend to house-hunt. Any chance I could stay with you a couple of days? It'll be great to see you.
Paula

Fiona emailed back a yes with details about her schedule, but her fingers slid off the keys limply. Paula had obviously received at least an oral contract for the new position, even though, according to Bettina, Dennis still fought for permission to hire. Fiona wondered if she had missed the meeting where the faculty vote had taken place to okay the search committee's recommendation. Two days ago, she would have assumed it would have been pro forma, but in light of Isabel's death and the news about Hannah Weinstein, all bets seemed to be off . . .

Darryl, wearing a denim blue cotton sweater and Levis, looked fit and lightly tanned. He greeted her with a warm hug, his dark blue eyes vibrant against the sweater. He pushed his sleeves up over husky forearms.

"You look terrific," he said, appraising her from top to toe.

Somehow, Fiona thought, when Darryl scanned her body it never felt obtrusive or leering, merely interested and appreciative. It was a wonderful talent, if that was what it was. She decided to simply enjoy it. "You too."

"It's so good to—"

"How nice to—" They broke out laughing as their words tumbled over one another.

Fiona's blonde complexion reddened easily and she felt it flaring now. It *was* good to see Darryl. At this moment, she couldn't imagine why she had ever stopped doing so. A little warning bell chimed in her ear—*slow down, girl.* She took a deep breath. "So how have you been?"

"Okay." He drummed his fingers on the table, a rueful smile creasing his cheeks. "Work is hell right now, as I don't have to tell you. Half my faculty have visited my office in the last two days. Let's see, that makes about two thousand tense minutes."

"Only ten minutes each? Not bad. You must have a good bedside manner."

"I wish. Seriously, I've not experienced anything quite like it."

They spent a few moments reviewing the horrible events of the past two days, chewing on the few details available to them, already so distressingly familiar as to provide no further nutrition, rather like a dog mouthing the tasteless shreds of a chew that had given up its flavor long ago. They ordered a bottle of Heron chardonnay and a plate of mussels to begin. Fiona picked up the pepper mill and rolled it at its base. "Darryl, what was your relationship to Isabel?"

For a moment Darryl looked genuinely horrified. His eyebrows went up. Seeing Fiona's absorbed face, he relaxed. "You mean chair to dean I hope?"

"God, yes." Darryl had something of a reputation among the women faculty for charm, flirtation, and the occasional fling. "Please don't be paranoid like everyone else seems to be."

"It is an epidemic," he agreed. "Well, I don't have to tell you how capable she was. Brilliant in many ways, really. But heavy-handed. And, ambitious—there was no secret about that. I wasn't happy when Miriam didn't assume the chairmanship, I mean the chair-personship, six months ago."

Fiona expelled a breath. "That was not a happy time."

He shifted his broad shoulders uncomfortably in his chair, as if the fabric of his shirt bound him too tightly. "I don't have to tell you your department's decision on that took me by surprise. But why the politics in Literature and Rhetoric should surprise anyone . . ." He shook his head. "Well, Isabel was making great headway as a fund-raiser, and in these times, that's a wonderful thing." He leaned in toward Fiona. "But I didn't like working with her. Everything was difficult, contentious."

Their waiter arrived with their wine, opened it, and melted away to another table.

"Thank God for this," Fiona said and they touched glasses. The wine, dry yet slightly buttery, rolled across her tongue. "I have to ask you something. About Paula Fabian."

"Terrific scholar." Darryl swallowed and then looked at her narrowly. "Just tell me you didn't accept my dinner invitation to get information."

Fiona laughed. "I promise, honestly. I'm just baffled about a few things. And a little scared, too. We don't have to talk about it if you don't want to. But I'll be terribly disappointed if we can't talk just for a few more minutes."

"Fire away. You realize I probably know less than you do," he said in a mock-grumpy tone.

"No one knows less than I do," Fiona said. "I get mostly third-hand information." Her mind touched on Bettina's theories, but he'd probably heard them from her already. Bettina was most likely the queen of gossip in both of their lives.

She reached for her glass. "Okay, back to Paula. I know the committee wants her—which is good news for me, Paula's one of my favorite people—even though Isabel apparently was trying to get someone else. Hannah Weinstein, I believe, who's excellent but not right for this position. Things don't seem decided yet, but I just got an email from Paula saying she's looking for a place to live."

"It's a midyear appointment—housing's tight. She needs to look now," he nodded.

"So she *is* hired? But we haven't voted formally as a department. Unless I missed something . . ."

"Fiona, the Tower wants Paula Fabian." The Tower, another name for the main administrative building, famous for a bloody sniper assault from its twenty-eighth-floor observation deck in the mid-1960s, also served as shorthand for the AU establishment. "I want Paula and so do most of you. Dennis told me about the committee's vote. Only Isabel stood in the way, really, and we're not sure why she changed her mind. Your executive committee met yesterday and approved the hire."

"My God, they met right after Isabel's body was carted away? They didn't waste much time!" Fiona felt her temper flare. "Damn it, why is everything so secretive? You used to be in this department, why can't we have a full faculty meeting and let the rest of us in on it!"

Darryl's forehead crinkled up to his gray-streaked brown forelock. "There's not a lot of time. Paula's very in demand right now—a lot of major universities want her. There just aren't a lot of African American scholars of her caliber."

Fiona said testily: "There aren't a lot of scholars like her period."

Darryl groaned. "I'm sorry, I've been a dean too long. I know she is superb, any categorization aside. She also fills a deficit; she's black and she's a woman and times being what they are, we can't ignore that. The legislature, the faculty, the public, we're beaten over the heads with how white this institution is and look where we are, for God's sake, on the border of Mexico. The state has a huge minority population."

He took a deep breath, smiled tentatively at Fiona. She noticed dark shadows under his eyes for the first time—sleepless nights? When she nodded encouragingly, he went on: "In any case, we need to move quickly. Lester and Froelich are stepping aside on this—even they know that with only one black faculty member, and one Hispanic, the Department of Literature and Rhetoric looks pathetic to the rest of the country. My God, I actually overheard some quota-maniac in the Tower boasting of a faculty member who was one-eighth Native American! Pretty soon the university will be hiring some kind of search firm to hunt down tiny fractions of faculty ethnicity, anything to trumpet our diversity. All of these desperate accountings make us even more of a poster child for lily whiteness."

He sighed, and filled a plate with mussels, which had just materialized on the table. "I told Paula things were on track and asked her to come back for another campus visit. For God's sake, I hope no one messes this up."

"Isabel would have done her damndest."

"Yes, she would have," Darryl said coldly. "That was obvious from a conversation I had with her Friday afternoon."

"Lord," Fiona said. "Everyone saw Isabel Vittorio on Friday. It's too weird. What bothers me is that I've heard no one, *no one,* express any real grief about what happened to her."

He nodded. "It's chilling. Absolutely. Remember that Christie novel, *Murder on the Orient Express*? It turned out there wasn't a single perpetrator of the crime—the whole carload on the train did the murder together. That's what this reminds me of: everyone had a grudge against this woman after her decade of ambitious carnage. It could be any or all of you . . . I mean, of us."

Fiona, taken aback, opened her mouth to demur, but Darryl was immersed in his thoughts. His voice turned wistful. "Do you know what, when she came here, I liked her. She was so bright, so energetic, so pretty, so charismatic."

He said the last word with a particularly mournful tone, as if lamenting the decline of an oft-visited monument. Fiona briefly wondered if there was any history between them of the romantic kind, both of them having rather generous reputations sexually. Bettina's voice echoed in her head: Dallying Darryl, Voracious Vittorio. She shook her head sharply; she really didn't want to go there . . .

The waiter materialized to take the rest of their order. "You can be sure she wanted to be dean someday soon," Fiona said.

Darryl picked up his wineglass with a steady hand. "Oh yes, I can be sure of that."

5

The great politicians, like Churchill or LBJ, seize their moment in history; they don't wait for it to be handed to them. Whether the country appears to be at peace or engaged in obvious conflict, trust me: they are waging war. Advancement demands strategic battles. Greatness requires transgression. Nothing is more thrilling to the public than controlled aggression and nothing—*nothing*—is sexier than success.

Isabel Vittorio, class lecture in political discourse analysis

Exhibit A: Isabel's diary, April 2002

April 13
Ran into Hannah Weinstein this evening in the downstairs lounge. Exclamations all around: so great to see you, didn't know you were presenting at this conference, etc. etc. The usual babble. Ages & ages since I've seen her. Since that seminar on discourse theory four years ago. The one at Rice. Must say BIG improvements in the body dept.—she's lost weight, picked up tone. Looks ten years younger. We make plans to have dinner.

April 14
Wish I could say it had been more suspenseful. Hannah hasn't had much of a sex life in a while. If I'm any judge— & I don't think I've lost my touch on that front. Still . . . all *very* nice. I'm right about the tone: nice legs, nicer breasts.

"Bella." Her voice low . . . & shy, too. "I always hoped this would happen."

Can't decide how I feel about the nickname. Bella—the one Mama gave me. "Why do you call me that?" Try to ask nicely. All the while tracing a line from her navel to her collarbone. Lovely. My head in one place. Body in another.

H. surprised by my question. "It's so beautiful, that's all." Her skin flushes a pretty pink. Then quickly—"I like it, it's soft, it's a part of you I don't always see."

Hmm. So she has a sentimental side. Don't know what to say. Just "Oh." Then sadness. Do I really seem so hard? Not always. Not with Mama. Back when we lived in Virginia. The old white house with woods all around. Her voice from the back porch: "Bella! Bellisima! Bellaluna—where are you? I'm coming to get you . . ." & then she crouches & lunges & hunts for me all over the yard. Ferocious growl—but funny, not scary—& then she finds me behind the tree. Always the same hiding place. I'm four or five then. Still a mite. Then the best part—her long arms scoop me up into her arms. I pretend to struggle. Then cry in a high voice: "The monster, the monster is getting me!" So delicious to pretend to be afraid. The more I cry, the more she squeezes me tighter. I squirm more, pretending to fight her & then—suddenly—go limp, a pretend-faint. Then the very best part—she carries me back to the house & I feel like the most precious, fragile thing. I loved that game, always, *always*—Mama's fierce grip, my little body, all safe, all hidden.

H.'s eyes on me then. Brown with tiny yellow flecks. "That's nice." I kiss her soft lips.

April 22

An odd thing. Back from the conference, I'm brushing my teeth or putting away a dish & feel Hannah—her voice, her eyes, her smooth skin. She lives in my thoughts. Thinking of H. makes me feel excited, happy. For the first time in years I feel possibility. Her voice sounds on the machine three times. I haven't picked up the phone & I haven't called back. Not yet.

Miriam won't speak to me in the hallway. Oh, she'll say hello. But gruffly, like it hurts her throat to mutter a greeting. It's the damned Chair thing. I never thought she wanted it so much—nothing from her those months when I began making noises about campaigning for it. She's so damned conciliatory & cooperative, how could I know what passes through that freaky mind of hers? Such a bitch dealing with her so-deserving/hard-driving/German-Jewish intelligentsia of a type. M. an absolute parody of the genre. This whole year since Sig deposed as Chair she's been acting head. From everything I noticed—off the charts on stress, impatient all the time—I thought she hated it. & she's done this wretched job once before. It's a snake pit & a horror. To think she cared this much!!

Yesterday, I run into her on the way to the mailroom. "Miriam, can we have coffee?" So hard to make the offer & then she looks at me like I'm a viper. How can this woman have changed—from a sweet creature to this harpy—since our fling umpteen years ago? In those days she seemed so soft, so malleable. Either I was desperate at the time . . . or maybe just suffering from some kind of weird culture shock.

This from M: "I'm completely tied up this week."

"Next week then?" I try to keep it light.

"Is-a-bel," the three syllables spool out slowly, separately—in that heavy way of hers, a touch of German somewhere in her speech. I don't remember—was she born there? Her parents were, I know. "Are you feeling guilty?"

Her words like a slap in the face. "Don't pull your psychobabble on me, Professor Held. I'm not one of your little mentees, your little ducklings you herd from room to room." Christ.

She chuckles then. Damn her. "Your temper, Isabel." She looks at me with those little eyes. Like polished pebbles. "It almost makes me like you." & she sails down the hall, if someone with such short little legs can sail. Maybe *waddle* a better word, like her ducklings.

April 24

H. calls again. That warm voice. It lingers on the air. I can feel it on my skin. I pick up. We arrange to meet—I have to go to Washington for the grants meeting anyway. I hang up & feel that delicious rush go through me. I'm not over the hill. I can still feel hot. I laugh at this, but it's lovely. Three more days. I need to have my head examined. Can I afford to fall in love? The next book is due June 1 to Cambridge. Fucking book. Fucking, yes. Book, no.

April 28

Washington beautiful. Hannah lovely. She's moved out of College Park & now has a townhouse kind of out in the country, that endless suburban sprawl in Virginia around the capital. Not like the real country near Farmville where we lived. But nice. I don't see much of the landscape though. Lucky me. H. & I spend most of our time occupied indoors. & eating. She's a fabulous cook. "You're too thin," she clucks, reminding me of Miriam. I blot that out in a hurry.

Then I almost choke on my baked halibut. "How is Miriam?" she asks—perfectly innocent face. I stare at her.

"I wouldn't know." I put my fork down, push my food to the side of the plate. "You haven't talked to her?" I know those two are old friends. How do I know that? Can't remember. Not from Miriam—she guards her precious past.

"Oh, yes, from time to time. We email. You know we once taught together."

Of course. Oregon or somewhere. "So why ask me?"

She laughs & her mouth opens in a perfect round O. She sees me notice her lips & blows me a kiss. Delighted with herself. "Because Miriam won't tell me anything. I haven't talked to her in ages. She's in some kind of funk. I asked Vivian about it but no help there."

"Vivian is the Alice Toklas to the great Gertrude Stein," my voice sours. "She protects her, screens her calls. Nothing must bother the genius at work."

The skin around H.'s eyes pleats softly. "Isabel, that's not quite fair. Vivian isn't a gatekeeper or a hatchet person, not like Alice was said to be." She finishes her food. Such a greedy eater.

"I know Miriam's upset about the chair vote." H. says slowly. Looks at me for a long time but I'm not able to tell what she's thinking.

I want to hurl my plate across the room. "She's so bloody dishonest. I asked her months before if she minded if I throw in my hat. She said: 'You're welcome to it.'"

"Did she?" H. takes a tiny sip of red wine, licks her lips. Her tongue very pointed & very red. "I think she was being polite. She didn't think you were serious."

"Oh, she knew I was serious." A twitch starts in the corner of my eye.

"Don't look at me like that, Bella," H. chides. "So icy. Brrr."

I throw up my hands. "Hannah, let's get something straight. If you want something, tell me. Don't pretend. Don't play coy games, like Miriam apparently did. Okay? I'm a very straightforward person. People just don't understand that. It's all up front with me. No bullshit. All right?"

H. half-stands and leans across the table, those luscious breasts dangling in front of my face. She kisses me, her tongue hot in my mouth. "I want something right now," she says.

editor's note:

Isabel's diary was found by Sergeant Crane: at the bottom of a pile of Edith Wharton novels in my office.* Only hours of tedious legwork, knuckle-grinding worry, and a bit of luck allowed me to discover who planted it there.

*How appropriate: Wharton always said she liked a good joke above anything else

6

The great female moderns all created a parallel universe. There weren't many accounts of untraditional women's lives to chart their way: they wrote the books
they wanted to read, and not only that, they wrote the lives they wanted to live.

Bettina Graf, class lecture, "Virginia Woolf and the Modern Sensibility"

On Friday Bettina brooded at her computer. She'd been stuck for
two months on a section of her Virginia Woolf book, one comparing
several stage and film adaptations of *Orlando*. She staggered to her
feet, stiff and clumsy after hours glued to her chair. What was the
point? Bloomsbury scholars spewed a continuous stream of verbiage
from their ivory towers; the field was mobbed—did the world really
need another critical study of this doubtless fascinating woman? Just
yesterday she'd received a notice from a friend at Smith about an upcoming conference in June 2003, asking if she wanted to contribute a
paper. Bettina envisioned the Woolfian armies swarming from both
sides of the Atlantic toward Northampton, their earnest eyes agleam
at the prospect of new discoveries about their idol's life and work.
And they wouldn't be dissecting the new work by Bettina Sedon
Graf, because she couldn't get the damn thing finished! Bettina
strode to her bedroom, right knee joint protesting, furiously pulled
on gray sweats and shoved her feet into a pair of running shoes. She
could barely contain her impatience to leave the house—well, really,

she needed to escape her office, the scene of procrastination and frustration—long enough to lace them up.

Outside, the October day was glorious. The weather had finally broken through the grinding heat of a long summer. Her mind sang—there is a world out here, it's big, it has real things in it!—as it relished liberation from the mounds of minutia to which it had been tethered all morning.

Bettina waved to her husband, working in his greenhouse, as she left the yard. Not for the first time, she envied Marvin, who after twenty-five years in the botany department at Austin U., had started his own business, Marvin Gardens. She looked back to see his bulky body happily bent over his seedlings. Marvin, in his element helping his clients design their yards and gardens, now gladly cooked meals and kept their Hyde Park bungalow afloat; the whole house bloomed under his green thumb. Their son, Carl, finishing college as a landscape architect, planned to join his father in the business. There were occasional money worries given all of this entrepreneurial activity, of course, but in general Marvin had made an excellent move.

Bettina, forty-nine and restless, contemplated her career options. On this fine day, her body slowly warming up as she walked briskly through her neighborhood toward the Hancock golf course, she couldn't think of a single one but didn't care as much as she had ten minutes before while chained to her desk. *Girl, you've just got to get out more,* she chided herself. Actually, she could think of several new occupations—landscape painting, consulting with older women on career changes, teaching yoga—but couldn't imagine earning more than ten thousand dollars a year doing any one of them. Given the cost of living in Austin, Texas, where inexpensive living was a long-gone relic of the seventies, it just wasn't an option.

At Twenty-ninth Street, under a half mile from her campus office, she remembered some papers she needed to grade before the end of the week. Why not walk there instead of driving over later, she decided. She detoured east toward the red-roofed mini-city that was Austin University.

Choosing the stairs to the seventh floor over the recalcitrant elevator—*keep those quads in shape, fifty is approaching,* she coached herself—she arrived only mildly out of breath. Quiet greeted her: it was six p.m. on a Friday, the one day of the week when there were no late afternoon graduate seminars. She controlled the apprehension that had dogged her in the hallways since Isabel's murder and strode to her office around the corner from the elevator. Catty-corner to her office was Miriam's office, the door of which was open wide. "Miriam?" she called. How lucky to find her colleague in; she needed to talk to her about summer teaching.

There was no answer. Bettina peered into her friend's office, which was smallish but had a large window with a view of the Tower. Miriam would most likely not move into the chair's office until the investigation into Isabel's death was wrapped up. On the desk lay a manila folder. Bettina entered hesitantly and stood in the middle of the office. What was she doing, uninvited, in Miriam's private space? Unable to help herself, she glanced at the folder, which had the intriguing label "minority hires." She nudged it open with a fingernail. Inside was a draft of a letter of appointment addressed to Paula Fabian. The next page was a memo from Isabel, dated the Friday before her death, protesting the procedures of the recent search committee: ". . . I intend to go all the way to the Provost if needed. This search, in my view, violates AAUP regulations. I demand that it be reopened." The memo went on, mentioning Hannah Weinstein and how she had been unfairly overlooked. But, most oddly, the names of the sender and recipient had both been crossed through with a black ballpoint, hard enough to puncture the paper in spots, leaving Isabel's name, as the sender, barely readable, and the recipient's name completely obliterated. It didn't seem like Miriam's style at all. Bettina picked up the folder; did it even belong to Miriam?

A noise in the hall stopped her. Bettina stiffened as a wash of fear swept through her. She put the folder back and eased out of the office. The sound was coming from the men's room around the corner. A moment later, Sigmund Froelich appeared, with his full head of gray hair and lined, but pleasantly attractive, face. Bettina, relieved that the person was someone she knew, raised a hand in greeting. Sig had largely recovered from a stroke last year, but his former rakish aura of agelessness was gone. Bettina sincerely hoped that his illness had relegated his once relentless pursuit of female graduate students into purely a spectator sport. As she felt fresh outrage over Sig's past unethical behavior, Sig turned his head in her direction.

"Bettina, what are you doing here?" He looked pointedly at his watch. "It's officially the weekend!" His eyes scanned her sweat suit and settled somewhere in her mid-chest.

"Hello, Sig. Have you seen Miriam?"

"Yes, Vivian picked her up about an hour ago. They were headed somewhere." He traced a vague arc with one hand and then looked at her hopefully.

"Why is her door open then?" Bettina asked.

"No idea. I was just leaving myself," he said, his face reddening slightly as he ducked into his office on the opposite side of the corridor, two down from Bettina's.

Bettina looked after him for a moment. The yawning office, sans Miriam, troubled her. She wouldn't be surprised if Sigmund had kept his master key from when he was chair. Had he unlocked Miriam's office, or had the door simply not latched when she left? Bettina acted quickly: she hurried back into her colleague's office, lifted the file from Miriam's desk, tucked it under one arm, and firmly shut the door. As a precaution, she rattled the knob to make sure the self-locking mechanism worked—which it had. Then she went into her own office, closed the door except for a crack, and waited. A few minutes later, Sigmund emerged with his briefcase, looked around, shut his office firmly, and walked to the elevator. Bettina both felt the vibration of the old mechanism grinding as it stopped on their floor and then heard its doors crank open and click shut. Bettina located the papers she needed. She secured them with a rubber band and placed the "minority hires" folder on top, deciding she would give the latter to Miriam for safekeeping. Perhaps she would read the file, however, in case it disappeared. Nothing seemed certain anymore—once a dead body was found in the state Isabel's was, stolen file folders and offices mysteriously left open seemed like trifles.

Collin Freed sat with Richard Lester in a bar a few blocks west of Helmsley Hall. God, but the man was a bore. Even though uneasy in the presence of his older colleague, supposedly the most erudite of nineteenth-century American scholars, Collin didn't feel he could refuse: he was up for promotion and tenure this fall, and Lester was a formidable political ally. The conventional wisdom in the department was that you had to have as a champion one of three professors, each of whom could muster enough votes for tenure if they put their muscle behind you: Lester, Miriam Held, or Isabel Vittorio. With Isabel gone, that left the two old adversaries: the lion of traditional scholarship or the priestess of feminist theory.

"Look, Freed," Lester was saying, his small, dapper head bobbing earnestly. "It's just for looks. The EC has already approved Fabian's hire. The faculty will vote to back the executive committee." His voice twisted slightly: "But I don't want that vote unanimous. I don't want Darryl Hansen to think he still runs this department." The dean had been chair of Literature and Rhetoric before assuming the Deanship of Liberal Studies. "So when the vote comes up for Paula Fabian, cast your vote against. It's that simple."

Collin made one timid attempt. He laughed uneasily. "Doctor . . . uh, Richard, don't you think that could make me look like a . . . a—"

Lester laughed. "A racist? Now why should it do that? You're going to vote for Weinstein. She's a Jew. No one can think you're entirely un-p.c."

"But I actually like some of Fabian's work. She has a terrific essay on film theory that I've used a lot."

"So keep using it. Lots of people produce good work; that doesn't mean we have to hire them." Lester focused on him intently. "Don't you care about this department, Freed? Don't you want to uphold the democratic process? What about poor Isabel Vittorio? Don't her dying wishes count for something?"

Collin felt a fat drop of sweat gather in the center of his chest and slide slowly down his stomach. "What do you mean, her dying wishes?" What was the bastard saying, he thought wildly, how would he know? Christ! He'd heard Lester murdered reputations, but . . . was he sitting and having a beer with a psychopath?

Lester's pale gray eyes were mild. "Purely a figure of speech, dear boy. Just a metaphor." Richard Lester took a sip of Scotch and made a mental note to call Sigmund Froelich when he got home, to tell him that Collin Freed was not to be trusted, after all.

Exhibit A: Isabel's diary, May–June, 2002

May 5

Classes ending. Tedious meeting with Hansen & all of the Chairs in the College. I find myself doodling, dreaming about H. & our time together over the weekend. A sudden lift in my spirits: so maybe I don't have to spend the rest of my life alone. Maybe at fifty-two I've found someone, *the* someone.

Weekend begins swimmingly. Until H. drops a bomb in the middle of our lovely time—about her affair with Miriam in Oregon. Eons ago but still turns me cold: can I never escape the eyes & reach of Miriam Held? The woman pollutes everything.

"Really?" I try not to react but feel one of those annoying twitches at the corner of my eye. We're out on her balcony drinking icy cold Pinot Grigio—quite delicious—& eating smoked salmon. My appetite kicks in around H. Have gained back two of the five pounds I dropped this year stressing out over the Chair position.

The question is, does she know that Miriam & I slept together when I first came to Austin? I study her keenly, her flushed & happy face, her huge glistening eyes. Should I bring it up? If I'm going to, now's the time.

"Miriam & I were fairly close at one time. Hard to

believe, I know." I open my mouth to say more but just then the phone rings &—unbelievable!—she races in to answer it. I'm so pissed off that when she comes back I don't say anything. I hope her lunge for the phone isn't some feeble hard-to-get ploy—a demonstration that other things are on par in importance to talking to me.

May 15

Another meeting with Hansen. He hints that Lit. & Rhetoric is under scrutiny for its Anglocentric hiring & promotion practices. He draws me aside: "For God's sakes. I've given you a new line—fill it with someone good. Please, think diversity this time. You've got fifteen percent minority graduate students & look at your faculty. The Legislature doesn't like what it sees."

I don't know why he bothers. The Lege doesn't give us a third of the money it costs to run this place anyway. But I placate him. I tell him I am actively recruiting & that several of the minority men in the Discourse Caucus have expressed interest in AU. A minor fib, but all I need do is get on the phone & I'm sure I can make it good.

May 16

Last night on the phone with H., a question spills out of my mouth: "Why did you & Miriam break up?"

H. sighs. A warm sound but I brace myself. "Why does anyone? Oh, I don't mean to be flip. I guess we were too young. Not long out of graduate school. Not ready for commitment."

I hear an edge of sadness. "Were you very sorry?" My voice small in my ear.

"Well, in some ways. Miriam is such an unusual person."

"How?" I hold my breath.

"I haven't met many people with her intellect who are also so insightful. & so kind."

"That's true." I have to agree but for some reason, I feel wretched.

She's silent. "But, Isabel."

"Yes?"

"We discovered we were meant to be friends. Really. Not partners. Things are the way they should be between us."

"I'm glad," I say & mean it. I know what she means about Miriam. She's so smart & yet so down-to-earth. When we were together, she sometimes made me feel petty & impatient. Like an immature shit. Even when I didn't want to be.

"Hannah, you're pretty special yourself. I wish you were here right now." Oh, yes.

She sends me a kiss through the phone. "I'll see you tomorrow, sweetie. I land at four."

"I'll be there, my dear Hannah."

June 1

Miriam promises to deliver Paula Fabian for the new hire. Unbelievable that she's preempting me like this. She's already talked to Hansen & half the faculty. They're all excited, already scheduling the courses she'll teach as if it's a fait accompli! The woman's nerve is just plain unnerving. I offer her an olive branch—consulting with her & courting her— which she treats like a thicket of poison ivy.

Maybe I should send her my c.v. to nudge her memory. She knows me well enough to know that I take my responsibilities as Chair very seriously. She's overlooking my record deliberately. But why? It's not her style to undermine another woman this way.

June 15

New position now official, joint appointment with Drama. It's very flexible: could be an artist/scholar, a dramatic theorist, a lit. person who also studies drama. The fact is it has to be someone with a reputation in gender & race. I email the position announcement to Hannah. M. & H. are still close friends. We'll see what H.'s application does to the precious Professor Held's loyalties. She claims to be a scholar of Tacitus—she'll see that she's not the only master strategist at work.

At home, Miriam picked up the phone to Bettina's low, confidential voice murmuring something about a file she was afraid was "unsecured."

"What? Wait, slow down. You forget my poor old ears," Miriam said. She put on her reading glasses—somehow this always helped with murky phone conversations.

"Hmm. Well, yes, I did have a file similar to that one."

She listened a moment. "A memo from Isabel threatening to go to the provost over an illegal search? No . . . I've never seen such . . . You'd better bring it by and let me look at it. Uh-huh. Twenty minutes is fine. I'll be here." Bettina lived only a half-mile north of Miriam.

Nervously, Miriam walked up and down the short hallway leading from her office to the living room and had barely gotten into a good pacing rhythm before the doorbell rang. Miriam herded her visitor into her study, Poirot hard at their heels, and the two women plunked into chairs around a small oval table. Poirot retired to his dog bed back in the living room. The field clear, Miriam's tortoiseshell cat, Alice, launched herself from her lair in the corner onto Bettina, her favorite of Miriam's friends, and began to box with the tasseled ends of a green and tan scarf draped around Bettina's neck.

Miriam clapped her hands. "Alice, you hoodlum. Off!"

"It's all right, I can balance Alice and a few papers," Bettina said over Miriam's protests. "Does this even look familiar?" Bettina pointed to the label of the file which she had disgorged from her bag.

"'Minority hires.'" Miriam stuck out her lower lip in cogitation. "No. On my desk I have folders about two recent search committees, one with credentials of the finalists for the new position, a file on Paula, as I've been trying to get her here for years, and of course one on the 'opportunity initiative' as we're ever-so-hopefully calling the new diversity hiring program." She touched the file label with a fingertip. "But no, this isn't my file. 'Minority hires.' Too generic for my filing system," she said primly. "However," she paged through the contents and pulled out two memos, and the draft of the letter to Paula Fabian, "I wrote these."

Bettina studied the two memos. Both were written to Isabel, reporting on conversations with Paula Fabian. "And did you copy the EC on these?"

Miriam looked bewildered. "Absolutely not. I assumed these were, well, not confidential exactly, but not for public view either. I was just letting Isabel know how very positively Paula viewed us. I assumed she would think that good news." She hesitated. "You know, last summer, Darryl reminded me—very gently—that I really must not bypass the chair in my communications with him about hiring. So I made an effort this fall to include Isabel in the deliberations."

"Against your better judgment?" Bettina inquired.

Miriam shook her head slightly, her lips pressed tightly together. "I felt I must try," was all she said.

The two friends pored over the two communications. "You assumed Isabel shared your enthusiasm for all Paula could give the department: fresh perspective, new leadership, connections with the African American Studies Center, the Women's Studies Center," Bettina spoke slowly and heavily. "But your arguments were seen differently: Isabel saw your efforts—and the prospect of Paula—as a threat to her own influence perhaps? An erosion of her power base?"

Miriam left the table and sat heavily in her worn armchair by the window. She stared out at the deepening shadows in her backyard, which was thickly wooded with pecan and red oak. "Her opposition to Paula—which really emerged only recently by the way—made no sense to me. Until I talked to Vivian about it. Did you know that Isabel had become intimate with Hannah Weinstein in the past months?"

Bettina shook her head in the negative. "No. I don't know Hannah, except on paper. And Isabel and I absolutely never talked to each other about our private lives."

"Well, it's hard for me to believe Isabel couldn't see Paula's attributes. And the two shared no research areas in common; there would be no competition there. It has to be that Isabel genuinely wanted Hannah for the position. They would no longer have to commute. Perhaps they are also collaborating on something together—some of their research indeed overlaps, although Hannah is also interested in performance."

"Oh, I'd say Isabel is very intrigued with performance," Bettina said with a laugh.

"Yes, if you mean the way she comports herself," Miriam parried, her eyes snapping with humor. "But I'm referring to the academic discipline of performance. As you know very well. But back to what I was saying: there are many advantages in having Hannah here, for Isabel and for us. Hannah is a good team-player. There's no doubt she'd be an asset to the department."

Bettina's green eyes drifted toward a paper mobile of tropical fish rotating slowly from the ceiling. "She would also be a senior faculty member under Isabel's control if she came—she would owe Queen Bella many chits for getting her the job. I cannot share your optimistic view of Isabel's motives."

Miriam raised her hands and let them drop. "I don't know." A house wren scurried across her wooden fence, stopped, warbled brightly, and then hopped away. "Sometimes I like birds better than people," Miriam said moodily. "They are direct: they call to attract a mate, to warn their offspring, to greet the day. They don't lie: they don't herald dawn and say, 'disregard that—just kidding,' for instance."

"Hmm, probably not." Bettina said absently as she sifted through the folder once more. She had just noticed a sheet stuck to another page at the rear of the file. "Look at this," she brought the sheet to Miriam.

Dean Hansen: I want to inform you about a serious lapse in ethical standards in the proposed hiring of Paula Fabian. One, she was never formally invited for an interview; two, the position was improperly posted: it was not listed in appropriate national venues but was strictly in-house, word-of-mouth or whatever you call something not advertised according to equal opportunity federal regulations; three, Dr. Fabian is being recruited on the basis of her race rather than on her academic credentials. As you well know, recruitment on grounds of racial preference—for either students or faculty—is illegal in the state of Texas under the Hopwood decision. A memo written by Dr. Miriam Held (dated August 15, 2002) specifically discusses Fabian's appropriateness for the position based on her African American heritage.

The letter was unsigned and dated Monday, October 14, the day Isabel's body was found sprawled on her desk in her office.

"Who wrote these falsities?" Miriam's hands trembled as she held the letter close to her face as if to sniff the identity of its writer. "Paula Fabian has an international reputation for excellence; racial preferences have nothing to do with anything. I wrote no memo discussing race. And this position was posted in three major national academic newsletters as well as the usual national print media."

"Miriam, listen to me. Accuracy and truth are beside the point: this letter is meant to discredit you and Paula Fabian."

Disengaging Alice, Bettina rose and strode across the room, her silk scarf streaming behind her. She paused in front of the window, the waning light highlighting a few silver strands twisting through her red hair. "It's someone—or maybe several ones—who wants to change the entire tenor of the department. Think about it: with Isabel gone, if you're driven into some corner of silence, that leaves only one female full professor in Lit. and Rhetoric—me. I'd be totally marginalized and so would gender studies. Paula would not come, so Larry Edwards would remain as the lone African American faculty member; with no support, he and his work would be shoved to the sidelines as well. They'll get rid of Carlos Lambros next, and they'll figure out a way to make me sufficiently miserable to leave too. Or maybe they'll just have my position axed somehow."

"Ach, it's like a pogrom," Miriam said. "A coup."

"They want to return to 1955 or some other idyllic date in the minds of whichever cretins wrote this," Bettina said hotly. "It's academic fundamentalism! Think about it: if we turn back the clock to erase multiculturalism, eliminate faculty who can teach gender, race, and sexuality, we can return to 'values' and 'standards'—forget relativistic postmodern thinking, poststructuralist perspectives, performative writing, *feminine ecriture*—"

Bettina was just warming up when Miriam broke in. "—Poststructuralism we can most likely live without," she said. "But seriously, it's ridiculous! They'd never attract graduate students to a program like that. Or new faculty."

"Oh yes, they would attract some—the population they want, as retro and reactionary as they are. It's part of the whole country's shift to the right: a lot of students would be more comfortable with the old canon; after all, if you have *the* list of Great Books, then you read them and can claim you are educated. There's nothing slippery about it: no choices to sweat, no critical thinking of your own to do. How many times have you had students say to you, 'Just tell me what you want and I'll do it.' It's a discomfort with ambiguity. The hope that even in the most complex of moral situations, there is the single, perfect right answer." She brushed her hands together in a gesture Miriam found very familiar: the master teacher dispelling chalk dust from her fingers after making a point.

Bettina took a breath and concluded: "Everyone wants to be spoon-fed. They want their choices black and white, thank you very much. But the world is full of shades of gray. Or fuchsia." She shrugged. "Life is tough all over."

Miriam studied the letter again. "I see what you're saying," she said slowly. "And yes, there are those in the department who would like to return to the way things were several decades ago. But that's not the point of this letter." She turned her face up to Bettina, squinting in concentration so that her eyes were narrow, shining slits of brown. "This letter isn't signed. It would never be taken seriously by Hansen unless it was. I doubt it was sent or will be sent to him."

She tapped the paper rhythmically with a pencil. "No, this person left this file on my desk. Deliberately. The copies of my memos, the note from Isabel. They're telling me they've been watching me, that they know what I know. They want to scare me." She lifted the piece of paper to the window where it became almost transparent. "This is a warning."

Bettina, ignoring a tweak of pain from her right knee, squatted in front of Miriam. "Not just to you but possibly a warning to Paula as well. And to all of us who support her. So what should we do?"

Miriam folded her legs tailor-style in her chair and grinned, showing strong, square teeth, rendering her a hybrid of canny Cheshire Cat and miniature Buddha. "Nothing. Go on as before." She radiated a calm alertness.

Bettina returned to her chair, her hunched shoulders indicating she did not share her friend's equanimity. "Miriam! I don't think that's wise. This could be serious, a hint of things to come. Isabel is dead, remember? She didn't get that way by herself."

Miriam turned her head slowly in Bettina's direction, her eyes slightly out of focus as she thought. "I said I would not change my outward behavior. Of course I will do something: I will use the power women like us do have: I will talk. I will not be silent. If something happens to me, there will be trails to follow."

Bettina's substantial chest heaved in a deep sigh. She lifted handfuls of hair from the back of her neck and resituated her scarf, its muted greens warming her peachy skin. She dropped her hair as if lowering a curtain. Chin jutting forward, she braced her arms firmly on her thighs, and pronounced: "I disagree. Talk doesn't even come close to being enough in this case. And we can't wait until something happens to you to flush this person out. We have to set a trap, and we have to set it now."

7

Fiona looked up from her book. "Where does the expression 'rat in a trap' come from?" she asked. "Rats are greedy," her father answered. "They're gluttons. One way to catch one is to offer it something it likes to eat. It can't help itself—it'll always eat more than is good for it. That's why rat poison works so well. You hide the poison inside something tasty and the rat will eat itself to death."

conversation between eight-year-old Fiona and her father, Bert Hardison, 1965

*F*iona drove to Bergstrom International to pick up Paula Fabian on Sunday. A high pressure dome had settled on Austin, and the mild, clear weather continued. Fiona listened to the golden oldies station and sang along cheerily to "Hotel California" as she drove out Riverside Drive to 71, the land flattening as she headed east. Austin, resting in the Texas hill country, rolling and rich with rivers and lakes, stood at a crossroads of climatological zones. A driver heading in any direction from Austin at the center of the state quickly discovers a terrain change: plains to the north toward Dallas, semi-tropics to the south on the way to San Antonio, dry-as-dust West Texas wending toward El Paso, and the richer soil of East Texas on the road to coastal Houston and the bayous of Louisiana.

Paula, a vision of elegance, already waited outside the baggage area as Fiona inched through arrivals: slender and tall (six one) with shoulder-length, glossy black locks and espresso-colored skin, she wore heavy silver jewelry around her neck and both forearms. As she stood in the sun, the rest of Austin indeed paled around her.

Fiona, wishing she hadn't traded in her much-aged and

much-beloved MGB, felt stodgy in her tan Toyota Camry. The apple-red "B," purchased to celebrate her early tenure when she was thirty-one, had only been reluctantly sold when Fiona's back began to rebel against its low-slung charms. Ah, youth, she thought as she popped the sedan's trunk and rushed out to greet Paula.

Steering away from university politics, Fiona gave Paula a short tour of Austin on the way back into her neighborhood, Travis Heights, just south of the Capitol and the river. Her guest was most excited to hear she had arrived early enough in the autumn for sun-set bat-watching on the famed Congress Avenue bridge, where the world's largest urban bat population (exceeding a million Mexican Freetail bats at its peak) ventured forth at dusk each night. In turn, Fiona's spirits surged at the opportunity to discuss benign night-seeking mammals rather than campus horrors perpetuated by ro-dents of a human, and far more dangerous, persuasion.

Unfortunately, Fiona destroyed the moment of respite herself. As they pulled up to the curb of her house on Alameda Street, she couldn't resist blurting, "Isn't it ironic that people are afraid of bats? They think they're blood-sucking vampires when they're really only interested in devouring pesky mosquitoes. Instead of a scourge, the creatures are altruistic!"

The word "vampires" apparently created a synapse in Paula's mind with the recent murder, and she immediately countered: "All right. Spill. Di-vulge. Should I be quaking even setting foot in this town after what happened to Isabel?"

"Do you want the long version or the short?" Fiona asked as she struggled with the house key and several sacks of provisions she had picked up on the way to the airport. Paula, who had one compact rolling bag, took the key from her and easily opened the door.

"Longest, of course. The unexpurgated version."

Dynamo peeked around the corner of the kitchen and peered at Paula, then scampered away as they approached. Her feline caution required time to vet the new guest.

"I think she's spooked by the sound of your wheels," Fiona nod-ded at Paula's bag. "She's very skittish."

Paula held out her hand to try to entice Dynamo, who now played hide-and-seek from behind the dining room table. "I'm afraid I only know dogs well," Paula said. "But don't try and change the subject."

The phone rang as Fiona dumped the grocery sacks on the counter. "Yes? Bettina! . . . uh-huh. Just picked her up. What? A party? Okay. She's here 'til Wednesday. So . . . Monday. Miriam says morale is horrid? Well, yes . . . Fine."

Fiona turned around with a smile. "You're in luck. Rather than listen to my boring recitation, you can meet all of the possible suspects and decide for yourself. Bettina is having a faculty party in honor of you, tomorrow night." She looked at Paula wistfully. "I wish you were just here for a social visit, a gabfest. Instead, you have to work, impress people, all that. And now this party."

"The party's a good thing," Paula retorted. "I need to get a sense of what the entire faculty is like anyway, see where all the dead bodies are buried." A mild ruddiness appeared under her dark skin. "Sorry."

Fiona laughed. "Some of the deadest bodies are still living, I'm afraid. Oh, you'll feel a vibe all right. So many you won't even know which frequency to focus on. Right now there are several factions. Bettina and I will coach you."

Paula put one hand on a slim hip and cocked her head to one side. "Please don't. Let me just do some quiet recon on my own. You'll see, I'll stay below the radar, and you'll be amazed what I'll be able to tell you after just one hour."

Fiona appraised her glamorous friend: even her voice, clear and low like a perfectly struck bell, set her apart. She doubted Paula could remain undercover for more than a half-second after walking through Bettina's door.

Monday morning Miriam was greeted by a small cadre of Isabel's students picketing in the courtyard in front of Helmsley Hall. A charismatic undergraduate teacher, Isabel had inspired some adoring followers. One of them, Reggie Bradley, a senior in the department, had been an occasional paid gofer for the slain chair. She seemed to be leading the group of protesters. Her sign said, "Murder most foul!" and her face was heavily made-up, one half smeared with black greasepaint, the other half with white. Tall and hunched, with bleached and raggedly chopped hair, she was a furtive and frightening reminder to Miriam of the uncharted landmines lying in wait everywhere since Isabel's death. Isabel's memorial service was scheduled for this coming Wednesday. Miriam would be glad to have it behind her.

Reggie planted herself in front of Miriam, so close Miriam could smell her breath, which had a stale, faintly metallic odor. "Conspirator," Reggie hissed.

Miriam tried to think of the young woman's loss and probable confusion rather than her own natural repugnance to the student's name-calling. She made an attempt as well to overlook Reggie's slavish devotion to Isabel, which had always seemed slightly inappropriate. During her five long years of undergraduate occupation at Austin U., Reggie had taken every course Isabel had offered, in addition to two independent studies. Far from discouraging Reggie's devotion, Miriam knew Isabel had paid her out of her own endowed professorship for vague duties over the past two years. She questioned Isabel's ethicality toward the young woman. In Miriam's view, as Reggie's advisor, Vittorio should have encouraged her to take a wider variety of courses and experience other faculty. She wondered also whether the monetary connection had influenced the quality of Reggie's dedication.

Miriam gave the angry young woman a steady look. "Why don't you come see me in my office," she suggested. "I'd be happy to talk with you."

"Ha! I'll bet you would." Reggie hurled at her. "Would I need a bodyguard for protection?" Miriam stared at her and out of the corner of her eye saw another poster waving in the air: "Dr. Held: Our Own Lady Macbeth."

Startled by this public accusation, Miriam stepped back and retraced her steps to enter the building from the other side. But as she opened the door, she began to giggle helplessly. The idea of her short, Jewish, lesbian, academic, and unglamorous self as Lady

Macbeth—the epitome of female heterosexual beauty and elegance, slavishly devoted to her husband's advancement—struck her as hilarious. She couldn't wait to tell Bettina and Fiona about the incident. Then, her step slowed. She did need to talk to Reggie Bradley. The young woman had been close to Isabel. Sometimes students, especially when they were in thrall to their mentors—observing and memorizing every crumb of information about those they had elevated to a pedestal—really might have noticed something no one else had.

Exhibit A: Isabel's diary, June–July, 2002

June 22
H. reluctant to apply for the position at Austin U. "Why not?" I ask cautiously. *Why the hell not?* I wonder.

"Isabel. We haven't been together very long. It seems premature. What if you get sick of me in a month or two"— & here she gives me an odd, arch look, that "your reputation precedes you" kind of a glance—"it would be horrid if I were in the process of moving to Austin to be in your department."

"That's cynical," I say hotly. "& it doesn't show much confidence in me."

She picks up my hand then. We're in her apartment again in Virginia, on the chenille sofa in her study. "Don't be mad. It's just that I'm not young any more. I know how quickly things can change. I'm just being realistic."

Dumbstruck am I. She's seemed like such a romantic— not the hard-headed realistic type at all. I'll have to regroup. Have I misjudged her? "I don't think that will h-happen," I stammer. To my surprise, I feel wounded—she doesn't trust me. I withdraw my hand.

She looks at me with her soft brown eyes. "I'm not right for the position, you know. Miriam will see that in a heartbeat. She misses nothing. I don't want to look foolish."

I feel relieved. "Oh, is that it?" I put my arms around her. "Hannah, my dear, it's not what you think. The position is flexible. I don't think the committee really knows what they want."

She laughs, her voice a high trill. "They want a theory-head, you know that. A high postmodernist. They don't want a discourse analyst like me. If you were applying, Isabel, even with your reputation, they'd put you in the stack headed straight for the nearest round file & you know it."

"I don't think that's true."

"Of course it's true! I study texts, I analyze them minutely. To the young turks in your department, I might as well be a new critic, living in the 1950s."

"Listen to me. The young turks don't have the power. The people who do—Lester, Froelich, Held, & even Graf—are old-fashioned scholars in the same sense you are. They're not into trends, & they're not just *theory-heads* as you put it."

She smirks at me. "How can you put Miriam & Bettina in the same breath as Richard & Sigmund? They're on opposite sides of the ideological fence. & I don't think Held & Graf think of themselves as old-fashioned either. Oh no. My dear, you'll never last as Chair at this rate."

I want to slap her. "Oh, you just don't want to listen. Forget it. Let's just drop it."

June 26

Things calmer between us. H. now says she'll at least think about the job. I was tough about it, telling her: "I don't know if I can see you anymore if you think I'm that capricious." That made an impact.

Of course, she's right. I've been capricious about sex most of my life. But that's not the point. People change. How dare she be so cynical so soon? Cynicism has always been *my* failing. It's so discouraging to find your own shortcomings in someone you care about.

July 10

"All right," H. says wearily after an afternoon of stony silence. "I'll apply. But it won't go anywhere. They won't look at me twice. The word is that this job is earmarked for Paula Fabian. I haven't a prayer."

Enthusiastic kiss & many smiles from me. "You're making the right choice, darling. You're the kind of sensible centrist the department needs." I laugh. "Actually, Bettina Graf, who usually utterly grates on my nerves, once said something incredibly insightful about interviews: she said as long as you drop a few key words & phrases like 'heteronormativity' & 'multiplicity of meaning' & 'normalizing ideologies,' everyone will think you're brilliant."

Hannah looks dubious at this. "& the drama part of the position? Will my foray into children's theatre be enough? I have the play & that book of essays on performance art."

"Actually, that department is low on critical analysis right now. I doubt their students know how to closely read a text." I make a note to talk with Dennis as soon as I head home to line up his support for Hannah. "Plus, what can Paula offer them? She works more within film criticism, really, than dramatic analysis. Believe me, you're made to order."

On Monday, Fiona escorted Paula on a brutal round of appointments: guest lectures, lunch with the dean, office hours with faculty, and a stint in her own senior seminar, "Literature and Film." There, Paula delivered a paper on class and the marked body in *The French Lieutenant's Woman* and led a discussion over sections of the film.

Fiona observed her three African American female students take particular notice of Paula. She guessed that even more than the other students, they scrutinized everything—Paula's clothing, her turns of phrase, her presentation of self and womanhood—with a special critical lens. They had to decide if Paula represented them or not, and if so, in which ways and to what ends.

One of the three, Pamela, a very talented writer, commented: "I always regarded the Victorian era in England as culturally foreign. With no connection to me or my life. So I resisted Fowles's novel. But, the book and film is really about the process of writing, of constructing stories."

"And the reliability, or lack of it, of storytellers," another student chimed in.

Paula nodded. "Fowles shows the unreliability, the undecidability, of all narrators. That's true in life too, isn't it? We all put ourselves at the center of our story, and arrange the details according to the impact they have on us. That makes us very unreliable."

These observations launched a discussion of the intricacy of narrative structure in nineteenth- versus twentieth-century fiction and speculations about early-twenty-first-century conventions. The students applauded Paula with genuine enthusiasm at the end.

"Good discussion. You got them thinking," Fiona said as they walked out of the building after class.

"Glad you thought so. They're good students," Paula replied. "It's funny how most people of their generation find Victorian England as far away as outer space. I think this is even truer for many African Americans who are more attuned to an oral culture than such a highly literate one. The humor particularly doesn't penetrate."

"Didn't you tell me once you've spent a lot of time in Britain?" Fiona asked as they hiked almost nine blocks to the fine arts complex where Paula was to take part in a workshop on cross-race performance.

"Yes. My mother was actually born in England, so the British sensibility never seemed that odd to me. And I've taught a couple of summers in our Oxford program. My husband actually fell in love with the place." She chuckled. "Brian's a hopeless fan of British t.v. He gluts on mysteries—his drug of choice at the moment is Inspector Barnaby."

"He should be here with you," Fiona said. "If you're going to look at houses and neighborhoods and all."

"We talked about that. But he promised our daughter that he'd be there for her school play. Alison was not happy with me leaving and missing it."

They stopped for a moment in front of the fountain near the theatre building, which gushed enthusiastically all over the sidewalk. "Oh, I do like this side of campus. It's so spacious and green and just so . . . well, big." Paula said. "This whole place was built on such a grand scale. And your libraries just make me drool. Promise we'll have time to visit the archives in the Research Center?"

Fiona looked across the street at the massive football stadium and nodded. "You can't beat Texans when it comes to thinking big. And that's both a good thing and a bad thing."

The two women laughed and Fiona said: "About the Research Center, Carter—you know, Dennis's partner—has promised you a personal tour. Now, that's one place where thinking big has really paid off. I don't think you'll be disappointed. The collections are really incredible."

Fiona checked her watch. It was three o'clock. "I'll pick you up at four and take you home. That way you can rest for a couple of hours before the party. Meanwhile, break a leg in the Drama Department."

A thunderstorm blew in at four, and just as speedily, withdrew. By six-thirty when they had to leave for Bettina's, the sidewalks were dry and the air washed clean of dust and damp.

Fiona squinted up at the sky as they walked to her car. "You can't trust the weather here. In Texas, it's equally likely that a sudden downpour will skip in a staccato rhythm to another location as it will stick around and sock us in for a week or so. It's a crap-shoot."

"Like Texas politics?" Paula offered.

"That's more predictable," Fiona grinned, "as crap-shoots go. Although, lately, the politics here have seemed like just plain crap to me. Schools getting cut, more testing, less attention to reading and writing, and all the blowhards boasting that everything's great 'cuz they're not raising taxes. We're getting Bushwacked all of the time— and I mean that with a capital 'B.'"

The two women slid into their respective sides of the car. As she buckled up, Paula said: "I live in Washington, remember? You don't have to tell me about the relentless grind politics can be. In fact, I'm plenty tired of living in such a huge city, especially one so obsessed with influence and power." Paula looked approvingly at the hiking trails along the river as they drove across the bridge. "Austin seems more manageable. Brian and I would like to get Alison to a smaller place, one with more community spirit. Brian wants to live somewhere where he can get involved in local politics."

"Austin still thinks of itself as a small town," Fiona said. "There's a special issue—and an election to resolve it—every five minutes. If you like to act locally, it's a good city." Fiona thought a moment. "I really like this place. And Texans think of it as the 'garden spot of Texas.' But I don't want to push too hard." Fiona struggled to represent other points of view. "Some of my African American friends grumble about the city. They feel the community's too decentralized. You'll have to snoop around and experience it for yourself."

Paula nodded. "That's what Brian tells me. He has family in Dallas so he knows this place some. I'm the one who thinks: Texas? And freaks. I guess I'm a typical northerner in that respect. And he says, 'Well, there's Texas and there's Austin.'"

"A cynic would say, 'Okay, but it's still Texas.' It's still too hot in the summer and Texans are conservative by nature," Fiona said thoughtfully.

"What do you say to that?" Paula asked.

Fiona shrugged. "I say there are trade-offs everywhere you choose to live." She made a face so that her nose crinkled. "If you find the perfect place, let me know. Until then, this is where you'll find me."

Bettina and Marvin's deck on Avenue F was aglow when they arrived. The day's light was fading, but Marvin had festooned colored lights in the shape of armadillos and wound them all over the bushes and the back of the house.

Paula disappeared into the crowd under the twin protective wings of Bettina and Miriam, headed for introductions and a multitude of short, intense conversations. Fiona poured herself a glass of white wine and strolled around the yard, nodding pleasantly at colleagues and friends. She admired a small burbling fountain in the center of the backyard and a new border of purple fountain grass along the property line, but avoided touching down in any of the small groups scattered around Marvin's landscaping. Instead, after one circuit, Fiona retreated indoors, patted the golden retriever, Barney, and walked through the living room and down the hallway toward Bettina's office in search of a book. As Paula's campus guide, introducing her for several events and delivering her to the day's appointments, Fiona had undergone a day so full of interaction that she didn't think she could talk to one more person.

The synthetic soles of her black slides glided noiselessly on the oak floors, but a murmur of voices caused her to halt mid-stride before she reached her friend's office.

". . . I don't think it's wise," a deep, hoarse voice was saying. "There are too many people here."

"That's why it's perfect," the other speaker, distinctly female but with a very low, almost tenor pitch, announced. "You want everyone here. They'll hear it and see it for themselves—it'll cut down on rumors later. Believe me, this is the best chance you have. If you don't act now, you'll regret it forever."

"It's not safe," the hoarse man insisted. Definitely familiar to her ears, his voice pattern tugged at Fiona's recognition. After a mind-wracking moment in which a signal seemed to bounce aimlessly from cell to cell in her brain without connecting, the voice registered: it was Richard Lester, with a bad cold. But who was he talking to?

"All right," Lester's companion, Ms. Tenor, said with a sigh. "But you're wasting a perfect opportunity."

After a long coughing spell, Lester replied irritably: "There will be others. Paula Fabian is perfectly capable of hanging herself."

Fiona froze outside the door. Paula . . .

The woman laughed, her voice musical. "You have a point there. It's obvious exactly who she is every time she opens her mouth. Her motives, her prejudices, her incredible narrow-mindedness couldn't be more transparent."

Fiona was stunned by the unself-consciousness of this limited person who projected her Lilliputian point of view onto other people.
Rather than risk discovery lurking in the hallway, she decided to
make a bold entrance and find out the identity of Lester's companion.
Lifting her feet in slow motion, she backed up soundlessly, and when
she reached the other end of the hall called: "Good boy, Barney!"

She then scuffed as noisily as she could back down the hall and
stuck her head into the door of Bettina's lair. Tension made her
breathing and heart rates speed up as if she'd sprinted a half mile.
"Oh!" she said with (she hoped) genuine surprise, "I thought I could
just hide away in here for a few minutes. Sorry to disturb. I hope I'm
not interrupting anything important," she fibbed.

She smiled cheerily at Lester, whose face first creased in alarm and
then went blank as he shot a look at the woman sitting across from
him. He shifted on the sofa, half-stood, thought better of it, adjusted
his tie instead, and said raspily: "Oh, hi, Fiona. Come on in. Nothing
important. We're just escaping the madding crowd." He managed to
scrape out a self-conscious laugh from his congested throat. "I'm not
sure you know Mary Morton from the Drama Department."

Fiona nodded at a solid woman in green knit slacks and a
black tank top that displayed beefy but toned arms. The woman's
face froze in a forced smile. She looked in her mid-thirties, Fiona
guessed. "No, we haven't met, but one of your colleagues is a friend
of mine—you must know Dennis Reagan."

Mary stood, revealing short legs and a thick torso. She grasped
Fiona's hand in her own rather clammy one. "Of course. One of my
favorite people."

Liar, Fiona thought. But as she released Mary's hand, she said:
"Mine too." Fiona recalled Dennis mentioning that Mary Morton
was the only person who had voted for Hannah Weinstein on the
search committee. That is, until Isabel changed her vote. She couldn't
recall any other information about her at the moment.

"Enjoying the party?" Fiona said, her heart still ticking at a rapid
rate, wishing she could just blurt: and what in hell are you two up to?

"Oh, yes. Marvin and Bettina are so sweet," Mary said, a blush fading on her very fair skin. "Bettina is such, well, such an original, isn't she? I've heard so much about her."

"There is no one like her," Fiona agreed, swallowing her reaction to the insipid descriptor of *sweet* applied to Marvin and Bettina collectively.

"Well," Lester croaked, getting unsteadily to his feet. "Mary and I were just on our way back to the throng. Mustn't ignore the guest of honor, must we?" He fairly lunged to snare Mary's elbow, and without a glance back at Fiona, steered her out of the room.

"Nice to—" Mary managed before she was thrust out the door.

"Delightful," Fiona called after her. As soon as the pair had retreated, she quickly shut the door. Unfortunately, the room had no lock; she might be interrupted at any time. She sat in the tatty peach wingback chair Mary had just occupied and studied the room. Nothing looked out of order, but it was hard to tell—Bettina practiced the pile method, and her office tended toward the chaotic. The mounds of paper on Bettina's desk didn't look either too neatly stacked or too hastily pawed through.

Fiona tipped her head back and stared at the ceiling fan rotating lazily above her. She rose out of the chair, scanned the bookcases, perched on one end of the sofa, drummed her fingers on its arm, and again surveyed the room. Her eyes strayed to a wastebasket to the left of Bettina's desk, which she now faced. As her eyes moved from the wastebasket along the floor, she noticed a wad of crumpled paper on the carpet, practically at her feet. Odd that she hadn't seen it before. Might it have fallen from Lester's pocket during his hurried exit?

She stretched out, scooped up the paper, and smoothed it out on her lap. Fiona concentrated on listening for interruptions from the hallway. No footsteps sounded; she heard only the click of nails and a soft thump as Barney lowered his bulk to the floor for a nap outside the office door. Fiona counted on him to bark and warn her if someone headed her way.

She discovered that what she'd found was really two thin sheets of paper twisted together. The first was a photocopy of a paragraph from an essay. Underneath the copy was written, in Bettina's looping handwriting: "This section of Richard Lester's 2000 book on Mark Twain sound familiar?" Below this was an identical paragraph from *Gender and Poetics* by Paula Fabian. Fiona had used this text in class and knew Paula's book had come out much earlier, in 1994 or so.

Fiona blew air out of her mouth in rapid puffs. Richard Lester, a plagiarist? And, one who had the poor taste (and, cynics would say, bad luck) to steal the work of the very woman his department wished to hire? Incredible.

The second sheet was standard inkjet printer issue:

To: Miriam Held
From: Bettina Graf
Date: Oct. 2, 2002
RE: Search

I am now almost certain that Isabel Vittorio offered the current position to two candidates. First, to Paula Fabian and secondly, before she had received a reply from Paula, to Hannah Weinstein. To protect the department, if this is even possible given what has occurred, I think the wisest course is to make Isabel's actions public, perhaps going so far as to publish Vittorio's letter to Fabian in the *Austin Journal Observer*.

Fiona stared at this second sheet stupidly. Was this true, that Isabel had already offered Paula the job before her death? This *was* news: if there was a paper trail of Isabel negotiating a faculty appointment with Paula, and then Isabel reopened the search and offered the job to Hannah, things were in a serious state. The department would be seen as violating not only ethical standards but federal equal opportunity hiring practices. She read the words again. The letter was not Bettina's style at all: too crude, too clandestine. She would never record her suspicions on paper like this; she would have just called Miriam and discussed them with her. Had Lester and Mary planted this paper in Bettina's study? Lester certainly wouldn't have wished to disseminate the accusation of plagiarism.

Puzzled that Richard Lester and Mary had left these documents, Fiona reasoned that she had interrupted them and one of them had tossed them on the floor in a reflex of surprise. In light of the memo, she wondered what Lester meant when he told Mary that something was too risky. Had she suggested he rush outside and confront the faculty about an illegal job search, discrediting Paula publicly in the process, to deflect any attention on the plagiarized passage? If he made Paula look bad enough, who would care that he had "borrowed" her research? Or, maybe he was too confident to even be embarrassed by Bettina's discovery. She could imagine his dry, acerbic voice proclaiming, à la T.S. Eliot: "Lesser mortals plagiarize. Great thinkers steal flagrantly."

She suspected he had plotted a way to sink the search itself, managing in the process to ridicule both Miriam's leadership (and her minority initiative) and Paula's professionalism. Perhaps the search would have to be terminated. . . . Fiona's head felt like it was swarming with wasps.

Fiona's thoughts chased each other for some time in an ever-deeper muddle of possibilities; when she finally checked her watch it said, impossibly, nine-thirty. The party was supposed to be a seven-to-nine affair. She opened Bettina's window and listened but heard no sounds of chatter, laughter, or music.

Soon after, footsteps sounded down the hall, and Miriam walked into the room, closely followed by Bettina. "Fiona, there you are," Miriam said, her face erupting in a smile.

Fiona handed Miriam the wrinkled papers. "I discovered Lester and Mary in here. And then I found this."

Miriam chuckled. Bettina joined her and their laughter chorused harshly in the small room. "Excellent," Miriam said.

"Oh, those two saw this all right," Bettina said. "Did you see how they made a beeline for Sigmund when they came onto the deck? They were fairly vibrating."

"I don't get it," Fiona said slowly.

"Just a little mischief, my dear," Miriam said.

"This isn't a real memo?" Fiona asked, pointing to the October 2 communication.

"Oh, no," Bettina said. "But something is very irregular about this search." She told Fiona about the file she had found in Miriam's office with its letter claiming a racial bias in the consideration of Paula Fabian. "There are alleged irregularities in Isabel's—and the department's—procedure."

"But, wait," Fiona said. "Let me get this clear for a minute: why would Isabel write a letter to the Provost about illegalities in the search when she was ultimately responsible?"

Miriam intervened impatiently: "This is the problem. Someone is making trouble. We are doubtful that letter was even written by Isabel."

"That's right," Bettina assented. "As for an offer of employment, we don't know what was actually promised or to whom. But we need to find out, and we don't want Miriam, as the current chair, to inherit Isabel's scandal if we can help it. Paula's reputation is at stake, too."

"Did Isabel actually send out such a letter—one making a real offer? It should be simple to ask Paula."

"Yes, Paula did receive a letter," Bettina said. "It wasn't a formal offer but it did make certain promises. But in light of Isabel's murder . . ."

Fiona was still in the dark. "Surely, you can ask Darryl. The dean has to know what offers were made—he had to have approved them. I do know the hire will go through; he told me that himself. But I'm still confused about what you hoped to accomplish by planting this letter in the trash so that Lester and Mary would see it." She looked hopefully at Bettina. "How did you know they'd come in this office anyway?"

Bettina fluffed her hair with a triumphal flourish. "I told Lester I had a first edition of *The Sun Also Rises* in my study. You know what a freak he is for Hemingway memorabilia." She smiled. "I think he's dating Mary Morton by the way."

"You're kidding," Fiona began.

Miriam's grip tightened on Fiona's arm. "Listen. We must stay focused right now. We think some correspondence is missing. Paula told me the letter she does have from Isabel hints at a subsequent letter—one to be mailed the Thursday or Friday of the week Isabel was killed—*that she did not receive.* Possibly someone else stole this letter."

"Ohhhh." Fiona hugged her arms to her chest. "And if you can find out who has it, you might find Isabel's killer."

"Exactly," Bettina said as Miriam nodded vigorously.

"This is madness," Fiona said, rubbing her forehead. "Letters sent, letters not sent; fake memos passed off as authentic and circulated, while other real ones are missing. How will we ever sort it out?" She stared at the white walls of the room as if their blankness might provide relief from this bombardment of possibilities. She thought a moment. "Does Paula know that Hannah was offered the job she is interviewing for?"

"That's part of our mischief. We're not sure that a formal offer was actually extended to Hannah. I think it's possible, but Hannah is being very closed-mouthed about the whole affair." Miriam winced at the word "affair" and began to pace a narrow path between Bettina's desk and the peach chair.

"How much have you told Paula? She's not going to want to come here if she thinks she's not the first choice." Fiona looked from Bettina to Miriam and was not reassured by the determined set of their faces.

"We haven't told her anything."

Fiona threw up her hands. "But now you've seeded this information about Hannah's offer in Richard Lester and Mary Morton's minds! They'll spread it everywhere. You have to let Paula in on it."

"Darryl and I offered her the job today," Miriam said calmly. "And she's accepted. I assure you she knows she is our first choice and that Isabel was up to some high-stakes high jinks. In the end, this will not reflect adversely on Paula."

"I'd like to discuss it with her all the same," Fiona said stubbornly.

"I can't keep a secret like this from her anyway. She's an old friend and she's staying in my house."

"Oh, all right," Miriam's tone was cross. "I'll go get her."

"Where is she anyway?" Fiona asked.

"Talking to Marvin. The party's over. The last guests are just wandering off." Bettina flopped down next to Fiona on the sofa. "Let's just do this and be done. Miriam, if you wouldn't mind bringing her back here. My feet are killing me." Bettina slid the footstool belonging to the peach chair under her feet.

Miriam bustled out of the office. Fiona turned to Bettina: "Why did you plant that note about Lester having lifted passages from Paula's book in your wastebasket? Now he'll have it out for her for sure. I don't trust him."

Bettina rubbed at a splotch on her cream-colored linen blouse. "Just trying to break up the logjam. He's a prime suspect in Isabel's death, don't you think?"

"Richard Lester?" Fiona grimaced. "He's vicious but only with that pedantic mouth of his. I can't imagine him actually using physical force."

Bettina was about to say something when Miriam rushed back into the room with a flurry of her short legs and arms. "Paula's not out there," she said breathlessly, leaning against the doorjamb for support.

"What do you mean?" Bettina said heatedly.

"Marvin's all alone, cleaning up. She left with Lester and Mary ten minutes ago. He said Paula told him that they were going to drive her to your house, Fiona, and she'd meet you there."

Fiona looked at Bettina. "You see what you've put in motion," she said angrily.

"Don't say that!" Bettina bolted to her feet. "Come on, let's go to your house. I'm sure we'll find Paula waiting for us."

"You gave her a key, yes?" Miriam said, with an intake of breath. She looked very, very worried.

"I did," Fiona said. "But she planned to go back with me . . ."

"Come on," Bettina grabbed Fiona's hand and lifted her to her feet with surprising energy. "Let's stop stewing and take some action. There's no time to waste."

8

Rash judgments provoke rash actions. In no time at all, the most sensible people can forget how to air their differences with civility and instead behave impetuously. And then what are we left with? Mayhem, confusion, idiocy. What's that quote from *Hamlet*? "I will speak daggers to her, but use none." Ah, I wish that were the usual impulse . . .

editor's note

Exhibit A: Isabel's diary, July 2002

July 21

It's the second session of summer school. No one around. The search committee won't review the files until mid-August—that's the very earliest. H. seems relieved. She & I meet in Albuquerque (on 19th) & drive up to Santa Fe. Huge reprieve from the heat: cold at night, terrific stars, dry mountain air. Yesterday, at lunch in the Plaza, she finishes a huge bowl of posole & puts down her spoon.

"This is divine," she says. "Let's stay on vacation. Better yet, let's retire & move here."

"Huh. Do you know how many tourists a year come to Santa Fe & say exactly what you're saying? Which is why small shacks sell for a million apiece here."

H. takes a bite of tortilla, then tears off a piece & tosses it at me. "Can't you give up being practical for once? Just think about it: we've both worked hard. I've already taught for, let's see, thirty years if you count graduate school. Isn't that enough?"

Thirty years. That puts H. around fifty-five, M.'s age. Hannah looks younger—face still round & unlined except for a scratch of crow's feet around each eye. "Well, I'm not ready for that. What would I do?" I feel a clutch of panic at the thought of retiring.

H. laughs, showing little, sharp teeth. "Take up painting, start meditating, open a business. I don't know. You can't be a Chair forever. What have you always wanted to do?"

I lean forward. "Let me tell you a secret: I love what I do. This is what I always dreamed of: research & writing & getting paid for it."

"But aren't you tired of teaching, Isabel? Tired of the young, expectant faces looking to you for answers?"

I swallow the last of my beer. It's lukewarm. "I don't teach that much anymore. Besides, if they're looking to me for answers, they're sorry out of luck."

"I doubt that's true." She looks away, at the other diners, the waitstaff bustling about with trays loaded with enchiladas & bottles of cerveza. She gives me the eye & sips her margarita. "I suspect they think you know the answers. &, I'll bet you give them that impression."

That little smile on those plump lips can be so annoying! "Fine, think that if you like."

H. speaks in a dreamy tone. "Isn't it funny that when you were in college, & were unformed & confused, you'd look at the professors & envy them their certainty, their maturity? Then, once you're a professor, middle-aged & burned out, you stare at your students & lust after their youth, that endless sense of possibility?" She dabs at her mouth with her napkin, raises a hand to a waiter, points at her margarita. "It doesn't seem fair."

I laugh. She's so spoiled & so content with herself. "Your age is showing, my dear. Of course it isn't fair. But I'm happy to be in the shoes I'm in, thank you very much." God, to think of eighteen again, the poor skin & nerves, eager to get out of the house & away from my father. Just desperate to have a life, any life as long as it was my own . . .

"Truth?" H.'s voice still dreamy & drifting. "I'd change with them . . ."—she leans forward & startles me by snapping her fingers in my face—"that fast! Responsibility, making & maintaining a reputation, it's all so wearisome."

"Perhaps you should change careers, not retire." I try to be low-key.

"Maybe I should try administration." Her eyes shine. "If I come to Austin, maybe that's what I'll do. How about I chair a department? I could become vice-chair of Literature & Rhetoric & then move into your position when you're ready to move up as Dean. Which will probably be soon."

I roll my eyes, ignoring the Dean reference. Besides, Hansen's term isn't up for two more years. "We call them associate chairs here. &, If you think you're sick of academia now, chairing will not warm the cockles of your little heart. Come on, let's drag our middle-aged, burnt-out asses out of these chairs & go for a hike in Washington Park."

July 28
The other day I ask Anna for Paula Fabian's file. "It's not there," she tells me nervously after the usual hunt & peek through the file cabinets.

"It's not with the other files for the new search?"

"Oh! I forgot. Dr. Held checked that file out two days ago."

"Anna." I try but cannot contain my impatience. "Miriam isn't even on the search committee!"

She gives me that woebegone look of hers, the fleshy bags under her eyes drooping onto her cheeks. The woman needs sleep—she looks utterly a wreck. "It's awkward. She was Chair, you know . . ."

I refrain from grinding my teeth to the nubs—as if I didn't know who had been Chair of the department! "Well, she's not now."

It's no secret that Anna is utterly devoted to Miriam. Just the day before I hear her in the hall, blushing & giggling at some witticism of Miriam's: "Oh, Professor Held, you always make me laugh!" Then she sighs, a huge outbreath of longing (I peg her as a queen of nostalgia without a doubt)—implying, I suppose, that working for me she's now stuck with a dour & unfunny person. &, irony of ironies, I have never heard Miriam Held say anything even remotely witty. . . .

Anna gives me a prim look. "Isabel, any faculty member has a right to look at the applicant files during a search."

Her insinuating "Isabel" rankles, given her crowing of "Professor Held" at every opportunity. But if I object she'll assume that I care a rat's ass about what she thinks of me, so I refrain.

Anna's just hitting her stride: "Besides, Dr. Held is on the Executive Committee & I'm sure needs to review the files for your discussion." Long-suffering looks as she pages through the diary on her desk, the pinky of her right hand salutes the air. "The EC meets August 26, you know."

"I know that perfectly well. Would you mind, terribly, Anna, bringing me that file in the next two days? Please. I must have it."

"Fine." Little girl voice, she's so put-upon, etc.

I resolve from that moment to make duplicates of the finalists' files & keep the copies in the bottom desk drawer—the one that locks. I can't have files just disappearing like this. Faculty are like children—insanely attracted to paper . . . more likely to shred, lose, or probably even eat the stuff than keep it in its proper place.

July 31

Reggie visits my office today. She's assisting me this summer, looking up archival material on Teddy Roosevelt, letters, memos, etc. Claims she loves research. She's so young, so eager. Those limpid gray eyes of hers, oh my. Quite flattering. Then I realize that she's probably this puppyish with all her professors.

"Thank you, Reggie. You're a great help," I say to her when she tosses on my desk a zip disk of notes.

"You think so?" A look of pure delight on her face. I've never seen her smile like that before—she's usually sunk in gloom.

"Absolutely." I dig through my desk—can't remember where I put the last zip she gave me.

"I'll see you in two weeks." I don't mean to be brusque, but am desperate to get back to work.

"Umm, Professor Vittorio?" Reggie lurks in the doorway, as if the space has a magnetic charge that keeps her inside its frame.

"Yes, Reggie." I look up from the desk in time to notice her staring at me. She looks to be in some kind of trancelike state. I pray for patience. Honestly, these students can be so spacey, so out of it.

"Is there anything else I can do for you today? I'm just on my way to the Union . . . Maybe a cup of coffee? Or a sandwich?" she asks. "It's no trouble." Am I imagining she sounds wistful? Hasn't the girl any friends?

"No, but thank you very much." I manage a smile but my face feels tight. "I really just need to get something accomplished today & I'm afraid I'll just have to buckle down & do that on my own."

Reggie scratches her neck & her face gets all pinched. "Oh, okay. I'll just be going then."

"Goodbye," I stand up & close the door as she leaves.

Marvin had just stuffed the last plate into the dishwasher when Miriam, Fiona, and his wife rushed into the kitchen. Bettina, her face an unhealthy shade of pink, cast a wild eye about the room. Marvin reached in his pocket and pulled out her keys. "I rescued these from the counter by the phone." He glanced at their unnerved faces and then dried his hands on a dish towel. "Why don't I drive us?" he said gently. "That way, the three of you can continue your conversation."

Moments later, having herded the three agitated women out of the house, he backed his four-door Ford pickup out of the garage. "Come on, get in. All of you." he added to Fiona and Miriam, who stood in a clutch of indecision halfway between their two cars. "Let's not waste time deciding how many cars to take!"

No one talked as they sped down the interstate and crossed the river on the access road. Beneath them, the water glittered under a bright half-moon. Miriam squeezed her eyes against an unbidden vision of Paula's body, weighted with rocks, being shoved from this very bridge into the Colorado River below. She wished they would go faster although she had to admit that Marvin, a Marine Corps medic during Vietnam, had a steadier hand at the wheel than she would have in this situation.

Fiona's one-story house across from a neighborhood park was dark. Marvin parked in her driveway and the group trooped along the path to the back door.

"Damn, I forgot to leave the deck light on," Fiona said. She ran ahead of them, covered the three steps onto the deck in one lunge and then stopped in front of the door. "I'm afraid to open it," she said.

The screen door stood ajar. Marvin flipped it open with one beefy shoulder and held out his hand for the key. Fiona handed the key to Bettina, who passed it to her husband.

"We'll go in," Bettina said. "You two stay out here, just in case."

Miriam exchanged a frightened glance with Fiona. "In case of what?" Fiona asked.

Bettina brushed her hand through the air at them impatiently, as if waving a flag of caution. "Be quiet," she said.

When Marvin unlocked the door and pushed it open, Dynamo hurtled through the opening and streaked past them, leaping off the deck and into the bushes that bordered it.

"Oh!" Miriam gasped, and stumbled forward, catching herself against the deck railing.

"She always races out like that," Fiona said, patting Miriam's back. She was relieved her cat appeared all right, at least.

Miriam and Fiona, ignoring Bettina's advice, followed Marvin and Bettina into the hallway and then turned right into the living room. Fiona flipped light switches as they advanced.

Marvin and Bettina moved quickly through the hallway toward the bedrooms and Fiona's office, while Fiona and Miriam checked the kitchen and dining room. The sudden whirring of the refrigerator was the only sign of life in either.

"There doesn't seem to be anyone here," Marvin said from the bathroom near the guest bedroom, his voice muffled.

A groan filtered down the hall from Fiona's office. "Is that you, Bettina?" Marvin asked.

"No, it's not me," Bettina said hoarsely. "I'm right behind you."

The four of them rushed into Fiona's office to find Paula lying on the rug in the middle of the floor, her knees drawn up to her chest. "Oh my God, is she bleeding?" Miriam asked.

Paula sat up slowly, her face groggy and puffy. Fiona knelt beside her and put a supportive arm behind her back. "Are you hurt? Would someone get a glass of water?"

Marvin had already removed Paula's shoes and was searching for a pulse in her wrist. "Strong and steady, a little slow," he said.

Bettina pressed a glass of water into Paula's other hand. "Drink this," she said. "Should we help you to a chair?"

Paula nodded, and Marvin half-lifted her easily into a leather recliner in the corner of the room. Marvin sat on the arm of her chair watching her closely. Fiona propped herself on the floor against the desk and Miriam and Bettina sank down on the sofa.

"What happened?" Bettina asked.

Paula swallowed half the glass of water. She rubbed her forehead and winced. "I'm not sure." She looked at her watch. "A little over an hour ago . . . ," she nodded at Marvin. "—I was still at your house when I started to feel a bit sleepy and spacey, you know that funny wrapped-in-cellophane feeling. After a bit I felt like I wasn't going to be able to stay awake. That was around nine-fifteen. Almost everyone was gone by then. Just then, Richard Lester and Mary Morton came up to me and asked if they could drive me home."

"What did they say exactly?" Miriam asked.

Paula's brown eyes still looked tired and unfocused. "Richard said something like, 'You look all in. Would you like a ride?' And I said, 'Where's Fiona?' and Mary said something like, 'She's tied up right now. We'd be happy to drop you at her house.' By then, I was feeling light-headed and I was afraid I was going to be sick. So I just said, 'I'd appreciate it,' or something like that." She peered up at Marvin. "That's when I told you I'd meet Fiona here."

Marvin nodded. "I should have noticed you weren't feeling well," he said. He tugged unhappily at the collar of his polo shirt.

"Why didn't you say something to one of us?" Bettina asked.

Paula looked from one to the other of the Grafs. "I . . . I don't know. I don't remember thinking anything," she said. "I guess I wasn't processing very clearly by then. I just wanted to lie down." She sat up straight and clutched her abdomen. "Oh, I think I'm going to be sick."

"Here." Marvin whisked her up out of the chair and they headed to the bathroom, Paula's feet barely touching the ground, before anyone else even moved. Coughs and retching sounded from down the hall.

"I think that's a good sign," Miriam said. "Maybe she'll get rid of whatever it was that poisoned her."

"'Poisoned her'?" Fiona asked. "Do you think so? She'd had a very hectic and long day with traveling the day before. Maybe she's just exhausted."

Marvin reappeared at the door. "I don't think so," he said. "She said she felt perfectly well until she suddenly felt very sleepy and disoriented. That doesn't sound like the gradual sort of running down you get from having a hard day. And it isn't how food poisoning presents either."

Paula came back into the room, her face slack and ashy under the usual warm coffee-color of her skin. "I've had food poisoning," she said. "This feels like some kind of drug, a sedative maybe." She eased her body back into the leather chair and stretched out cautiously. "I feel much better now."

"We all ate the same food," Miriam said slowly. "I think I tasted every one of the dishes," she said, "as usual. I couldn't resist. So I don't think it was in what she ate." Frowning, she asked, "What did you drink?"

Paula thought a moment. "I didn't drink the wine that was open on the counter when we first arrived. I remember walking into the kitchen and asking if there was any Scotch."

"I don't remember that," Bettina said, her face pale and concerned.

"You weren't there. Actually, none of you were. Someone else said, 'Oh, I know where it's kept' and brought me some." She looked thoughtful. "It was someone I had just met." Her eyes fluttered shut for a moment. "That nice young man with light brown hair and glasses." She looked hopefully at Fiona.

"Was he wearing a red bow tie?" Fiona suggested.

"Yes."

Bettina stood excitedly. She moved to the window, shut the shades, and then sat on the edge of Fiona's desk. "Collin Freed! One of Lester's toadies. He made you that drink."

"But wait," Marvin said. "We didn't have any Scotch in the house. Remember, honey?" he turned to Bettina. "I was taking inventory and I said we were out of Scotch. But it was late in the day and we had everything else, so you said 'Don't worry about it, it's a wine crowd.'"

"Ohhh," Miriam struck the side of her head with a fist. "I brought the Scotch—it was single malt. I knew you'd have wine and beer and I didn't feel like either of those."

"You?" Bettina turned to her. "Then you drank some of it too?"

"Yes, when I first arrived. I had one drink."

"So Collin Freed put something in your drink?" Marvin asked Paula.

"I don't know," she said. "He just brought it to me. I asked for a Scotch and soda."

"I can't believe it was Collin," Fiona protested. "I saw him earlier in the day and he was most excited about Paula's job talk tomorrow."

"There's your motive," Bettina's voice was hard. "Paula's job talk. Whoever did this wanted her to either have to cancel tomorrow or certainly not be at the top of her game. How could she be, puking her guts out the night before? Or passing out and getting a concussion? Any of several people could have made that drink. Maybe Collin didn't mix it but just played fetch and carry. I have a feeling that it's Lester who is behind this. How else did he have the impeccable timing to offer you a ride at that moment? Why was he still there when everyone else had left? Fiona, tell them what you overheard in my office earlier."

As Fiona summed up her encounter with Mary and Lester, Miriam fumbled in her purse for a handkerchief. She pressed the fabric to her face and throat. "This is getting serious. We're not just talking about accusations on paper and missing correspondence anymore. Paula could have been really harmed."

"I'm feeling much better now," Paula said, her eyes at last wide open. "I'll be fine. It really might have been nothing." She laughed shakily. "I'm fully capable of feeling exhausted and disoriented all on my own."

Fiona shot a warning glance at Miriam, who was about to say something more, one that said "enough." Out loud, she said, "Paula, let me get you settled. I think you should try and get some rest after the evening you've had."

Paula looked up gratefully. "I would like to go to bed, I think."

"How about some herbal tea or hot milk?" Fiona suggested.

"Tea would be nice."

Fiona took Paula's elbow. "The rest of you are banished to the living room. Paula's room is next door and I don't want you keeping her up."

Marvin, Bettina, and Miriam decamped the interior entirely and retreated to the back deck, where they continued to talk in low voices. Dynamo materialized in the shadows and lay down near Bettina's chair, her ears pivoting as she tracked their voices.

"Whether Paula feels better or not," Miriam said wearily, "I'll have to report this to Sergeant Crane. Someone not only tried to knock Paula out of commission, but they used my Scotch to do it."

"I'm not sure you should go to the police. At least not yet," Bettina said. "You're in a difficult position. That 'minority hires' file was found in your office, the Scotch Paula drank tonight was yours, you offered Paula a job that some of the faculty obviously don't want her to have. If we could give the police something concrete first, it would take suspicion away from you entirely."

"Suspicion! Of me? That's absurd," Miriam protested stoutly.

Bettina spoke sharply: "Miriam, wake up! You had a conflict with Isabel, over the chair job, and now she's dead. You had an affair with Hannah Weinstein who has applied for this job; she was involved with Isabel; you were once involved with Isabel. It could look like you are trying to push Hannah's cause all the while pretending to aid Paula. And now this attack on Paula: with liquor you brought into the house! You're being framed."

"It looks like that's what someone is aiming to do all right," Marvin said, his big hands resting on his knees. "This is just a hypothetical: who would profit if you had to resign as chair because of a conflict of interest—real or unreal—over this search?"

"Or because you're a prime suspect for murder!" Bettina added in spite of Marvin's restraining hand on her arm.

Miriam looked dazed. "Well, I'm not sure it would be any one person. But certainly Lester, and Sigmund Froelich, who will not welcome someone as politically savvy and frank as Paula in the department, would perceive that as a victory. And I have no doubt they would be delighted to get rid of me entirely." Miriam paused. "I would like to say, 'over my dead body,' but in light of the past two weeks, I'm too superstitious."

"And Lester might seize the chair position in that case," Bettina said. "Paula would most certainly not be hired."

"And Hannah Weinstein?" Bettina ventured. "How does she fit into all of this?"

"I'm not sure," Miriam said. "I wish I knew. Something is very strange on that front. Why have we not heard from her?"

"Won't she attend Isabel's memorial on Wednesday?" Marvin asked.

"Of course! She almost has to," Bettina said her voice warming with excitement. "Unless . . ."

"Unless?" Miriam echoed.

"Unless she killed Isabel."

"Bettina! You can't be serious." Miriam clapped her hands down onto the arms of the Adirondack chair she sat in. The slap of flesh against wood cracked unpleasantly in the still night air. Dynamo's fur rose; she hissed and leaped off the deck into a wispy stand of Mexican feathergrass.

Marvin laughed and then said soberly, "But in police shows, the murderer always attends the funeral. He—or she—can't resist seeing the reactions of others to the deed. Apparently."

"Or is too proud of having caused the death—perhaps the killer fantasizes of standing up at the occasion and confessing in a rush of, what, pride? Paranoia?" Bettina joined in, and then touched Marvin's hand. "Murder is the ultimate act of hubris, wouldn't you say, darling?"

"It always comes back to that, doesn't it? Someone killed Isabel." Miriam closed her eyes and then squinted as if a bright light suddenly exploded in her face. "There's no way to escape the finality of that act. It's like a monstrous creature with far-reaching tentacles, wrapping itself around all of us. We're all implicated."

As she said this last sentence, Fiona stepped out onto the deck. "That's funny," she said. "Darryl said something like that at dinner the other night. He mentioned that Agatha Christie book, you know the one made into a movie, the one that takes place on the Orient Express. It turns out there's not one killer. Instead, a whole group of people is responsible for the death of the victim. He said everyone surrounding Isabel had a motive."

"You don't have to wield the knife to have a hand in someone's death," Marvin said quietly.

"Good Lord," Bettina said uncertainly and reached for his hand.

"But this is someone we all know that we're talking about," Fiona protested. "I just can't get my mind around that."

Marvin needlessly smoothed his blond buzz-cut. "Isabel aroused strong emotions. Envy and fear. She pitted people against each other. A climate of suspicion can change everything. I saw that in the war. It incites people to think things—and commit acts—that would never occur to them normally."

In the silence, they heard the sharp cry of a nighthawk and the answering call of another. Miriam stared at a bright planet cresting the horizon. "I have something to confess," she whispered.

"Yes?" Bettina leaned forward.

"I saw Isabel on that last Saturday—before the Monday when she was found—at about one in the afternoon. We had an unpleasant disagreement about the new position. And I haven't told the police. I'm too terrified what they will think of me."

"Ah," Bettina nodded, her voice a mixture of relief and excitement. "I also saw her Saturday, right before you did. Does that make both of us prime suspects?"

Miriam's brown eyes were lusterless in her pale face. "Yes, but we seem to occupy a crowded field."

9

Isn't it fascinating that when one person from an underrepresented group takes a baby step forward, say, gets a competitive position, some entrenched and privileged person cries "Inferior qualifications!" or "Limited candidate pool!" Yet, when a member of the same group as the privileged person is given a job or wins an award, the same person falls all over him- or herself saying how qualified and deserving that person is.

Actually, it's not fascinating. It's utterly boring and predictable. The Way of the World is pretty dull, really.

Paula Fabian, on the treadmill at her health club, talking to a friend

At home, Miriam's feet slid soundlessly over the floor as she stepped from the bedroom, where Vivian slept soundly, into her office. She couldn't sleep; she couldn't stop thinking.

Marvin's claim that Isabel had created a "climate of suspicion" particularly troubled her. For while Isabel might have been guilty of zealously hoarding power and making autocratic decisions, others around her augmented this culture of paranoia and envy as well. Unhappily, Miriam recognized that she and Bettina had recently contributed to that very culture by trying to incite one or more of her colleagues into revealing their motives at the party. Their conspiratorial approach abetted the habit of communicating by innuendo and insinuation, the very behavior which so irritated them when practiced by certain of their colleagues.

It was increasingly obvious to Miriam that Isabel's death, while very possibly committed by a single individual, nonetheless resulted from years of enmity and dishonesty involving a number of people. Social environments, like weather patterns, took shape over a period of time, gathering mass and momentum only when the right ingredients enabled a potent alchemical shift. In fact, Miriam suspected that the motives around Isabel's murder might possibly predate the victim's tenure at Austin University.

Not only had Isabel not shared warm memories of her mother or her past, but Miriam recalled how Isabel typically spoke disparagingly of the places she had lived before Austin. Miriam wondered if Isabel was one of those people who employed a scorched-earth policy about their lives: in each location, they made enemies or created a crisis that became untenable, propelling them to move on to the next place. The past became a repository of old grievances, bitter skirmishes, and unresolved relationships. Isabel had left Miriam at the first sign of distress, and she had never looked back. There was no attempt at resolution, only a desire to get away. Miriam smarted still from Isabel's abrupt departure. Who knew how many hurt or angry people littered the landscape of Isabel's forward march?

Seated at her desk, Miriam drew out the notebook from the bottom right drawer. She picked up a pen and drew a border around the next empty page, doodling distractedly within its margins. How did Paula's visit threaten the person who murdered Isabel Vittorio? That was the question—unless the two events were unrelated, which Miriam found almost impossible to believe. She began to jot down a few scant details, free associating on the page in a style similar to Gertrude Stein in her experimental work, *Tender Buttons:*

A room. A square room. A room is white, white and light. A desk, a chair, a cabinet. Something and a chair. Something on the chair. A body. Just a body. At home. In a home. The body not at home.

Another room. In another place. With a body. The body is, not was.

Two bodies in two rooms at two times. One is and one isn't. Do they like? Are they alike?

And where? Where did they live? Before one died and the other didn't.

106

Miriam stopped writing. Had Paula and Isabel known each other in the past? Perhaps they had a history she knew nothing about. She stepped over to her bookcase and drew out a members' directory of the Modern Language Association. Looking up the two scholars, she found that Paula's Ph.D. degree was from Northwestern, Isabel's from Stanford. The directory didn't list their B.A. or M.A. degrees. Miriam switched on her computer; she had summary bios of all faculty in her department in a file marked "fac c.v.s" and a file of pertinent facts on the finalists for the current search. She manipulated her mouse for a few minutes. There it was: Isabel received her Ph.D. in 1980 and taught for five years at Indiana University. Paula Fabian, a good ten years younger than Isabel, received her B.A. degree in 1982 — from Indiana. Miriam tapped a pencil on the desk. It was certainly possible the two had known each other there, even that Paula had taken classes from Isabel. The early eighties seemed far away. Then, she and Hannah were teaching together in Portland, Oregon, blissfully far from these people and events.

Indiana. Miriam turned to a fresh page in her notebook, selected a red pencil, and wrote the word down in capitals. Interesting. Both Sigmund Froelich and Richard Lester had known each other at that institution, as colleagues in the English Department. She opened another file on the desktop: Sigmund had arrived at AU in 1985, Lester in the fall of 1982. She wrote "1982" next to "Indiana" and drew an arrow between them; she then penciled in an equal sign on the other side of "1982" and wrote down the names of Isabel, Lester, Sigmund, and Paula. They had all lived in Bloomington at that time. She thought it had been perhaps an auspicious year in the heartland.

Miriam noted the digital clock on her desk: eleven-thirty p.m. She hesitated, then picked up the phone to call Dennis, whom she had talked to earlier in the evening at the Grafs' party. The two of them had hunkered down in a corner of the kitchen and combed over Dennis's recollections of the search committee meetings, hoping to unearth any overlooked detail that might have had an impact on Isabel's death. As chair of the committee, he of all her colleagues would have studied Paula's file; he might know about her associa-tions at Indiana. When he'd left the gathering, Dennis had made her promise to call him if she needed to talk.

"I mean it, Miriam. Call me whenever. I'm not getting much sleep these days anyhow. I've shut the ringer off in our bedroom—Carter's had a cold and has been hitting the pillow early—and I'm reading late in my study most nights. So if I'm up, I'll answer from there. Otherwise, I won't hear the phone."

To her relief, Dennis answered on the second ring. "Dennis, I hope I'm not calling too late . . ."

"Nope. Just settling in with a mystery. How about you?"

"I'm afraid the evening has provided me one of my very own." In a rush, she recounted the night's strange blend of frantic search and grim speculation. "I'm trying to trace Paula's college career at Indi-ana. I've just realized that she was there at the same time as Isabel and Sigmund and . . ."

"Call Blake," Dennis said impulsively. "He was there when Sig was chair. He didn't last long, no thanks to Sig, but if there's any dirt to be dished, he's your man."

"Of course! Why didn't I think of calling him sooner?" Their old friend, Blake Burnois, was the current editor-in-chief of *The Gazette of Higher Education*. With his wealth of connections and prodigious taste for gossip, Blake could be viewed as a one-stop researcher's res-cue for those on the hunt for trivia in the tiny world of academe. "This shows you how distracted I've been," Miriam sighed. "All this stress has made me a dullard."

"I'm surprised he hasn't called you himself. You can bet that by now he knows more about this story than we do."

"Excellent, my dear Dennis. He won't mind if I call this late? It's almost one a.m. Washington time."

Dennis laughed. "His evening is probably just beginning—he's not an old married fart like me."

Disconnecting from Dennis, Miriam felt an uplift of hope as she punched in the next series of digits. She was slightly disappointed to reach the recorded Blake rather than him directly, but she enunciated clearly: "Blake, it's Miriam. I need your help with something . . . it's kind of a long story . . . I'll be at home tomorrow by—"

"Doctor M, I presume?" The crisp baritone came on the line sounding fresh and alert.

"Blake. Thank you for picking up." Miriam felt absurdly grateful.

"Ah, for you, anything." She heard the rattle of ice cubes. "Actually, I am dying to talk to you, my brilliant friend. Has all gone haywire down in Longhornville? Murders instead of sex, mayhem in place of rock-and-roll. What's happened to my divine river city?"

Blake's reckless cheer lightened Miriam's mood. "You can imagine what it's been like since Isabel died."

"Dying is one thing, my sweet, being murdered another. You can tell Uncle Blake: who did it?"

"Your guess would be far better than mine at this point."

"Why didn't you tell me you required my services to solve the crime? All you needed to do was ask. It's Sigmund, of course."

Miriam laughed. Blake had a simmering dislike of Sigmund Froelich dating back to Indiana when he had been a lowly lecturer, one of fifty fired through a reorganization plan initiated by Sigmund. "I don't think so. But maybe. You knew Isabel when she was at Indiana, didn't you?"

Blake sighed. "Regrettably. She and Sig were pals. They were a power couple, bedfellows in the political sense only, of course."

"And Paula Fabian was an undergraduate student in that department at the time, yes?"

"Paula. Indeed, yes. She was, pardon the expression, the golden-haired girl." Blake giggled. "Sig didn't like that too much, of course. Isabel either. They liked their golden girls to have fairer complexions. But Paula was sharp, a brilliant debater, top of her class. I hear you might have a crack at wooing her away from Georgetown."

"It looks like we might. But," Miriam pressed, "was Paula Isabel's student?"

Blake thought a moment. "Had to have been. Vittorio's "Discourse Theory" class was a requirement for seniors. Lord!"

"What?" Miriam felt a surge of hope.

"I almost forgot. I have a date in thirty minutes and I don't even know what I'll wear," Blake said, a manic note creeping into his voice.

"A date? At this hour?"

"Dearest, some of us are not over the hill. Not yet. We're nearing the shank of the evening."

Miriam, feeling the adrenaline ebb from her body after an eternally long day, longed for bed. "I am over the hill, Blake. Thank goodness. Enjoy yourself."

"I'll kiss him goodnight just for you, M. Gotta go." The ice cubes rattled one last time. "Oh, but one more thing . . . almost forgot. Check this out: Paula was Richard Lester's research assistant her last semester at Indiana. The word was that he borrowed some of her work, passed it off as his own. Embarrassing, no? Stealing from an undergraduate? And this is the funny thing about it: Isabel stuck her neck out defending Lester at the time. Ms. By-the-Rule-Book jettisoned the rules. No one knew why. Paula threatened a grievance and somehow Vittorio persuaded her to drop it."

"It's odd that you should mention that, as a matter of fact," Miriam began.

Blake broke in: "Everything about it is odd. Our man Lester left Indiana after that. In fact, the next fall found him making a soft landing at your august institution. Coincidence? It might be if we believed in them, but you and I know better."

"Blake, do you recall—"

"Better dash. Can't keep my date waiting. This could be Mr. Right."

Miriam lapsed into a stern, parental tone, one she often used with Blake, who, at forty-five, had never met a balanced life he cared to live: he careened between grand enthusiasms and the slough of despond. "Blake, you must give that up. How many Mr. Rights have there been by this time?"

"I've heard thirteen is the charmed number."

She laughed. "Only thirteen? Why do I doubt you?"

"Because, dearest M., you know I can't count. Ciao."

On Tuesday morning, Miriam attended a brief meeting of the entire Literature and Rhetoric faculty to consider whether or not to hire Paula Fabian. The pro forma vote was overwhelmingly in Paula's favor, as expected, except for a curious negative vote from Collin Freed.

An hour later, Anna ushered a sullen-faced Reggie Bradley into Miriam's office. Officially, Reggie needed the chair's signature to switch to a different faculty supervisor for an independent study. Now that Isabel was no longer available, Miriam arranged for Fiona to take over supervision for the class. Miriam had made use of this formality to schedule a meeting with the young woman.

With her goth-like mask scrubbed off, the student looked young and a little scared. Reggie slouched in the chair opposite Miriam's desk, her shoulders hunched protectively over her small breasts in the manner adopted by many tall, thin coeds. Her eyes darted from blue walls to gray carpet to loaded bookshelves, avoiding Miriam's face.

Miriam spoke quietly, opting for a careful blend of concern and reserve; she mustn't push Reggie at all. The young woman had slender hands with ragged, bitten nails. The fingers danced a nervous jig on her knees. A painful-looking rash bloomed on her throat. She appeared ready to bolt at the slightest provocation.

"Doctor Hardison will be your temporary advisor as well as your supervisor on this course," Miriam began.

"I've already talked to her," Reggie said in a flat voice, her face showing no trace of either enthusiasm or dislike.

"That's good. I think you'll find her—" Miriam hesitated, wishing to be enthusiastic but not wanting to sound Pollyannaish about Fiona.

"She's okay," Reggie said. Her gray eyes once again made a circuit around the room, and then settled on a print of O'Keeffe's *Road Past the View*. She blinked. "She makes it look good," she said ambiguously.

"What?"

"New Mexico. I hate the place."

"Are you from there?" Miriam asked.

Reggie ignored the question. "I took Doctor Hardison's class last year, film and lit." She shrugged. Miriam noticed that although her white t-shirt had a calculated tear around one shoulder, her black Levis were new and pressed.

Miriam came out from behind her desk and sat in a chair adjacent to the student's. "Reggie, I know you had a fairly long acquaintance with Doctor Vittorio . . ."

Reggie's eyes immediately ceased their survey of the room, but she carefully avoided Miriam's face.

"I'm sure this is a difficult time for you," Miriam began again.

Reggie's affectless pose deserted her. She glared at the older woman, her neck stretched and rigid, her cropped hair a spiky crown. Miriam was reminded of an angry swan prepared to protect its offspring, and braced herself for a vicious outburst. But to her surprise, Reggie's face crumpled and she began to sob. She covered her face with her hands; her shoulders trembled and tears leaked through her fingers.

Miriam placed a Kleenex on the student's lap and said sympathetically. "Of course you're very upset." With difficulty she refrained from the innocuous remark, "We all are," which, while true in this case, probably would not matter to Reggie at the moment.

Cautiously, Miriam placed a hand on Reggie's shoulder and when the girl tilted toward her, encircled her arm across her back, supporting her while she cried. "It's a terrible thing, what happened to Isabel," Miriam said soothingly.

The girl cried harder, swiped at her face with the Kleenex and turned an imploring face toward Miriam. "You don't understand," she said.

"No," Miriam clucked. "No one understands what you're going through. But I'm very sorry, very." She patted Reggie's back.

"I . . . I . . ." Reggie mumbled something Miriam couldn't hear.

"What, dear?" Miriam leaned closer.

A huge sob shook Reggie's thin frame. "I LOVED her," Reggie said.

"Yes. Oh, I see," Miriam said and gave her another Kleenex.

"You . . . can't . . ." Reggie choked out the words.

Miriam waited while another squall of tears erupted on Reggie's face. What could she possibly say to this young woman? That it might not be love she felt for Isabel but infatuation, that it was easy to feel oneself in love with someone one admired as much as Reggie probably admired her advisor? But love was magic; pedestrian words like the ones Miriam had just thought would be as unappealing as scattering dross next to diamonds.

After a bit, Reggie was quiet. "No, you don't see," Reggie sniffed. "There was no one like her." Her head lolled against the back of her chair. "I'll never care about anyone like I did her." She began to cry again, this time silently, her mouth a tortured oval.

Miriam dialed the counseling center and told the receptionist she would be bringing a student in. "Let's go for a walk." She grasped Reggie's elbow to better help her up out of the chair. "I would feel better if you talked to someone about this. Someone who is better trained than I am," she tried for the most matter-of-fact tone she could muster. She told herself to make no sudden movements, to keep her voice low and mild.

Reggie's shoulders stiffened at Miriam's touch. She stared at Miriam with bloodshot eyes. "No. I can't." She looked around the room nervously. "I'll talk to you, but I can't talk to some stranger."

Miriam reflected that she herself had been a stranger just ten minutes before, but she nodded understandingly at Reggie. "That's fine. Then sit back down. Let me make you some tea."

Reggie picked up a blue back pack which she'd dropped on the floor when Anna had shown her in. "I can't." The tendons in her neck stood out as if a scream hovered in her throat and it was only sheer will power that kept it from erupting into the atmosphere. She gulped air. "I have a class." She lurched to her feet and made for the door. "I have to go!" she said frantically and disappeared.

"Reggie . . ." Miriam called after her and then sat back heavily in her chair, her spirits low. With all the good intentions in the world, she hadn't said the right thing. Even though she knew there really wasn't any way to alleviate the young woman's misery, Miriam felt she had failed her, had driven her away. Somehow this young woman, with poor social skills and a seemingly fragile emotional balance, would have to find her own way. Miriam feared for her. She stared down at the backs of her hands, the skin rougher and more lined than she remembered it; she noticed two small spots of a darker pigment on her right hand. She was much older than Reggie, yes, but she remembered that blind, aching, consuming love she had felt in her teens and twenties. It had blotted everything else out. In one's life it was like a total eclipse of the rational sun by the beckoning, ardent moon.

She sighed and went back behind her desk. She would need to speak with Reggie again, and she resolved to alert Fiona immediately about the student's need for counseling. Miriam swallowed painfully, her throat hot and dry. Had Isabel known how blindly Reggie had loved her? Had she been responsible with this young woman, only a girl, really, or had she used her—to reassure herself that she was still a magnet for young minds and bodies, to rekindle her flagging, middle-aged desire? Miriam shook her head. She hoped Isabel had kept some distance, had used good judgment. But in her own heart, Miriam felt a stirring of dread. The Isabel she had known was brilliant in her zeal for theory and analysis, but in gauging the raw emotions of the human beings in her orbit, she had been obtuse. So dazzled was Isabel by the stars just out of reach that the earth beneath her feet went unnoticed; it was just something to trample on.

That afternoon Paula delivered a lecture to the faculty and graduate students in both Literature and Rhetoric and Drama. While initially advertised as part of her interview, rumors flew that Paula had already accepted a position on the faculty, so the talk now had an added aura, a kind of "coming out" gala. Despite her rocky stomach and unsteady head the night before, Paula appeared cool, poised, and decisive as she spoke on "Permutations of Masculinity in Toni Morrison's *Beloved*." The room, which contained a hundred seats, held an overflow crowd (including the dean and the provost), and the audience spilled into the aisles. A lively discussion—spearheaded by sharply diverging views over whether or not the Nobel laureate relied on stereotypic depictions in drawing her male characters—continued after the scheduled time of the event. Dean Hansen had introduced her proudly as a "most impressive new addition" to the faculty, and at the reception afterward there was a press of bodies around Paula as people rushed forward to congratulate her.

Several reporters jostled for position, wielding videocams and microphones to record the most glamorous star presence Austin University had lured into its fold since a Nobel prize-winning physicist had been hired a few years before. A much-publicized lawsuit had made hiring in Texas on the basis of race illegal, which had upped the ante—and the interest—in the acquisition of minority students and faculty. By any measure, Paula Fabian was a catch. Only the late Barbara Jordan herself, a figure without peer in the state of Texas, would have inspired more stares and applause from this particular audience.

Miriam received a glass of Chardonnay from the waiter at the faculty club. She allowed herself a deep breath and a luxurious swallow of wine. She relished a warm surge of satisfaction that this illustrious woman had been hired despite Isabel's obstruction and death, regardless of the opposition of a bloc on the faculty, and in the face of a potential threat on Paula's life. She lifted her glass and silently thanked every celestial power she could think of. She turned and surveyed the room, which buzzed with conversation and that unmistakable synergy when a crowd senses a change in the tide or a resurgence of possibility: by any measure, Paula Fabian was enjoying a triumph. On her way to join the throng around the successful candidate, she passed a table where Sigmund and Richard Lester sat talking.

"You win some . . . and then other days you bide your time," she heard Lester saying to Sigmund, making no attempt to lower his voice as she passed by.

"Professors," she nodded to them as she approached. Sigmund raised his chin, beamed her a hard-eyed smile, and looked away.

Lester's short gray hair bristled with gel. His taupe jacket, a soft weave of silk and wool, hugged the contours of his square shoulders and narrow waist, and new horn-rimmed glasses handsomely set off his regular features. While her colleague had always dressed neatly, Miriam assumed that Lester's newly dapper appearance was the handiwork of Mary Morton, who was at least fifteen years younger than he. Her eyebrows rose as she noticed a large silver and turquoise bracelet encircling his wrist. Lester had certainly undergone a sartorial renovation since his divorce from his second wife a year ago.

"Professor Held," Lester said, bestowing on her a shrewd appraising glance. "Most impressive," he added, enigmatically.

"Hello, Richard." Miriam wasn't sure if he referred to Paula's lecture, her acceptance of the position, Miriam's own role in getting Paula hired, or something else. She decided to take the high road. "*She* is most impressive," she said firmly. "We are unbelievably lucky that she still wants to come here." She refrained from adding, *in spite of overt and covert threats from unnamed members of the faculty.*

Having dispensed the requisite amount of civility and attention upon the two senior colleagues, Miriam continued on her way, her usually brisk stride slowed by the realization that she really didn't know if Lester or Sigmund had any part in the recent acts of aggression. Even more disturbing was the knowledge that if they were not involved, she was more at sea than ever. At this perplexing time, she wished she lived inside a Dorothy L. Sayers novel and could make an emergency summons to Lord Peter Wimsey and Harriet Vane. But since so-called real life was more bizarre and less manageable than fiction, there was no hope from that quarter either.

At four o'clock Wednesday, the university held a memorial service for Isabel in the Opera Lab Theatre in the Fine Arts complex. As they passed the circular fountain in front of the building, Vivian placed a detaining hand on Miriam's arm. "Wait. The sky, the fountain, the perfect day. It's all so dramatic. It's like nature has come out for Isabel."

"Almost as if she had stage-managed it herself," Miriam murmured wistfully, thinking of Isabel's uncanny instincts, and that she would never have opportunity to observe their brilliance again. On this sun-drenched day, the green-tinged water churning against the cornflower-blue sky provided a dazzling backdrop for Isabel's service.

Vivian seemed reluctant to leave the display; her lean face tilted toward the sky. In a dreamy voice, she added: "Isabel had such a talent for beauty, didn't she? I did admire that."

As the two of them entered the foyer of the small theatre, Miriam felt a light touch on her arm.

"Doctor Held, may I speak to you for a moment?"

Miriam looked into the pale blue eyes of Sergeant Crane, a broad-shouldered woman barely taller than she was. Sergeant Crane's brown hair curled around her head shaggily; a pair of burgundy wire-rimmed glasses framed her eyes. She had, Miriam noticed, a lovely complexion, her skin smooth, unlined, and lightly tanned.

Miriam replied quickly to cover the flutter of anxiety provoked by Crane's appearance. "Certainly. Vivian, I don't believe you've met Sergeant Susan Crane." The two women shook hands. "I'll meet you inside," Miriam murmured to Vivian and then pivoted to accompany Crane.

They found two chairs in an alcove near a small women's restroom in the basement that Miriam knew was rarely frequented.

"Doctor Held . . ."

"Please call me Miriam."

Crane nodded. "All right, Miriam, I'm afraid that you haven't been entirely honest with me."

Miriam looked at the younger woman sternly and waited. At this moment, she couldn't remember exactly what she had divulged to the detective in her earlier interview, and she thought silence, which worked well in getting her students to reveal their intentions quickly, by far the best policy.

Crane obligingly continued: "I've just been told that someone made an attempt on Professor Fabian's life on Monday night."

"Someone did try to drug her, it appears. We can't be sure of that, though." Miriam laughed shakily, instinctively downplaying recent events. "But to call it an attempt on her life is an exaggeration, Sergeant."

"Please call me Susan." Crane adjusted her eyeglasses with both hands. "This is a very frustrating case, Doctor Held . . . Miriam. The rumor that academics love the sound of their own voices doesn't seem to be true. The people who work in your building are suddenly too shy to talk to me."

"Then who told you that Paula fell ill after the faculty party?"

Susan Crane shook her head. "I can't tell you that at present. But I can tell you that I absolutely must request that you report any and all unusual incidents to me. From this point on. Is that clear?"

Miriam shut her eyes for a moment. What did the woman know? "Susan, everything at present feels so utterly unusual I don't even know how to make such a deliberation."

"I understand that you were once involved in an intimate way with Isabel Vittorio," Susan Crane said unexpectedly.

"Yes, a very long time ago. Twelve years ago." Miriam said stiffly, alert to any indication of prejudice about same-sex relationships in Crane's attitude. Detecting nothing definite beneath Crane's neutral tone, she said with as much authority as she could muster: "I can't see how this could be significant."

"Everything is significant," Crane said sharply.

Miriam made a decision. "Then you know that Isabel was also involved with one of the two finalists for the new position in our department."

Susan looked at her steadily. "Yes, and this woman, Hannah Weinstein, is another very close friend of yours as well, someone who lived with you some years ago. Doctor Held . . . ah, Miriam, you must see that the connections among the three of you are . . ." she paused delicately, "let us say, unusual."

"There are other connections equally as unusual: you are no doubt aware that Isabel worked previously with both Richard Lester and Sigmund Froelich at another university." Miriam omitted Paula Fabian's name from the Indiana roster.

Crane nodded as if this detail had little importance.

Miriam stared at her, stung by the injustice of what seemed to her to be Crane's focus on her to the exclusion of more pertinent details. She waved her hands in the air impatiently, like a traffic monitor flagging down a speeding motorist in a school zone. "I cannot help that these two women are part of my past, in both cases my very distant past. What is much more important, I would think, are allegations of fraud over this search which are patently untrue! Professor Fabian has been accused of academic blackmail—of bargaining her race in exchange for a job. Who stands to profit by discrediting her and questioning the integrity of those of us involved with the search? These are things you should be investigating, not my dry-as-dust past attachments!" Miriam sputtered, almost choking on her own saliva in her agitation.

Susan Crane's head jutted forward and when she spoke, her voice was quiet but tense: "Doctor Held, Isabel Vittorio was found not only dead in her office, but nude. Were you aware of that?" Her light blue eyes were riveted on Miriam as if to record and store the slightest reaction.

Miriam blinked, her face suddenly pale. Utterly shocked, she stammered. "N-no, I wasn't. Really, no details have been told to us, I—"

Crane continued in a hard voice, "Her nudity implicates someone who knew her well, a current or former lover perhaps. It is not surprising, therefore, that we are interested in those who have had romantic attachments to the victim."

Miriam could only stare at her.

"There is about this case a certain, shall we say, lesbian intrigue. You are a lesbian as well as someone who has had a romantic connection with the deceased. You also fought—and sometimes lost—key political battles with her in past months. Your relationship was complex. Complexity breeds passion, Doctor Held," Crane said shrewdly.

Offended, Miriam blurted, "Sergeant Crane, I am used to being targeted as a lesbian faculty member at this institution. I will not be intimidated. Using the phrase 'lesbian intrigue' romanticizes a sordid crime, in my view."

The detective dismissed her remark. "Please, let's not be academic. Now, as to your other point." Crane crossed her legs, which were encased in well-cut black trousers. Miriam noticed that the detective wore very sensible low-heeled shoes. "I have heard that there is the equivalent of a 'poison pen' making allegations impugning you and Doctor Fabian and questioning Vittorio's conduct as well, but no one has turned such letters over to me," Crane said pointedly. "If you have any such letters in your possession, I expect that they will be turned in to me tomorrow by noon at the latest."

Miriam studied the blue and gray weave of the carpet under her feet. Crane's tone irked her; the woman obviously did not comprehend the intricacy of the forces surrounding the case. Disliking the defensive note in her own voice, she nonetheless countered: "I did not give you those letters because I did not want to grace them with that much credibility!"

Crane's mouth hardened in a firm line. "You know better, Professor Miriam Held. You are a researcher, and, according to your colleagues, a very brilliant one—you must know more than most how a seemingly incongruous detail can be of vital importance." Her face reddened as if she were in danger of losing her composure. She took off her spectacles and massaged the bridge of her nose. "Everybody associated with this case seems to be scribbling all the time—notes, letters, plots. It's incredible how much you people *write*. And yet no one admits to so much as putting pen to paper. If I didn't know better, I would think the lot of you were trying to obscure a quick solution to this case."

Crane resituated her glasses and checked her watch. "And now, I don't want to miss the ceremony upstairs. I believe that Doctor Weinstein was due to arrive ten minutes ago." She stood, made a slight bow, and walked off with a determined gait.

While short, Crane exhibited a certain athleticism and Miriam guessed that the detective took obstacles in her stride, if not easily then with little hesitation. Crane would not be one to conveniently fade away in the face of resistance. Like Miriam herself, expecting results, she would most likely get them.

Relegating thoughts of her possible adversary to the back of her mind, Miriam rose to her feet quickly as well. *Hannah . . .* she had forgotten that her old friend naturally would want to attend the ceremony, but Miriam didn't feel she had adequately primed herself to encounter her under these circumstances. She felt a wave of distaste at the thought of Hannah's involvement with Isabel and then, a prickle of alarm. What condition would Hannah be in? What could she possibly say to her under the circumstances? Miriam realized she had waited too long to make contact. Given her earlier silence, any overture to Hannah might now be viewed cynically by her friend.

She made her way to the stairs, shaken. The thought of Isabel's disrobed body horrified her. Images of Isabel, proud, seductive, handsome, floated through her memory. Miriam stopped and stared out a window that opened onto the lawn at ground level. A squirrel hopped into the shadow of a pecan tree, a fat nut in its mouth, and began to devour it. Miriam envied the creature its clarity: It was hungry, it found what it needed, it ate. Miriam's own insides felt empty. Past passion was a very dead thing. Once she had known Isabel intimately. The Isabel the detective referred to, crushed and broken and naked, that Isabel was unrecognizable to her.

Her mind looped back to an image of Isabel twelve years ago. Carrying a tray of coffee for both of them, Miriam had halted in the doorway of her bedroom, arrested by the sight of her lover. Isabel stood in front of the window, smoking a cigarette with the early morning light behind her. She was wearing a blue robe in a thin, clinging fabric, carelessly belted, that lightly graced her knees. Cool and distant, with her brunette hair and slender body, her Roman nose and molded lips, she had reminded Miriam of a forties movie star, backlit by soft light. That Isabel was gone, fading from her memory month by month, losing resolution like an old photograph. Even in memory, all life eventually drained away, leaving only coarse-grained dots and smudges to mark that it had ever been. Ashes to ashes, she thought, her mouth feeling dry as dust.

Heavy with melancholy, Miriam turned from the window. She knew now without any doubt that Susan Crane thought her implicated in Isabel's murder. Crane could not know that Miriam was constitutionally incapable of physically hurting anyone she had once cared for. Crane had no conception of how little violence or fury lived in Miriam's heart. Who Miriam really was, the depth of her feelings, held no interest for the police. Crane and her cohorts only wanted a solution. Crane told Miriam the detail about Isabel's nudity in a calculated attempt to startle Miriam into revealing what she knew about Isabel's murder. Dread and gloom clouded Miriam's brain as she registered her captivity in an insidious cycle: the only way to mollify Crane was to volunteer details that the detective desired; yet, Miriam could not reveal what she did not know, which only cemented Crane's conviction that Miriam was a withholding and obdurate suspect.

At the top of the stairs, winded from anxiety as well as hurrying up two flights of steps, Miriam collided with a tense-faced Daphne surveying the lobby. "There you are. Come at once." Daphne, dressed austerely in a midnight blue, ankle-length dress, steered Miriam into the rear of the auditorium where Vivian was holding seats for them.

"I have a very bad feeling about this," Daphne whispered into Miriam's ear. "Look who the speakers are."

On the stage were Sigmund Froelich, Richard Lester, Hannah Weinstein, and Dean Darryl Hansen, among several others. Miriam noticed a large band-aid over Hannah's left eye, only partially covered by her bangs. "The woman sitting with Hannah is Isabel's sister," Miriam said, indicating a striking woman of about sixty with silver hair, wearing a dove-gray silk suit and a double choker of pearls around her slim neck.

"Well, it makes sense that Sig and Lester would make some remarks. They worked with Isabel a very long time, both at Indiana and here. And of course Hannah would want to be present. I'm surprised she would feel composed enough to speak, but why does this disturb you?"

Daphne turned her mismatched cat's eyes on Miriam. "I am certain that one of those three—Froelich, Lester, or Weinstein—either killed Isabel or knows who did."

"How can you be so sure?" Miriam felt sick to her stomach. "Have you heard something?"

"No one has to tell me anything," Daphne said tensely. "The signs are all there for anyone to read. Is Paula still here?"

"She had to fly home this morning. Why?"

"Thank goodness. She would be in danger here, now. You must dissuade her from returning while the killer is at large."

"At least you don't think she's one of the suspects." Miriam felt the gnawing of her own anxiety in her body like a strange kind of hunger.

"That isn't funny."

"I didn't mean it to be."

Daphne grasped her arm. "Listen. I've told Susan Crane that Richard Lester is in Paula Fabian's debt—that her research, used without her permission, has augmented his reputation. His plagiarism is a secret he has kept for years but now the news is spreading. Paula's very presence throws this fact in his face. Nothing matters more to him than his standing professionally. Nothing. It's his life."

"Yes, but how did you—"

"Shhh. Sigmund is about to speak."

Miriam noticed Sergeant Crane sitting on the aisle in the third row from the stage, a notepad resting on her knees. Dennis and Carter were in the middle of that same row, their heads in a level line, looking, in their physical closeness, strangely vulnerable. In the very first row, Reggie Bradley, in a black cape with a hood, gazed raptly at the stage, a stream of tears cascading down her face. Miriam felt a stab of guilt: had Reggie made it to the counseling center? She must find out.

Sigmund Froelich stood at the microphone in the center of the stage, his large hands gripping the sides of the podium so tightly they looked utterly bloodless. He surveyed the room, his shaggy white hair flying as his head swept from one side to the other. "Colleagues, friends," he turned to Isabel's sister, "and family. We gather here to mark the passing of a remarkable woman, one I considered a dear and special friend. Indeed I consider our friendship perhaps the crowning jewel of my long career." He cleared his throat, wiped his brow with a light blue handkerchief, and then smiled tenderly at Isabel's sister. She bowed her head briefly.

Sigmund took a deep breath and began again: "We shall miss Isabel Vittorio because of her wit and her wisdom, because of her brilliance and style. She was the kind of leader who actively participated in making Austin University the premiere institution it is today."

Two rows ahead, Bettina turned around and caught Miriam's eye. Bettina's forehead creased and she shook her head slightly. She turned back around and whispered something to Fiona, who sat next to her. Miriam interpreted Bettina's gesture as one of disbelief at Sigmund's expression of loss, but Miriam knew that he had been genuinely fond of Isabel; even Blake attested to their long closeness. Or perhaps Bettina judged Sig's manner excessive. In any case, Miriam felt certain that Sigmund's grief was sincere, that, for once, he had been touched, and deeply.

Sigmund summarized Isabel's achievements, mentioning the titles of her six academic books, her presidency of two major organizations, her many awards, and, finally, her extraordinary dedication to students and to colleagues. With a hand that trembled slightly, he then carefully folded his notes and put them aside. After a long pause, Sigmund's voice, with its over-rich baritone, rose in volume. Miriam, listening numbly, thought that Bettina had been right when she'd dubbed his oratorical style the "voice(over) of God." She struggled to pay attention.

He leaned into the podium, a white lily drooping from the lapel of his dark blue suit. "However, today we come not to praise Isabel Vittorio, but to set her at rest." He scanned the room searchingly and straightened his shoulders. "But none of us, none of us, including our dear departed Isabel, will ever be at peace until we find the perpetrator of this heinous crime, until we identify this monster who cut down a fine woman and a brilliant scholar in her prime." His voice cracked, awash with tears: "I demand that her murderer come forward now!"

Startled, the crowd ceased its usual rustlings and coughs for several long seconds. Then, murmurs broke out into several sections of the room. Ten or so people left the theatre hastily. The room began to pulse with agitation as if the speaker had taken off his clothes or thrown up. Miriam, dazed, saw the room shift in a series of frames, as if watching a jerky, silent film: Sergeant Crane stood up and made for the aisle; Reggie Bradley leaned forward and almost toppled out of the front row; Darryl Hansen materialized at the edge of the stage by the curtain as if to veil from public view the entire proceedings; Richard Lester rushed forward and grabbed the microphone from Sigmund.

"Please, resume your seats," Lester began in a commanding, level voice. "My colleague has been overcome by his feelings for his dear friend." Lester raised his hands and then allowed them to flutter slowly down to his sides, as if blessing the audience. "Please." He cleared his throat, nodding encouragingly as people straggled back to their seats. "Please, let us continue. Graciela Brown, Doctor Vittorio's sister, would like to read a poem in honor of the departed." Isabel's sister looked around with a bewildered air and clutched her purse. An uneasy silence fell once again in the room.

Graciela stood up hesitantly and made her way to the podium. She placed a slim hardcover volume on the wooden lectern in front of her. But as she opened her mouth to speak, Hannah Weinstein brought her fists to her ears. "Stop!" she screamed. Lester swirled around and Graciela put out a hand as Hannah made a strangled sound, fainted, and pitched forward onto the stage. Her body hit the wooden floor with a smack. The sound seemed to reverberate and echo in the room, resounding in Miriam's ears over and over again like a hammer thwacking a two-by-four.

10

All actions have implications. Every human thought reveals motive. Each life has consequence. Occupy your place on stage like you have purpose and meaning. Let's not delude ourselves: acting isn't living. But it's your job to make an audience work like hell to tell the difference.

Dennis Reagan, remarks in introductory course in acting

Exhibit A: Isabel's diary, August 2002

August 7

Reggie drops by today, a week before her appointment. I'm on the phone with my editor at Cambridge, begging for just a little more time on the wretched book manuscript, when I see her hovering around Anna's desk.

"Just one moment, Barbara." I put down the phone & go to close my door. Anna catches my eye & I frown at her, my eyes cutting to Reggie. Anna just shrugs [*what, me worry?*]. Her incompetence astonishes . . .

"All right, all right." I return to Barbara who seems the sanest person in the world given the crew in this office. "November 1. Absolutely. I promise. Let's see, how about I offer you my firstborn. . . . Too unlikely at this stage? You wouldn't want it anyway?" We both giggle. Barbara—with *five* children—not too eager. Another kid no higher on her list than adopting is on mine. "Okay, the time share in

Florida then, two years running. It's yours if I renege this time. You strike a hard bargain. Ha. Yes, that's why I like you too . . ."

We ring off. I take off my jacket. I am sweating this conversation for real. Sort of like being in a sauna for a half-hour.

Anna buzzes my office. "Miss Bradley says she must see you this afternoon." So self-satisfied, that "this is a public university, serve your constituency" officious bullshit tone of hers.

"Send her in." Reggie my cross to bear. I look at my watch: three-thirty. H. due in at four-thirty. Am itching to go to the airport. "Tell her I have fifteen minutes."

"That's really not my job, Dr. Vittorio." Miss Prim strikes again.

I get up to go out & give her hell when Reggie's hopeful little face appears in the doorway. I manage "Have a seat. I'm a little rushed today."

She looks at me, blushes, & smiles. "I'm sorry to bother you," she says & then waits.

I don't think you are sorry at all. Sometimes students make me want to scream: they come in unscheduled, demanding time, lying through their teeth that they're so sorry to interrupt, when that's precisely what they do want to do, & then, after *interrupting & disrupting* any coherent thought you might have had, they have the utter nerve to sit there with nothing to say!! As if they've come to sit at the feet of an oracle & I'm supposed to, on demand, spout wisdom or truth or whatever it is their little brains need at the moment.

"How can I help you?" I say instead of *God damn it . . .*

She looks around, confused. "Oh," she says. "The independent study . . ."

"Yes?" I rack my brain about her research, something about the history of women's suffrage speeches—?

"You know, I'm, well, I'm like, trying to analyze the

speech that Elizabeth Cady Stanton made . . . you know, the famous one in front of the New York Legislature . . ."

"I'm familiar with that one," I say, stealing a glance at my watch: three-forty.

Reggie grimaces & covers her mouth with her hand. "Oh, duh. Well, yeah, of course you are—I'm using your book on the great speeches after Seneca Falls."

"& what seems to be the problem?" I prompt, squirming in my chair. It's so ungodly hot in the room. I need to get Anna to call physical plant & have the thermostat checked. I turn back to the student across from me, still there, sitting mutely. At the moment, urging Reggie to get to the point, I feel like a hybrid of a vocal coach and a dentist extracting an embedded tooth.

She makes another face, twists her mouth to one side so that she looks like a strained fish. "I'm just so stuck. I was wondering if you would take a look at this draft, it's about half of the paper." She retracts a grubby-looking pile of papers from her backpack & holds them out, her precious offering . . .

"I'd really prefer to read the entire essay once you've finished." But she looks so utterly crestfallen, the papers dangling limply from the fingers of one of her chapped hands, that I reach out & take them from her. "Oh, all right, let me have a look at it."

I page through the calendar on my desk. "Let's talk again next Thursday. At two."

"That would be great." She writes the date down on her wrist with a felt-tip pen. Other dabs of ink etch the wrist like a tattoo.

"Excellent. I'll see you then." *Finally.*

"Oh," she says, "I almost forgot." She brings out a gray card from her backpack. "My roommate & I are having a party next weekend. I wanted to invite you." She lays the card on the edge of my desk.

I look at the card, lying there like a smudge on my desk. "Thank you, Reggie, that's very kind of you. But I'm traveling next weekend."

She squirms. "Oh. Well, I just wanted to let you know we'd love to have you come over."

I nod. "That's fine. & now, I'm afraid, I'm out of time."

She takes an agonizingly long time gathering her things: the tatty blue backpack & the water bottle & a stack of books & a sunglasses case that falls on the floor. Waiting for her departure, my body jangles with energy. For the first time in months I think of my uncle's land in Wyoming & riding hard all day when we were kids—the *freedom* & *openness* & *bliss* of it. Not like my life now—too urban & constrained.

Finally, all her things in a pile against her chest, Reggie stands at the door & extracts one hand from the mess. She waves. "Bye."

"Goodbye." The second she oozes out the door, I get up & shut it. I lean against it, impatience screaming through every nerve. I'm stunned at Reggie's invitation. Don't know why, but feel absurdly guilty & embarrassed & oddly touched—I remember the kind of social awkwardness Reggie seems to feel. But I am the Chair of her department. I must be almost two generations older. I wonder . . . I took her to lunch last semester to thank her for her research help. Maybe the lunch led her to believe we were friends? The last thing I want to do is fraternize with undergraduates. Either I'm sending off the wrong signals or else this girl is completely oblivious, or else . . .

August 9
H. & I in my house. In bed, sipping wine. "I have a student who is a potential problem."

Her round face looks sympathetic. "Poor dear. Boy? Girl?"

"Her name is Reggie."

"A crush, do you think?" Hannah puts her finger in her wineglass & drips a few drops between my breasts. Then she licks them. "Um," she says.

I rest my hands on either side of H's. face & pull her up to face me. Her greediness makes me smile. "I'm a little worried," I say. "There's something, I don't know, *unbalanced* about the girl."

Hannah looks at me seriously finally. "Most undergraduates seem a little unbalanced, to us. I guess they are: hormones, unresolved family issues, the usual late adolescent stress. But trust your intuition. If this girl seems like trouble, protect yourself." Thinks a minute. "A friend of mine at Maryland is so afraid of a student right now—threats, weeping, tantrums, following her around, you know, giving her the heebie-jeebies—she's refusing to teach a class the student is taking. Bad business. The hidden side of teaching. No one talks about it."

I don't want to hear this. "Protect myself? It's not so easy. She's my research assistant & she's taking an independent study from me this summer." I sit up in bed, clutching my knees, my stomach in knots. "I should have seen this coming. She's taken an awful lot of classes from me." I see Reggie's face, in a trance state of attention, always in the front row in class, watching me. Disturbing.

"Honey, you don't know how attractive you are," Hannah says, pushing her brown hair off her forehead. "Especially to someone insecure. In her mind, you probably are her role model, her mother, her fantasy all wrapped up together."

"Ugh." Horrid thought. "I don't want to be any of those things to any of my students. Most of them have mothers already, I hope, or a reasonable substitute & plenty of fantasies without me. Role model I guess I can't help." I take another swallow of wine. "Maybe you're right & it's time to retire." What a misery.

Hannah kisses my neck. "This is probably not a good time to think about it."

August 15
Reggie now leaving little notes in my mailbox—things like "you're the best, Dr. V." & "you make me happy" & yesterday, flowers "from your admirer, RB." Yesterday this letter arrives at my house:

Dr. V.,

I can't thank you enough for your time and attention this summer. I love working with you and I feel like I'm learning so much. I feel like you take such an interest in me. No one's ever made me feel this special—I feel like you really see me for who I am. I'm wondering if we can continue to work together in the fall. Your Reggie

p.s. I thought about you all day yesterday.

I realize I must talk with her. This fantasy bubble she's living in must be pierced. I email her & suggest an appointment. She comes in at three today.

I cut right to the chase. "Reggie, it's very thoughtful of you to give me flowers, & —"

Pure happiness on her face. "I'm so glad you like them!" she says. "I saw those peach roses & they reminded me of you."

"Yes, they're very nice." I pause, reject a veiled way of telling her I am uncomfortable about her gift—like "you really shouldn't spend your money on me"—for a blunter approach. "But I don't expect you to give me gifts for doing my job. I don't think it's suitable that I accept them. &, I don't think it's appropriate for us to continue to work together in the fall." I'm very firm.

She looks alarmed, but is quiet, & I press on: "As your advisor, it's my duty to recommend what I think best for your course of study. You've taken four classes from me, & two independent studies. You need to experience other professors here. It's an excellent department." How flat-footed, but what else can I say?

"I know. & I've taken lots of classes from the others. I just really need what you have to offer right now."

I try to speak gently. "I think you're making me into something I'm not," I say. "I'm your professor, Reggie, not your friend."

"Fine." She jerks herself erect & stands, all gawky arms & legs. She slings her backpack over one shoulder. "I think you're making a mistake," she says. "& I feel like you're accusing me of something. Like I'm, I don't know, after you or something. Which is crazy. That's in your head, not mine. I should report you to the Dean."

I stand also. This sense of purpose on her part heartening. "Go to the Dean if you like. That's your prerogative, of course. I'm sorry you feel I'm accusing you of something I'm not. I'm asking you to be realistic about who we both are, that's all. That way, neither of us will be disappointed in the other."

She doesn't say anything. Face burning red, her mouth twisting to one side, she flees the office.

I sit back down. Whole thing worse than I thought. Something underneath it all—not affection but *ANGER*. Creepy. But—too much to hope for?—maybe she'll be too embarrassed to pursue me further. &, if she talks to Darryl, I'll just explain it all to him. My behavior impeccable & he'll see that. Meanwhile, I need to keep careful notes about Reggie's behavior from now on.

August 24

Anna takes her sweet time about delivering it, but last Friday, I read through Paula Fabian's file. I'd forgotten . . . Paula's so accomplished. What a coup for this university to hire her. M.'s right on this one.

But can I work with her after that ghastly business at Indiana?

---

editor's note:

The following separate document was found lying within the pages of the diary, typed rather than handwritten and, to my eye, more carefully considered. On loose sheets, it was folded in three, and secured in the diary by a paper clip. As if its writer wished to guarantee its authenticity, the typewritten account was signed, by hand, in Isabel's script.

August 25

In the early '80s, I advised the Honor's Program in liberal arts. Paula Fabian had a job as Richard Lester's research assistant, exploring theories and criticism on American humor, Mark Twain in particular. Lester chaired Paula's senior honor's thesis committee as well; I was second reader. In the first draft of her thesis project, Paula had made an incredible new leap about the performance of race in *Huck Finn.* The maturity of her work was extraordinary in an undergraduate, even in an honors student. She was weeks from graduation and well on her way to her next triumph when Lester intervened.

"You what?" I said to Lester that day, twenty years ago, when he came into my office, his usual ooze of confidence replaced by a sheen of sweat along his hairline.

"I borrowed excerpts of Paula Fabian's essay on *Huck Finn.* I just wanted you to know: what Paula is saying about me is true."

"But why? Why would you compromise yourself like that? You're a wonderful writer, Richard. I don't get it."

He'd sat down, his spine curving forward helplessly. I hardly recognized him—Lester, cocky, with quasi-military posture, had always been such a martinet. "I don't know. I was going through one of those phases, you know, feeling stuck, uncreative, like I'd never have a fresh idea in my head ever again. And there it was: this beautiful work that dovetailed into my own without a seam. I thought no one would notice."

I felt a pain behind my left eye, which I knew would spread across my skull. "You thought no one would notice you stealing the work of a young African American woman, probably the brightest person in her class, the president of the student body, I might add the first female black student body president at this institution, a paragon of her race? Someone who's already been offered full fellowships to do doctoral work at five major research institutions? Tell me you're kidding. Please."

"I'm not kidding." Lester's even features leached into the pale parchment of his skin.

"She's filed a grievance," I said. I tossed a file across my desk; it landed at the edge and flipped open, the contents spilling across Lester's lap.

He picked up one page and held it up to the light. He squinted at it and let it fall to the floor. "Yes, I know."

I walked over to him and pulled up a chair next to his. I picked up one of his hands, the skin clammy, fishlike. Lester had been under incredible stress; his first wife had instituted divorce proceedings and had taken their two children with her when she left. Her leaving was overdue. Lester at this phase of his life had a history of having affairs with graduate students and leaving the charge card receipts for his motel liaisons on the kitchen table for her to find. The red ink, in their finances as well as an obvious flag of infidelity, had finally driven his wife away. "Richard, did you try to seduce this woman? Is that what this is about?"

He jerked his hand away as if my touch was the hot stove of truth. "I think she's attractive, for a . . . Well, I . . . I may have teased her occasionally, even flirted with her once or twice." He swallowed. "But no, I didn't. It was all perfectly innocent."

I winced at this choice of words. How could Lester appreciate that for a young woman dependent on him—as a mentor and guide, for grades and recommendations—that "flirtatious" and "innocent" didn't go together?

"That is debatable, but we'll save it for later. So, if not that, then what?"

"Isabel, you and I go back a long way." His eyes were round and pleading in an attempt at boychik charm that Lester, at thirty-nine, had about used up. He just didn't know it yet. "I need your help. Please."

I didn't say anything. My mind raced back over the ten years I'd known Lester. He'd been instrumental in my career. He'd helped me get the position at Indiana, and after that, tenure. He was the best friend of my advisor at Stanford. I could say that my work merited my job and tenure on its own, but we both knew he had paved the way. I closed my eyes, wishing I could erase him and my debt to him.

"Isabel," his voice was tight, as if forced through a narrow tube. "I'm ashamed of this . . . but Paula, she's so young, so confident, she's so goddamn good. She's going to be a big star."

I opened my eyes to see that his had filled with tears.

"It's really going to happen for her, Isabel. You'll see. She's going to have the kind of career that I . . . well, that most of us only dream of. And with the backdraft her race will give her, the incredible opportunities, she'll be unstoppable. It's . . . it's incredible to contemplate."

The pulsing in my head was raging. "Let me get this straight: you envy this young woman . . . this *girl?* You, Richard Lester, an accomplished, respected, white man, a full professor at a prestigious research university, are jealous of this young black female who is only twenty-one years old and has published nothing?" I felt my voice rise to match the ache that now clamored at the base of my neck.

He just sat there, shaking his head. He ran a hand through his hair, which clumped around his head as if he'd slept on it for days. Then he whispered, "Yes."

I couldn't believe what I was hearing. It was beyond pathetic. As I turned this confession around in my head, into a small corner of my awareness came the face of the valedictorian of my high school class, Rachel Stein, a plump Jewish girl. Brilliant. In spite of the grinding hours I spent, the extra assignments, she was always several jumps ahead of me, and I graduated second in my class, not first. I had admired her brains, yet I resented her. I swallowed and Rachel's face disintegrated. "Get out of my office, Richard. You disgust me."

"Isabel, please, the disgrace . . ." He raised his head, his skin gray, and licked his lips. "I'm begging you."

I didn't trust myself to speak. I watched him put his hands on the arms of the chair and push himself up with effort. Then, I said: "I'll talk to Paula. I might, just this once, be able to get you out of this. But don't you ever, *ever* ask me to clean up one of your messes again."

I had a long conversation with Paula the next day. Or, rather I made a speech; she said nothing. I told her how original and incisive her work was. I offered to direct her honors thesis, since Lester, of course, would be removed at once from the project. And I promised I would write the blurb for the first book that would undoubtedly result from her work. That she could count on me for recommendations went without saying. Then, feeling like I was drowning in the muck of my own words, I made excuses for Lester. I explained about the divorce, his midlife crisis. I told her confidentially that I feared for his emotional health if he were publicly pilloried for his "breach of protocol" (it was all I could do not to choke on this euphemism). I asked her to drop the formal grievance and leave the job of disciplining Lester up to the department and the college.

She listened very carefully. At the words "midlife crisis" her chin came up and she said: "My grandfather worked for General Motors for thirty-five years. He didn't have the luxury of a midlife crisis."

But in the end, she told me she would drop her grievance against Richard Lester to avoid tearing the department apart. The politics around race would be not only unpleasant but would, she volunteered, tokenize her in a way she wished to avoid. Most of all, she said pointedly, she would drop the charge out of her deep regard for me.

She barely stayed around for my choked expression of thanks, which was painful for both of us. On her way out, she paused at the door. She studied the office as if she might never see it again, and then turned to me. Never will I forget the look, filled with contempt and even pity, that she leveled at me that day.

After the memorial, Vivian, Daphne, and Miriam found themselves outside the theatre in the bright sunlight, blinking and disoriented as if they'd just emerged from a movie with a labyrinthine plot. What had happened?

Miriam turned back toward the building, observing the people pouring out in ragged clumps. "Where have they taken Hannah?"

Bettina and Fiona caught up to them. "Hannah is on her way to the hospital. Sergeant Crane is with her. And so is Darryl," Fiona said, clenching her fist around a mangled Kleenex.

"Which hospital?" asked Miriam.

"Austin General," Bettina said.

"I must go there as well," Miriam said, giving Vivian's hand a squeeze and hurrying toward her blue Subaru, which was parked along the curb in front of them.

Bettina watched her friend go. "What can she possibly do at the hospital?"

Vivian turned her aquiline nose toward Bettina. "She hasn't talked to Hannah since Isabel's death. She's extremely worried about her."

"Vivian, I'm glad to get a chance to talk with you without Miriam." Bettina steered Vivian away from Fiona and Daphne onto a bench that bordered the sidewalk.

"But Daphne, Fiona, and I are going out for dinner," Vivian protested.

"Fiona and I will wait here for you," Daphne called to her.

Bettina removed an oversize pair of sunglasses. "Do you know if Hannah was in Austin the weekend of Isabel's murder?"

"Lord, no. I've spoken with her on the phone once. And that was before the memorial. I don't know if it had even been scheduled at that time. She was still in shock. We didn't talk logistics," Vivian said, smoothing her skirt over her knees. "Come to think of it, there was one odd thing about her call."

"What?" Bettina leaned forward.

"Well," Vivian phrased her words carefully. "She didn't say much about how she felt—in the sense of grief, I mean. But she was very worried about her position as the lover of Isabel."

"You mean that the police may suspect her?"

"I assume so." Vivian looked at Bettina expectantly. "She seems frightened and secretive. What do you think?"

"I barely know Hannah," Bettina said. "I met her when she interviewed here in September and that's it. However, of course she is a suspect, and I assume she's been interviewed by the police."

Vivian nodded. "I'm sure Miriam will find something out."

"That's what I wanted to talk with you about. Miriam is in very great danger, I think."

"Miriam can take care of herself very well. You know that," Vivian said fiercely. "I don't think anyone would dare attack her."

Bettina shook her head vigorously, her curls glinting in the sun. "It's not so much that she will be attacked that worries me. The police are scrutinizing her; perhaps her more than others. She told me she spoke with Isabel at one o'clock that Saturday. In Helmsley Hall. Did she come home right after?"

"Bettina, I have been over this with the police. Twice," Vivian said wearily. "Yes, she was home at two o'clock that day. And then the two of us went to the art fair. It's ludicrous that they suspect her, but what can we do?"

"Vivian, think. Is there something we've overlooked? Something that would clear Miriam."

Vivian shrugged helplessly. "I don't know what that would be. If Hannah knows something, she certainly wouldn't tell me."

"Do you have a key to Miriam's office?"

"Well, yes."

"Excellent. Let's go over there now."

Vivian turned pale. "I don't think we should. It's an invasion of Miriam's privacy."

Bettina dismissed this with a shake of her head. "But things are not normal at the moment, and all of our privacy is being invaded. We must act and act quickly—desperate times and desperate measures and all that. Miriam's life is at stake. I want to see the files for both Paula and Hannah. They're in Anna's office, adjacent to Isabel's. I'm sure those offices are locked, but I happen to know that Miriam keeps a master key in her middle desk drawer."

𝕸iriam left the hospital and drove home, stirred from her state of distraction only when she noticed that the border of pansies she had planted along the side of the drive, and babied through the warm autumn, had bloomed at last. Then she slumped back once more into recounting her visit with Hannah. She had kept the distressed woman company while she waited for an examination room.

By the time Miriam had arrived, both Sergeant Crane and Darryl were nowhere in sight, and her old friend was not particularly communicative. "I'm so sorry to make such a fuss," she murmured, her customary energy extinguished by grief. "It's all so terrible. Poor

Isabel. And those people onstage who didn't understand her, who made her life a misery. They didn't support her when she was drowning, but then . . . never mind. Hypocrites! I just couldn't listen anymore."

"You don't mean her sister as well? She made Isabel's life a misery?"

Hannah shook her head. "They haven't been in touch."

Miriam mulled this over. She couldn't remember ever hearing Isabel talk about Graciela Brown, but then Isabel had never discussed her family with her. She decided to leave that subject alone. "Hannah, this is very important: were you in town visiting Isabel that last weekend?"

Hannah's forehead erupted into furrows. She hesitated, and then said: "The police know, so why shouldn't you? Yes, I was."

"I'm surprised the police let you go back to Maryland." Miriam drew a slow breath. "I mean, under the circumstances . . ."

"'Let me?' There's not much danger. I'm on a very short leash."

"Yes, but still . . . in a murder investigation, to let you leave the state. Unless, of course, it was an emergency . . ."

Hannah smiled faintly. "It was an emergency. My sanity."

Miriam found Hannah's attitude very unsettling. "What do you mean?"

"Think about it. Now that Isabel is . . . gone, I have no friends here—" she looked pointedly at Miriam, "—no family. The person I most loved has been brutally murdered. I'm sick, frightened. When it all sank in, all I wanted was to go home." She closed one eye as if it pained her; moisture seeped out from under its lid. "Where would you wish to be?"

"I see." Miriam sat quietly a moment, acknowledging the extremity of Hannah's situation, and how poor a friend she herself had been. "It must be horrible."

"'Horrible,'" Hannah echoed dully. "You have no idea. I used to have only sketchy notions of what it would be like to feel like a criminal, Miriam. I can now say that I know in excruciating detail. They searched every inch of Isabel's house. They took my clothes. They removed my lecture notes." Her eyes drifted away from Miriam's face and focused somewhere over her head. "They even took my sleeping pills." She laughed softly. "But they let me go back to Virginia. With psychological handcuffs attached. Police cars patrol my house regularly."

Miriam flinched as Hannah's eyes turned on her in a rage. "I'm so sorry, Hannah," she managed.

"Yes. Everyone's sorry. But not everyone was caught in what they call compromising circumstances."

"What do you mean?" Miriam touched her own forehead. "Your head injury? You're obviously hurt . . . is this a result of—" Miriam faltered.

Hannah shook her head, her lips compressed firmly. "I promised I would discuss nothing. It's a condition of my 'probation' or whatever you want to call the mercies the police are casting my way."

Miriam fell silent. "I understand. Can you tell me if you know what or who was bothering Isabel before her death?"

Hannah massaged her head with soft, short-fingered hands. "So many things. Oh, this headache. I really am not feeling well."

Miriam encircled Hannah's shoulder with her arm. "It's a terrible time. I know it must be so difficult . . ." She swallowed her guilt over pushing Hannah in her time of extremis. In her own desperate need for information, she prodded: "Can you just give me a hint of what one of the things troubling Isabel might have been?"

"She was in a lot of pain for one thing. Her back was flaring up. Bad enough for her to be taking her pain pills. I was very worried about her. And then, there was pressure from a student . . ." She licked her chapped lips. "I mean, from students and various faculty. . . . Oh, please don't ask me to talk anymore about it right now. I just can't." Her face lifted gratefully as a nurse summoned her to a consulting room.

At home, Miriam let Poirot out into the back yard and half-heartedly threw a few tennis balls for him to fetch. Inside, she made a pot of tea and retreated into her study. She drew out her notebook and flipped through it as if fanning the pages might release new possibilities, might tease fresh solutions from an implacable conundrum.

The pages stirred the air, but her own mind remained blank with fatigue.

Forcing herself to focus, she turned to a fresh page. Pills. Isabel's back. She remembered Isabel mentioning it once, very dismissively. An old injury, from falling off a horse when she was young. She wrote Hannah Weinstein's name in the blank space and underlined it three times. Hannah's reticence intrigued her. Was she the jealous type? What if she discovered that Isabel was having an affair with Reggie Bradley, for instance—might Hannah have been provoked enough to act?

She cogitated over this scenario, seesawing back and forth: on the one hand, it was unlikely, because everything about Reggie Bradley screamed instability. Isabel was no fool. And, she prided herself on her advocacy of students. Still, Isabel was prone to flattery . . . and capriciousness. In the midst of mulling over Isabel's sense of ethics versus her lascivious proclivities, the doorbell rang. She left the notebook open on her desk and hurried to answer the door.

"Hallo," she said as she opened the door only to find herself confronting Susan Crane on her doorstep. "Sergeant Crane. This is a surprise."

"May I come in?" Crane asked pleasantly.

Miriam's eyes fluttered; she thought of the notebook lying open in her study. "Of course." She opened the door fully and stepped back to allow the compact frame of the policewoman inside.

Miriam led her through a short hallway and then right into the living room. "Please take a seat. I'm having some tea. Would you like some?"

"Thank you. That would be very nice."

Miriam smiled tensely. "Just a moment." She hurried into the kitchen, filled the kettle once again, and turned on the burner. "I'll just go find my own cup," she called, and bustled down the hallway to her study to retrieve the tea and slide the notebook back into its proper drawer. She entered her office, which sported its usual paper clutter, and tried to imagine how it would look to a strange pair of eyes. Perhaps she should just leave things as they were. After all, a

142

notebook lying open in the private sanctum of an academic was hardly shocking. She picked up her teacup, her hand hesitating over the notebook.

"Nice office," said the calm cool voice of Susan Crane behind her. "You have a wonderful library."

Miriam turned around, startled. "You frightened me," she blurted, spreading her fingers to cover the page that was open.

Crane took a step toward her. "May I see?" the sergeant asked, her eyes drawn to Miriam's desktop. "I'm very fascinated by how writers work."

"No," Miriam said, closing the notebook and clutching it tightly against her chest. "I'm afraid it's private."

Susan Crane smiled at her, the blue eyes innocent. "Come now, Doctor Held, let me see it. I can have your office and your home searched, you know. I don't think we need go to those lengths, though, do you?" She put out her hand, palm up, to receive the thin volume.

A potent brew of embarrassment and terror coursed through Miriam's system. The scholarly part of her brain, critical and detached, dismissed her jottings as ridiculous and poorly written; the reptilian part, desperate for survival, wanted to hiss and strike at Susan Crane's outstretched hand. "It's nothing," Miriam said, groping for a way to regain some control in her own territory.

"Ah," Crane laughed. "It's the 'nothing' that I find the most interesting. Always. Please," she extended her hand further.

Miriam leaned backward and crushed her diary beneath both arms as if to flatten it into obscurity. The notebook was hers and hers alone. She had a fleeting memory of a scene in the film *The Remains of the Day* when Anthony Hopkins, as head butler, refused to let Emma Thompson, the housekeeper, look at a book he was reading. The unshared book marked their irreconcilable difference: his fear of intimacy, her desire for connection. When Hopkins dismissed her from the room after she finally snatched the book from his arms, Thompson reluctantly backed off in deference to his superior position. In this case, Miriam felt the tug-of-war but not

Crane's retreat; indeed, she felt like a petitioner in her own household. She realized that to protest further would only increase the notebook's importance, so she handed it to the detective, feeling an acute sense of loss as its small weight fell from her hand.

"Thank you," Crane said gently. She leafed through it with a light-fingered hand. "'Death of a Department Chair.'" She raised her eyebrows, which were sand-colored and slight. "How amusing. Playing amateur detective?"

Crane eyes scanned the first entry and then slowly closed the journal; her fingers firmly grasped its spine. "Interesting that the mode of the murder is so similar to that which actually happened." She chuckled ambiguously. "In murder as in real estate, it's all location, location, location."

When Miriam didn't respond (was this remark intended as wit or simply macabre?), Crane cleared her throat and tapped a short fingernail on the book's cover. "I did tell you earlier that you weren't being entirely honest with me, Professor Held. I have recently found out that you met with Isabel Vittorio at one o'clock on the crucial Saturday. As you might know, the coroner puts the time of death between one and three o'clock that day, on October 12."

Crane paused as Miriam attempted to absorb this information, then continued, brandishing the diary: "You either are a very prescient person or you cause events to happen. I think I'd like to hold onto this if you don't mind."

Miriam's mouth tightened. "Susan, those entries were begun to amuse myself at a faculty meeting one day, long before Isabel's death. I assure you I had no idea that such an event would ever come to pass."

"It's quite a coincidence, though, isn't it?" Susan Crane's pale eyes shuttered slightly. "Especially if, as you're saying, these writings predated the murder. Amusing? I confess I don't get the joke."

For a moment, dismay at Crane's misunderstanding of her meaning overshadowed Miriam's growing sense of peril. She addressed Crane as if she were a disappointing pupil. "Oh, must you be so literal? You must know that I don't mean that Isabel Vittorio's murder was amusing in any sense! At the time, the prospect of such a thing

144

actually happening seemed utterly a fantasy. I suspect you have never suffered through a dull faculty meeting."

Crane flipped open the notebook, then closed it with a snap as if to secure her mind against Miriam's plea for empathy. "No, I haven't sat in a faculty meeting of any kind. You have obviously never been on the serious end of a murder investigation, either. Perhaps if you had, you would be more careful about what you say. And write. And fantasize about."

The two women glared at each other. A moment later, Bettina's excited voice called up the hallway: "Miriam, you won't believe what we found in your office!" She burst into the room carrying another notebook, this one flat black and spiral bound, and then halted in the door frame when she caught sight of Sergeant Crane.

"Oh," Bettina said, breathing as if winded. "I assumed you were alone," she directed her comment to Miriam.

"As you can see," Miriam gestured to Crane. Perplexed, she asked her friend, whose usual ebullience had deserted her: "What is that you're carrying?"

Vivian, arriving close behind Bettina, put a protective hand on Bettina's shoulder when she saw the detective. Forehead crinkled and nostrils pinched, she telegraphed an anguished look toward Miriam. "That's what we wanted to ask you." Vivian struggled for a dismissive tone: "But, obviously, we can talk about it at another time." She prodded Bettina and the two of them edged into the room. With the set of their faces reflecting hard thinking as they sought a plausible subject to talk about (anything but the notebook), they looked like guilty schoolchildren. Miriam was reminded of the old joke about the elephant in the living room that everyone sees but pretends to ignore.

Watching this mute dance of avoidance, Crane's eyebrows again climbed skyward. "May I?" she asked, extending her hand once again.

Vivian and Bettina looked helplessly, first at each other, then at Miriam. Miriam, assuming it was one of many student notebooks in her office, urged: "Go ahead. Give it to Sergeant Crane. I've never seen it before." Miriam said this last with perfect confidence.

"It seems to be a diary," Vivian said, almost shyly. "It was in a stack of books in your office."

Miriam, utterly baffled, looked at her partner, her face flushing. "I suppose it's a very long story, why you and Bettina were in my office?" To Bettina, she said: "You seem to be making a habit of this."

In a small voice, seemingly on the verge of tears, Bettina replied, "I'm so sorry, Miriam. We were looking for your master key and . . ." Slowly and stiffly, as if the joints in her hands pained her, she passed the book over to the detective.

Crane opened the spiral-bound document and flipped through it quickly. Then, she went back to the first page and poured over it. "Yes, it is a diary." She raised her head, her face animated with a wolf-like hunger. "It's Isabel Vittorio's diary." She raised an index finger as if to make an accusation, but then thought better of it, and lightly tapped her chin instead. She turned toward Miriam, her mouth settling into a severe line. "And how coincidental it should be found in your office, Professor Held. Yet another in an incredible series of coincidences. Now, I think we should all sit down and have a long talk."

---

editor's note:

I do not mean to vilify Sergeant Crane in any way. While she did not typify the obtuse variety of detective often depicted in fiction, I did find her during the investigation to be utterly prejudiced against me. I often wondered if I reminded her of someone particularly repellent in her own life: an older female relative, perhaps? Or, possibly, that most misunderstood of creatures, her eighth grade teacher of English?

That night, in bed, Miriam was too agitated to sleep. The day's events sputtered and stalled on an endless series of reels spooling inside her brain: the green water spraying into the air and cascading back into the fountain's pool, Sigmund's white hair flapping over his face at the podium, Hannah's body crashing to the stage, Susan Crane's face staring at her with unbridled suspicion. "Ohhh," Miriam groaned, turning for the fiftieth time in the sheets. What she neglected to say, comments she wished she had made, churned inside her mouth in a similar jumble as she ground her teeth in her agony. "I just stood there, flat-footed, while Crane insinuated I was capable of murder!" she ranted.

Vivian, jolted into full wakefulness by her partner's turmoil, reached out and touched Miriam's sweaty forehead. "Honey, let me fix you something—how about some hot milk or a hot toddy?"

Miriam pulled the pillows from beneath her head, punched them as if they were responsible for her predicament, and stuffed them behind her back. She maneuvered various body parts, which were nerve-charged yet devoid of energy, into a sitting position and lay back with a gasp. "I can't drink anything. Or eat. Or sleep. All I can do is think. I'm ruined," she said, her voice cracking.

They had, of course, gone over this ground many times in the evening, first with Bettina and a quickly summoned Daphne over a scrabbled-together dinner, then on into the night alone, until they had given up with exhaustion and retired to bed. Vivian, deeply worried and fatigued, now said only: "Crane has entirely circumstantial evidence—the placement of the diary, your notebook. By themselves they're meaningless."

"But don't you see, it all adds up? All of these . . . coincidences—because I lost the chair to Isabel and was involved with her romantically—point the finger of guilt at me." Miriam shifted her weight as a pain shot through her lower back.

Vivian propped herself next to her unhappy partner with care. Knowing that Miriam disliked being touched when her nerves were screaming, she left a few inches between them. "I know you," she said, projecting all her feeling into her voice. "You're tough and you're strong and you're a fighter. Sitting and talking about this won't help. We need a plan of action. If you have something to do, you'll feel better."

Miriam's eyes watered as she turned to Vivian, her face looking very young and frightened. "Will we ever feel better again, Vivi?"

Impulsively, Vivian wrapped her long arms around her. "Yes, my sweet. We will."

Hearing the forced note of bravery in Vivian's voice, Miriam started to cry. "I'm terrified," she said.

"I know," Vivian said. "Me too."

She sniffed and shuddered and then, for perhaps the fifth time that night, Miriam blurted out: "What if you all give up on me? How long can this go on before no one believes in my innocence? What will I do then?"

"Shhhhh," Vivian said, hugging Miriam more tightly. "That isn't going to happen. Everyone who knows you trusts you. Completely. And we'll stick it out. Someone is playing games. Deflecting suspicion on you. We just have to find out who it is."

"But why?"

"I don't know," Vivian said wearily. "But they won't elude us forever. They'll slip up. They'll leave clues. We will find out why and who and how."

After a few minutes, Miriam disentangled herself. She groped for the Kleenex box on the table by the bed, removed a tissue, and blew her nose thoroughly. She lay back on the pillows and stared at the ceiling. "I wish I knew the answer," she whispered.

In the near-dark of the room, illuminated by a bright three-quarter moon, her partner sighed. "There is one. We just need to find it. Or wait until it reveals itself."

Miriam stirred. Her voice flared with ragged energy: "Something just came into my head. When Gertrude Stein lay dying, she asked Alice: 'What is the answer?' The story goes, when Alice couldn't answer, Stein's last words were, 'Then what is the question?' That's what we have to learn. Why did someone kill Isabel? If we untangle the threads of that question, we'll have our answer."

Exhibit B: Fragment of audiotaped conversation between Hannah Weinstein and Sergeant Susan Crane, October 15, 2002

SC: You said earlier that you woke up in Isabel's office, on the floor.

HW: Yes.

SC: Where was Dr. Vittorio?

HW: At the desk.

SC: Sitting?

HW: No, of course not—she was unconscious! She was sprawled across it. Her hair was matted with blood . . .

SC: Was she alive? Did you try to take her pulse?

HW: No . . . yes . . . I didn't know if I had a pulse myself . . . I . . ."

SC: You were unwell?

HW: Blood was in my eyes. It was everywhere. I couldn't see. My head was bursting.

SC: But you got up and walked away?

HW: Did I? I couldn't have. I would never have left her . . . alone. [*groan*] I don't know. Somehow I found myself at Isabel's, but how . . . I don't know.

SC: Someone brought you there?

HW: They must have.

SC: Who is "they"?

HW: [*hoarsely*] "They"? Oh, well, I assume someone . . . I . . . I don't know.

SC: Did you see someone in the hall outside of Isabel's office?

HW: No . . . You mean after? Wait . . . there might have been someone . . . yes, I'm sure there was. . . . [*groans*] Oh, but I can't remember.

SC: Did you drive back to Dr. Vittorio's house?

HW: [*no answer, quiet breathing*]

SC: Dr. Weinstein?

HW: I don't know. You don't understand. I thought I was dead.

SC: But you aren't dead. Do you ask yourself how did you survive when Isabel Vittorio didn't?

HW: [*whisper*] It's all I think about.

SC: [*long pause*] Did you kill Isabel Vittorio, Dr. Weinstein?

HW: I loved her.

SC: But did you kill her?

HW: KILL? What do you—No! I would never . . . I couldn't have . . . How? . . . No! No!

SC: Are you sure?

HW: Sure? [*sad laugh*] I'm not sure of anything. Not even if I'm really here. Am I really here, Sergeant Crane?

11

Keep your wits about you when dealing with those who might cause you harm, as in the old proverb: "He needs a long spoon who sups with the Devil."

Isabel Vittorio, in a class on the great speeches in Shakespeare,
explaining a reference from The Tempest

Exhibit A: Isabel's diary, September 2002

September 9
No sign of Reggie since classes began: oh, bliss. But then Thursday she appears at my office door (no warning & not my office hours). Her little face—surly & resentful—stares at me as I work my way through a stack of mail. She says nothing, silence the biggest demand for attention, I always think, so I keep reading the letter in my hands. When I finish, I put it back in its envelope, place it with the others, & look up. Reggie is fussing with the books in the small bookcase near the door. In the middle of the top shelf is a row of red hardcover books for my history of rhetoric class— collections of Cicero, Saint Augustine, Plato, the sophists, etc. On each end of the row are large, marble horse head bookends. They're ivory in color, solid in weight. Can't even remember when I got them. Very comforting all the same. A reminder of my old life.

"Yes, Reggie?" I try to relax as I look at her grim face. Luckily, the door is open & Anna is puttering around in the anteroom. R. lets her fingers slide over one of the bookends & then walks forward. She stands—inert, wooden, in front of me. I don't ask her to sit down.

"I'm here for my independent study." Stubborn tone.

I control my temper. "Reggie, we don't have a conference course scheduled this semester. I thought we agreed you would take courses with other faculty."

She flushes. "Yeah, that's what you told me to do but I still have an incomplete from the summer."

I'd forgotten. After she sent the flowers & we had our little talk, she disappeared, never turned in her final paper. "Ah. Well, then, let's get that dispatched, shall we?" My voice too perky.

R. stares at me, her upper teeth clamp down on her lower lip. She bites down so hard I can see a bright ooze of blood around her front teeth. She notices me flinching & licks her lip. She smiles. I shudder. She tosses her backpack on the floor but remains standing, arms tight across chest. "So, what do you want me to do?"

I page through the calendar on my desk. "How about you turn in the paper by September 20. That's a Friday. Can you do that?"

"Sure." R. cocks one hip, puts one hand in her jeans pocket & fiddles with her cell phone with the other. The phone swings from a case on her belt loop. "How long?"

"The same length we agreed upon in June," I say, trying for calm. I reach behind me & open the middle drawer of the file cabinet. Here." I give her a copy of the agreement for the independent study, signed by both of us.

She stifles a yawn & barely regards the independent study contract, her eyes flicking over the signatures. "Check." She drops the paper on my desk. "The 20th." She hefts the backpack over one shoulder & heads for the door. Her heavy boots thud against the floor. She fingers one of the bookends again on her way out. "D'you ever ride?" She pauses at the door, eyes narrow.

"Yes." Why do I feel cautious about even admitting this to her?

"Are you any good?"

I thought of the trophies at home for show jumping. "Fair." I hesitate, decide to let that be enough.

R. doesn't turn around, but laughs: "I can just see you. Have gun will travel." She puts a hand in the air, finger & thumb pointed to make a gun. "Pow," she says. Laughs. An uneasy sound, like a car sputtering before it turns over. As she walks through the outer office, I hear the jangle of her phone.

September 15

Last night I walk across the street to my car, get in & am just turning the ignition when a blue minivan cruises past, giving me a glimpse of Reggie's thin face at the wheel. This is a coincidence, maybe, though I parked in a faculty lot. But yesterday, I lean down to pick up the newspaper from my front steps & when I straighten, I see the same van, or what looks like the same van, disappear around the corner.

I start leaving the phone ringer off at home at night after several hang-ups. When I call Hannah & mention the calls, she says: "Bella, just get caller i.d. & then you'll know who it is. Stop being so stubborn. The technology's there—use it."

"I'm feeling a little frightened." My hand begins to cramp before I notice how hard I'm clutching the phone.

"Honey. I'll come down there," Hannah said, in that slow, heavy way she has, like warm maple syrup. More & more, I regret the geographical distance between us. "Or, better yet, come up here. Come straight away."

"I'll have to wait until next weekend."

"Don't wait. Come at least by next Thursday. You need to get out of there. What's going on in the department?"

I groan. "I almost forgot; this Reggie Bradley business has me so distracted. It's official: you & Paula Fabian are the two finalists for the position. That's the real reason I called. We need you to come down here in the next ten days & do an interview. Can you?"

Her voice loses its soothing timbre & tightens some. "Of course. But this job thing still bothers me. I don't think I'm right for it. & I feel like you're shoving me down the faculty's throat. To tell you the truth, I'm embarrassed."

To my surprise, I feel wounded for some reason & tears well up in my eyes. "Hannah, please. When you come, I'll tell you the whole story. There's a history here you don't know about; something you really need to know, okay?"

"All right. Let's see . . ." Her voice muted a moment & then she speaks clearly: "How about I come the Wednesday after next, the 25th?"

I calculate. Paula is arriving on that Monday, which makes Hannah the last impression the committee will get. "Perfect," I say. *Bulls-eye.*

September 18

Spend two days worrying, obsessing, etc. A part of me wants Paula hired, wants a second chance to show her that I'm not just a lackey of the good old boys. I especially want to fly in the face of Lester, who must be writhing at the thought of having Paula as a colleague. Just as he predicted all those years ago, her career outshines his own.

Siding with Lester, helping him cover up his theft, has haunted me for twenty years. It stands as my moment of weakness, my bête noire. Lester has paid me back for my discretion & loyalty by getting me hired at AU. If I can hire Paula, I'll have a second chance to win back her respect. &

yet, to have Hannah here, to have a lover & an ally, someone I can count on . . . I want that very much. The department politics not quite a wash: Sigmund & Lester will be happier with Hannah, although only marginally. The Dean & younger faculty clamor for Paula. Is there a way I can stay on the fence by coming out strongly for both candidates?

Finally send Paula a letter—my persuasive best—outlining what we can offer & saying that I genuinely hope she'll consider the position at AU, that I hope we can put the past to rest between us: "If you accept a position on this faculty, it would give me an opportunity to overcome the horrible impression you must have of me from our acquaintance of twenty years ago." I cross out that sentence, change "if you accept" etc. & redo the letter to read, "If we were fortunate enough to be able to welcome you onto our faculty, I would work tirelessly with you to build the kind of program that would attract the best graduate students." I offer her a pool of funds earmarked for recruitment—to improve the balance of minority students.

I consider the risks of sending such a missive, on the eve of her & H.'s official visits. If H. thinks I'm playing both ends against the middle, she'll be furious (*understatement*), but I'm in a huge bind. Pressure from the Dean about Paula at every turn. If I can give him this star professor, filling two of his diversity categories, it'll buy me some time as Chair to exert my leadership. Otherwise, Hansen will try to run the department from the Dean's office. I FedEx the letter. Paula sends back an email message saying that she looks forward to her interview.

September 26

The interviews are both well-attended & generate buzz, but without a doubt both the folks in Drama & our shop give their most spirited approval to Paula. H. not an idiot—sensing her audience is committed elsewhere, she telegraphs a conflicted look to me during her formal lecture, part "what's the use?" & part "what have you gotten me into?"

Afterwards, back at my place, H. breathes a sigh of relief. "I'm glad to put that behind me. Really, Isabel, I don't care about the job. Commuting is a nuisance, but we can do it. It keeps us from being bored," she says, trying to tease, but her heart isn't in it. Her eyes grave & a little sad. "Frankly, I don't like the way things feel here politically. There's a lot of tension. Who needs that? It's not good for me. You either."

I ask her not to withdraw until the search committee meets. "Trust me," I plead, but really, I have so little faith in what I'm doing myself. I'm being outflanked. If Paula arrives, her influence will be enormous. I can see it already—she & the Dean & many of the faculty & students will form a coalition with momentum behind it. If I manage to hire H., the loss of Paula will dash expectations & spirits—I'll be seen as a pawn of the old guard & the old order, a Chair without vision or leadership. I'll be just another ineffectual pundit, spewing her opinions like a noxious cloud of hot air.

I'm not sure how I've done it but I've outmaneuvered myself. I've set up an endgame that's left me no room to run. It all gives me an unfamiliar feeling: I'm sick of the games, the jockeying for position. Seems an exercise in futility: like a jump so high & hard to maneuver it isn't worth risking my mount or myself. I want to leave it behind—the Chairmanship & the university. To start over. To get out while I still can.

September 30
Reggie appears at my door today—at home. Crying & with a huge scrape on her forehead.

"You're hurt, what's happened?" The girl in bad shape.

She looks bewildered. On the other side of the street a bicycle is crashed on its side across the curb, its back wheel spinning in the air. "I'm not sure. I think a car backed into me. All of a sudden, I was thrown off my bike."

"Come inside." I bring her into my kitchen. We sit down & I clean up the raw patch on her face. I put water on for tea. I don't ask why she just happens to be riding her bike on my street in the first place.

She watches me take out cups & measure the leaves into the pot. When I sit down again, she says, "I'm sorry," & begins to cry again. She's much more appealing without all the defensiveness & the anger. She blurts out: "It's all my fault."

"What's your fault?"

"I just take up your time. I'm in the way. I know you don't want me here."

I feel a flash of the old annoyance. But the girl—dirt streaking down her face, eyes bleary from crying, nose running—looks so pitiful I can't stay angry. "Reggie, what's going on?"

"My girlfriend & I broke up," she says, misery leaking from every pore.

"I see. How long were you together?" A lame question, but what else to say?

"It doesn't matter." Sullen voice. But then she throws her arms around my neck & sobs. "I just want to be c-close to you."

God. She looks like she needs someone to cook her some good meals & tuck her in for a long rest. What the poor thing needs is a mother. I want to ask her what her family is like. Her misery is so palpable, it threatens to soak into my bones. But I don't dare to get involved. Not the way she feels about me already. & her neediness, her desperation, her pale hungry face, it all makes me want to turn away. It's too familiar. I've come too far & I won't, *can't* go back.

I pat her back & then manage to pull away. I hand her a

tissue & try for a reassuring tone. "Reggie, I think you should talk to someone, someone other than me. I don't know how to help you."

She jerks as if stung by a huge wasp. She stands up, her neck juts out & shouts down at me. Her voice boils with rage: "You're just like everybody else. Always fobbing me off on other people. What do you know about feelings? What do you know about love? You're just a giant brain. Thinking, that's all there is for you. Well, think again! If you don't let yourself feel, you're just going to be dried up. & old. & used up." She knocks over a chair as she runs out of the house. Through the wide open door, I hear metal scuff against the pavement as she rights her bike & in a second, the grind of the gears. Then it's quiet.

The news of the discovery of Isabel's diary spread as quickly around the campus as if a solar flare had erupted into the sky during a lunar eclipse. In the department, the halls came alive with rumors and corner strategy sessions. Miriam anticipated fall-out and was almost relieved when the axe fell after only two days.

Sigmund Froelich made his move at the very next faculty meeting, the Friday after the memorial. Miriam had just begun to conclude the meeting by asking if there was anything else anyone wanted to discuss, when he began to speak: "I think in light of police scrutiny and public attention during this murder inquiry, we might appoint an interim chair."

Bettina immediately countered: "But we have an interim chair," she gestured at Miriam. "Why would we need another?"

Sigmund pushed a lock of gray hair off his forehead. He smiled sympathetically at Bettina. "Professor Held is under a great deal of strain at the moment. I happen to know that Sergeant Crane has been in her office three times this week. The evidence is circumstantial, but until she is cleared absolutely we must have a chair who is not distracted."

Looking stunned, Fiona nonetheless objected forcefully. "Miriam is the best judge of that. If she wants to step aside, that's one thing, but I would hope the faculty will support her in whatever way she desires." She looked around the room with, for her, an unusually challenging gaze. A number of those assembled immediately dropped their eyes as if they found the surface of the table riveting.

Carlos Lambros, his dark eyes startled, raised his head and looked at Sigmund with a stubborn stare. "I agree with Fiona. We must support Miriam." He turned toward the end of the table and addressed her: "Tell us how we can best help you."

No one else seconded Lambros's gesture. There was a long and awkward silence which Miriam finally broke with a brisk: "I appreciate that, but Doctor Froelich's point is a good one. I would welcome relief from administrative duties at present. Thank you, Sig."

Sigmund beamed and bestowed his most beneficent patriarchal nod of approval at the gathered assembly. "That settles it," he said. "I nominate Doctor Lester to fill in, until Doctor Held wishes to return."

"I would be happy to take this on," Lester said gravely. "Of course I regret the necessity for doing so."

Bettina shook her head and glared at Collin Freed, stunned into helpless silence by the face of her disapproval. She gathered up her notepad and pen. "I don't like this," she said defiantly. "This room reeks. Of disloyalty and expediency. I need some fresh air." She left the room.

The skin around Miriam's eyes crinkled with strain, and her face was very pale, but she was otherwise composed. Avoiding a vote, the result of which was too uncertain, she said: "Unless anyone objects, I suggest we revisit this arrangement one month from today." As if a gavel had been struck, the rest of the faculty filed out of the room.

Lester remained behind. "You took that with grace," he said to Miriam, who methodically layered into her briefcase several manila folders, her reading glasses, pens, and a daytimer encased in leather.

Miriam snapped the front buckle on her brown leather bag. "I try not to waste my energy on battles I can't possibly win." Her mouth thinned in a bittersweet smile. "I suspect there will be others in the near future that will require my concerted effort."

She checked her wristwatch against the wall clock and frowned. "In the meantime, I suggest you get in shape. My friend Daphne tells me that one can never be prepared enough for a sneak attack. Think, Richard, if this faculty has so little loyalty to the barely departed Isabel and such small belief in my innocence—at present I may be the suspect du jour, soon it will be someone else—how much trust and commitment will they accord to you?"

Miriam slipped quietly from the room, inwardly fuming about Lester and Sigmund's move to seize the chair position. Her only consolation was that she had seen it coming and had rehearsed her response to it, thanks to Bettina's repeated warnings.

She scurried down the back stairs from the seventh floor to avoid meeting anyone, and hurried to her parking lot. She unlocked her vehicle, threw her briefcase in the backseat, and was bending to assume the driver's position when she straightened back up. On second thought, she decided to walk over to a small café west of campus and have a coffee.

Cloudy skies and a drizzle of rain cooled the air. She reached the café and slid into a booth in the back. When the young waiter arrived, she ordered an espresso and a slice of blueberry pie. She hoped that caffeine with a side of sugar would restore her good humor and creativity.

She savored her late-afternoon treats while doodling on a grocery receipt she'd found in her purse. Miriam found it almost impossible to think without a pen in hand and paper in front of her. Leaning back in the booth, she remembered how her mother, Bette, had sketched on almost anything at hand—the odd scrap of paper, cocktail napkins, unused margins in newspapers, and, of course, on drawing paper as well. Often, when the young Miriam sped through the kitchen to grab a piece of fruit or a jar of peanuts, she'd see her mother wielding a pencil or a crayon. When she asked her what she was doing, her mother replied: "Oh, just thinking." Miriam's father had affectionately called his wife a "doodlebug."

But Miriam's mother, in her early fifties, had blossomed from a doodlebug into a serious artist. Miriam's father, Paul, had not lived to see it, having died in a freak car crash when Miriam was only ten. By the time Miriam was twelve, she experienced her seemingly ordinary mother transformed into a person of consequence: at fifty-two, Bette, working in oil pastels, had her first exhibition of landscapes. Miriam recalled the raptures of pride she'd felt in her mother's accomplishments. Haunting the galleries of Bette's early shows, eavesdropping on observers' comments, she'd reported back to her mother her interpretations of what viewers of the paintings had said. This early undercover activity became a serious pursuit to Miriam, an only child, and she sometimes rehearsed in her room so that when she performed the gallery devotees for Bette, she'd get their walks and gestures just right. Bette, delighted by Miriam's antics, referred to these early impersonations in subsequent years as her daughter's first foray into "research." Wistfully, Miriam hoped her father somehow was able to see how brilliant and successful his wife had become, and how clever his daughter.

She stared down at her slip of paper and saw that it was filled with an abstract design, all sharp angles and twisting lines. She covered the paper with one hand and looked over her shoulder.

"May I join you?" a deep voice asked. It was Carlos Lambros, his broad forehead crinkling as he smiled his kind, lopsided smile.

"Oh yes, please," Miriam said, pushing her empty pie plate aside. "I was just going to order another espresso."

Carlos was dressed in an olive green, long-sleeved shirt of very soft material and cream-colored, fine-gauge cotton slacks. Miriam admired how his clothes, simple but well-cut, draped his solid body attractively.

"How are you holding up?" He sat across from her and crossed his arms. "What a bleak day this is."

"Oh, it's not so bad," Miriam said. Thinking of her mother had cheered her. She, too, felt like she was having a resurgence in her fifties, and she had sudden confidence that someday the events of this dispiriting afternoon would prove to have little consequence.

Carlos shook his head, his dark silky hair falling around his face. He brushed it off his forehead. "You're a brave woman. It was like a pack of hounds braying for fresh kill in that room today. I think I'd have had heart failure if they'd been after me."

"Ha! I don't think so." Miriam leaned over and patted her colleague's forearm. "You had the courage to speak up, which is more than most of them did. Thank you for that."

He dismissed her gratitude with a wave of his hand. "Miriam, I'm seriously worried. I've emailed Hansen that I can't stay in a department that has Richard Lester as its chairman."

"You won't have to. This investigation can't go on forever. And when it ends, Lester will have to withdraw."

"I didn't think you should have made it so easy for him today." Carlos said, his deep brown eyes pensive.

Miriam nodded. Had she been in anyone else's shoes, she might have agreed. But, to her, Lester's blatant pounce for power had been revealing and instructive. Pressured by his increasingly rampant greed, he seemed to have abandoned all caution. She wanted to uncover the source of his confidence. To Carlos, she only said: "It didn't seem worth fighting. Not today." She frowned briefly. "We didn't have enough soldiers to support us. But don't worry: we may lose the skirmish but win the war."

"That's what I want to talk to you about. I've been talking with Paula . . ."

"Yes?" Miriam said as he paused.

"I didn't want you to think I'm going behind your back," he said apologetically, his caramel-colored skin pleating around his eyes.

"Oh, no, go on. Paula is an excellent strategist. And she is now an official member of our faculty as well."

"Good," he said boyishly. "That you don't mind, I mean. Paula is ready to go to the dean with something that will immediately discredit Lester. She told me she had intended to let it go since she was joining the department, but in light of today . . ."

"Ah, you mean Richard's theft of Paula's work? I know about that."

Carlos exhaled, relieved. "She has proof."

"Yes," Miriam hesitated. "Carlos, I would like to ask you and Paula to hold off, just briefly. I have a feeling there will be a break in this case very soon"—she said this with more authority than she actually felt—"and I don't want Lester alerted by a confrontation with the dean just yet. If you can just trust me on this for awhile, say, a week or so?"

"Miriam, absolutely. We just want you back in the chair's position where you belong, that's all." Carlos's chin went up aggressively. Miriam seemed to recall that his résumé included a stint as a collegiate wrestler.

"I'm very glad to have you on my side, Carlos. Believe me."

"You can depend on me. You've gone to the mat for me more times than I can count," he said stoutly, and their eyes met in a kindred moment of shared purpose.

By the time Miriam made her way back to her car, her entire system was supercharged with espresso and resolve. Miriam felt a new buoyancy as a result of Carlos's generous support and comradeship. It pleased her that the younger generation still found her a worthy leader. And God knew she needed their physical vigor and fresh perspective. Like an exhausted commander rejuvenated by fresh troops and materiel, she felt ready to fight another day. She even took slim comfort in the realization that setting aside the effort of running the department had its positive side. She intended to spend the time exploring every possibility of how Isabel had met her death. She would start by visiting Daphne to jump-start her intuitive process. A logical assault on the mystery had so far yielded only limited results. Other weapons and approaches were obviously required.

12

When the weather turns against you, go to war as if your life is at stake. Fight with every weapon at your disposal: fertilizer, artificial light, change of location, fungus remover, poison. Anything to promote growth and retard rot.

Marvin Graf on his gardening website, Marvingardens.com

The Sunday after Isabel's memorial, Miriam, Vivian, Bettina, and Fiona met in the evening at Daphne's house for potluck. As soon as they had consumed a hodgepodge of salads, fresh bread, chicken casserole, and chocolate-pecan ice cream (this last a home-made concoction of Marvin's he had festively packaged and sent with Bettina), they assembled in Daphne's consulting room. The soft room, with its cream-colored walls, longleaf pine floors, and various multicolored rugs, enclosed Fiona like a snuggery after the raw aura of suspicion haunting Helmsley Hall of late.

"Are you all ready for this?" Daphne inquired, a sphinxlike smile rippling across her features. Dressed in a roughly woven, pearl-gray robe that fell in an unbroken line to the floor, her wild silver hair clasped severely behind her head, she assumed the role of high priestess with both gravitas and hauteur. One hand raised for si-lence, she led them into the room individually, placing each woman at an assigned seat at her round cherry table. Next, she prowled the room with ritualistic slowness as she closed the blinds, shut off all lights, and then rotated her body in a full circle, pausing to salute each of the four directions. At the very last, she turned on a low wattage lamp in the corner of the room, which spread a soft glow around the edge of the table. After her preparations, the very room, shrouded in an artificial twilight, took on an aspect of expectancy.

After Daphne assumed her seat, Fiona broke out nervously, "Are you sure this is wise? I mean, a séance. What if we bring something into this room we're not prepared to deal with?"

"Then we shall be very lucky," Daphne replied. "Think of this as merely exploration, a fishing expedition if you will, rather than a séance, which has connotations I'd rather avoid."

Fiona puzzled over what those might be, but such was her anxiety she preferred not to ask. The atmosphere teetered between the known and the unknowable, leaving her off-balance. The supernatural unnerved her. As a child, watching a horror movie disrupted her sleep and dreams for weeks. She didn't feel confident that her nerves, exposed and raw from the past days, were up to the challenge of psychic "explorations."

"Arthur Conan Doyle was a devotee of spiritualism," Miriam said crisply into the silence.

"Yes, and?" Bettina replied testily.

"Nothing. Just that he had a great head for mysteries and plots. It adds a touch of legitimacy to the proceedings for me, that's all."

"I don't see why it should," Bettina remained obdurate. "He wasn't much of a businessman. He tried to kill Holmes off after all—aside from Harry Potter, only the best-known character in the history of fiction. That makes me doubt his acumen entirely."

"Ladies," Daphne said in a warning tone as Miriam opened her mouth to reply. "You're polluting the atmosphere with this sniping. Now, everyone, join hands. Oh, but wait, I almost forgot." She withdrew her hands from the circle and placed her pack of tarot cards onto the table, fanned through them, and selected the Queen of Swords, a striking, dark-haired woman who sat sternly on her throne. "This is to represent Isabel: a woman of great intellectual gifts, strong, powerful, but perhaps too eager to do battle. You see the storm clouds gathering around her as she sits on her throne?

Also, around her feet the earth is barren. She lacks the gift of fecundity. This was a sadness for Isabel, I believe. She had brilliance, but not creativity. Most important, the queen looks angry, vengeful. We shall meditate on this card to bring her spirit into the room.

"Now, again, join hands. Concentrate on the figure's sadness and need for revenge. Buried within this grief and yearning we shall find the clue we are missing. Now, I will lead us in several cycles of deep breathing."

While Daphne counted sonorously, the women breathed obligingly. Fiona found herself quickly light-headed. A nervy rush went up her spine when Daphne said in a low voice: "Isabel, we invite you to join us. If you desire your death avenged, you must help us. The person who did this to you eludes us. We need you to speak."

Fiona felt a blood vessel pulse in her forehead. She had an almost uncontrollable urge to rub the spot but her hands were held fast by Bettina on her left and Miriam on her right. Her eyes jittered from one woman to the next, amazed that her four companions appeared so relaxed, their eyes lightly closed, their necks gently curved forward like graceful birds. Perhaps she should excuse herself; her agitation would surely jinx the proceedings.

"Isabel . . ." Daphne repeated, drawing out the three syllables on a single clear note, almost like a soft mallet striking a metal gong, and indeed the "bel" echoed throughout the room.

Fiona found herself growing sleepy as Daphne repeated the word once more. And then again, until the name became a mantra that circled and enclosed the room with its rhythm and resonance. "Isabel," Fiona whispered to herself.

"Yes?" a voice said.

Fiona jerked awake and looked wildly around the room, finding four sets of eyes riveted upon her. She opened her mouth to say "What is it?" but instead she murmured: "Ask Miriam. Ask her to remember what happened that other time, the other young woman."

"Miriam?" Fiona repeated, to her relief sounding like herself again. But, then in a moment, she hissed: "Miriam, be careful! You're the one he wants . . . or is it a she?" A reckless and alarming laugh rumbled in Fiona's throat.

166

"Who, Isabel?" Daphne said urgently. "Who is he?"

"No, not 'he.' I'm sure she said 'she'!" Bettina said.

A guttural sound came out of Fiona's mouth, half-choking, half-chortling. Fiona tore her hands out of the grasp of Bettina and Miriam and raised them to her neck. Her face reddened, her eyes watered and fluttered erratically. Fiona thought her throat would burst one moment, but in the next she sighed deeply. The air departed her lungs in a rush, leaving her empty and starving for oxygen. After a moment, she was able to inhale again and found herself capable of speaking. "Oh. How terrible," she gasped, breathing in great gulps. "I must have choked on something."

Again, four pairs of startled eyes rested on Fiona; the women perched apprehensively in their chairs, waiting. After a few seconds, the tension snapped and Vivian jumped up to get water. "Here," she said, returning with a huge glass, thrusting it forward with such energy that water sloshed down Fiona's v-necked top.

"That voice," Fiona whispered. "Whose was it?"

"It was coming from you," Daphne said. "Most remarkable."

"Me?" Fiona blinked rapidly. "But I heard it outside of myself, in my ear but not. Does that make sense? But when I opened my mouth to speak my thoughts, I found I couldn't." Softly, she touched her throat. It seemed impossible, yet she had heard something. Perhaps, overly excited, she had simply put a voice to the expectations in the room? Hastily, she covered her confusion: "Tell me: I don't remember what I said."

Daphne rose and found a pad of paper. "Quickly. We must write down every word before her message is lost to us." Crowding around her, Bettina, Miriam, and Vivian pieced together the fragments they had heard.

"That business about 'he' and 'she,'" Vivian said. "Was that a joke?"

"Sometimes the spirits do amuse themselves at our expense," Daphne said. "But I'm not sure that's what she was doing. Perhaps Isabel isn't sure what happened herself." She looked up, her unmatched eyes curiously bright. Fiona felt the glare of the tawny cat's eye to be especially unsettling.

"Oh, no," Miriam burst out. "What hope do we have of finding the solution then? Surely no one else will know. Except for her killer. And that person will never tell."

Fiona broke in: "I don't understand. Why would Isabel speak through me? We had absolutely no connection and very little contact." She felt sheepish that her mutterings—maybe just a waking dream—influenced her friends' thinking. But she kept quiet; if what she had said incited their creativity, well, who was she to put a damper on their enthusiasm? She certainly had no solutions of her own.

Daphne shook her head. "You were the most susceptible today for some reason. In this room at this time, you served as the portal— the point of entry. I don't know why." She focused on Miriam and prodded: "Think, Miriam. What did the spirit mean about 'that other time' with the 'other young woman'? And who is the young woman this time?"

Miriam moved away from the table and sat down, cross-legged, on the Navajo rug, its red and black pattern streaking out from around her body like waves of energy. "There is a young woman who was close to Isabel, Reggie Bradley. I have spoken with her twice. The first time she seemed to accuse me of having some responsibility in Isabel's death, but I have come to think that is just a ruse. She later told me she was in love with Isabel."

Bettina turned to Daphne. "Let me pull her picture up on the university website. I think I know her."

Daphne gestured toward her computer at the other end of the room. "Help yourself. But the other time? What does that mean?"

Miriam scrubbed her face with her fingers. "Twenty years ago there was an incident with Paula Fabian, at Indiana, that Blake Burnois told me about. I've told all of you about that. Possibly she is referring to that—certainly Isabel's maneuvering over Paula is a central part of this case. But I wasn't aware of that history before Isabel's death." She passed a frustrated look to Vivian who joined her on the floor. "She must mean something that happened before I met Vivian."

"Yes, when you and Isabel were together briefly," Bettina agreed. "It must be then. Let me think back, too. What female students were in Isabel's orbit twelve years ago?"

Fiona, who had joined Bettina at the computer, said: "Wait. There was a graduate student who worked closely with Isabel and Sigmund, the one who was studying Churchill's speeches with Isabel and World War II poets with Sig." She snapped her fingers and rushed over to Miriam, her blonde hair flying around her face. "What was her name?"

Miriam gave her a bewildered look. "I don't know who you mean."

"Of course you do! Oh my God, don't you remember, she had the most awful crush on first one and then the other . . ." Fiona stopped, staring at Miriam who looked miserable. "What?"

"I think she *was* playing a joke on us," Miriam said. "I think she is referring to Vivian. Reggie Bradley loved Isabel who did not return the favor. I fell very hard for Isabel and she did not reciprocate, for very long anyway. Is she making fun of me once again, about being a spurned lover . . . ?"

"No," Daphne said curtly. "That's not it. While that event in your life has great importance to you, for Isabel it is all in a day's work, I'm sorry to say. Expedience is her trademark, not sentimentality—she would not dwell on the past unless she herself were wounded. Fiona, what happened to this young woman whose name you cannot recall?"

"She got a job at Maryland, tenure track. That detail I remember." Fiona tapped her index finger against her head and then announced: "Farraday. Her last name is Farraday."

"Maryland," Daphne repeated. "Where Hannah Weinstein teaches. That might be it—she's tying Hannah in."

"But Hannah is already tied in," Bettina protested.

"Yes, but 'the *other* young woman' also implicates Reggie Bradley," Daphne said. "Somehow Reggie and Hannah are connected to what happened to Isabel."

"Well, yes, on the one hand how obvious. On the other, these connections are positively labyrinthine. Too oblique for literal-minded me," Vivian said. "There's a reason I find technical writing comforting." She leaned against Miriam's shoulder.

"It is a puzzle. Exactly. Even if Isabel is being a trickster, making us all doubt our pasts and our motives, I think she must be referring to Paula as the past young woman. And what happened with Paula?" Daphne asked.

"Isabel felt she betrayed her. Richard Lester put her up to it, but there's no doubt she let Paula down, badly," Miriam explained. "She failed as a mentor. Perhaps Reggie Bradley felt betrayed as well." She gripped Vivian's hand. "Betrayal is the root of all of it. What if Richard Lester felt that after all of this time, Isabel was going to betray him, for example? By hiring the one woman who was at the root of his academic disgrace. And certainly Hannah Weinstein must feel betrayed as well—Isabel did not support her for the new position."

"Except at the very end," Fiona said slowly. "Remember? Dennis told us that on the Friday before she died Isabel reversed her position and threw her support behind Hannah. That is our clue, that switch that she made at that late hour."

"Isabel, Hannah, Richard Lester, Reggie Bradley." Daphne intoned the names thoughtfully.

"Once again, everything revolves around Hannah," Vivian said. "The strangely absent Hannah . . ."

Daphne nodded. "I wish we had Isabel's diary. Too bad Bettina and Vivian had to surrender it to Sergeant Crane."

Bettina's face looked pensive and closed for a moment, but then she unexpectedly beamed a smile at all of them. "Yes, but not before I made a copy." She went to her briefcase and drew out a sheaf of papers. "I've noticed how documents connected to Helmsley Hall have a way of being swallowed of late and so I took precautions."

"Hallelujah! You are an excellent woman." Daphne swooped toward her, her robe undulating around her ankles as she walked, gathered up the papers and spread them out on the table. "Let us study the final entries first."

Exhibit A: Isabel's diary, October 2002

October 3

H. & I argue—awful, awful scene. She flies home after her interview last week, stews for a few days, & then bounces back to Austin today in a state. The search committee this morning voted for Paula, with only Mary Morton from the Drama Department voting for Hannah. The EC plans to meet next week. "You knew the department had made up its mind. Absolutely. Why did you put me through that charade of an interview?" She storms around my back deck, pacing up & back, her voice shrill, raving. I begin to worry that the heads of neighbors will peek over the fence to see what the commotion is.

"Hannah, please. I'm in agony about this." I tell her the whole story of Paula & Lester & Indiana. This does not mollify her.

"That's supposed to make me feel better? That you're using me as a pawn in your attempt to make amends with my rival for the position?" She pulls at her hair. "I am such an idiot!" She looks at me with those soft brown eyes. "Isabel, you used me. I didn't want to apply for this job. & now I feel like a fool."

She is quiet then & that makes me feel worse. Her eyes look far away. An ache slices through me. She must not leave me . . . "Hannah, my sweet Hannah. I feel terrible. Can't you see I'm conflicted horribly? I want you here. I'm selfish. But then there's this political reality . . ."

"Just stop," she says, voice like sandpaper. "Don't make it worse. & I don't want to talk about how you feel right now. I'm trying to tell you that I feel terrible. & expendable. & like you used my love for you."

I stare at her. "Yes, I said love," she says. She picks up her wine glass & looks at the pale amber liquid lapping the sides of the crystal. "You're so lucky, you know that? People feel strongly about you whether you try to win them over or not. Even when you don't deserve it." She smiles bitterly. "You arouse passion, Isabel. Maybe that's it, not love, because I see how you are disliked as much as you are admired. Be careful, passion is a dangerous emotion." Suddenly, her voice loses its energy. "Oh, let's talk about something else."

I do my best to distract her but, really, what else is on our minds? I feel the truth in what she says. I'm a political animal. Always putting my position—& my career—first. I wonder . . . is it too late for me to change?

October 5

H. still here. Something alarming this morning: as we have coffee at the little table in my bedroom I think I see a face at the window.

"Do you have someone coming to mow the lawn?" H. asks lazily, pouring cream lavishly into her cup. She takes a generous bite of a croissant. A smear of butter glistens on her lips. Her good humor—& her appetite—have returned thank God.

"No. The service comes during the week only, once every week. It's Saturday. & they were just here last Wednesday." I stand at the window. A blue van is pulling away from the curb. "Oh, Lord. I think it's that wretched student again!"

"Reggie? She must have it very bad for you, Isabel. I warned you about passion. It's a double-edged sword. Don't forget Judith beheading Holofernes."

I can't place the reference at first, but then—a twinge of dread. I remember, on a trip to Florence, seeing Donatello's stunning sculpture of the brutal murder of Holofernes, the voluptuous torso of Judith rising over the slain warrior, her erotic posture countered by the sword in her hand. I try to be flip: "That's a heterosexual drama. & Judith was rescuing her people from the Assyrians. Neither detail seems to apply here."

She smiles coyly. "Most homosexuals have no other models for their histrionics but heterosexual ones. The whole concept of *drama queen,* which is ascribed to gay men, is straight out of the femme fatale tradition—very straight. I think . . ."

"Hannah, please. Save your celluloid closet discussions for Fiona's film & lit. class. Didn't she ask you to come & speak?"

The flesh trembles under her chin as she draws her head back. "I went to her class during the interview. I thought we weren't going to talk about that anymore."

God. I'm in a rut of saying the wrong thing, each time, every time. I fill our cups with coffee. "Getting back to Reggie. I'm afraid she might be crazy." I realize with a stab of certainty that Reggie really is insane. So far, everything is fairly minor—following me, the notes, the phone calls—none of it really huge. But I know in my gut without a doubt she is dangerous. "Last year an honors student, maybe even a friend of Reggie's, accused Bettina Graf of sexual harassment. It wasn't true but it caused a lot of trouble for Graf. & she's married to a man & has two precious offspring. Maybe they're horrors or sprogs, who cares? The point is she reproduces, she's straight. If even she's suspect, think what this could do to me!"

"Has this young woman said she's going to file a formal grievance? This is more serious than I thought," H. says.

There are worse things than a grievance I think. Much worse. A stalker, an unstable wacko scaring me half to death . . . "Nooo. That hasn't even come up. Yet. But that's because she's still hopeful of getting my attention. She did babble something about talking with the Dean at one point but didn't do it. I'm worried. I can't afford a charge like that

173

right now." My heart feels like it's doing laps at a speed trial at the thought of it. God, why didn't I see this coming? I've been vulnerable: a known lesbian without a permanent partner. Just a sitting duck for an unbalanced person like Reggie, desperate for a maternal figure.

"She's confusing desire for a mother with a need for sexual intimacy," I tell H. "Poor boundaries—the oldest lesbian trick in the book."

"You've never heard of a straight young woman looking for a father figure in an older man?" H. says. "Of course these are old tricks—it hasn't gotten any easier to be female in the last century or so. Don't be so hard on women."

I stare at her. She's right. I hold women to a higher standard. No wonder I'm so often disappointed.

"Why don't I talk with her?" H. offers.

I turn to her slowly. "That's it. You."

"What?"

"If she knows how involved I am with you, she'll have to back off."

"Well, maybe not—"

"No, hear me out. Hannah, I want you to move here & live with me. I'm tired of the Reggie Bradley's, the speculative looks of students, the demanding petty faculty, one political battle after another. I want to change my life. I want stability, I want permanence. Let's be together."

H.'s brown eyes are suddenly opaque. "Isn't it a bit late for that?"

"What? Why?" I lick my lips, my mouth suddenly parched.

"The way you handled this job. Your ambivalence with me. If you really had wanted me here, things would have turned out differently."

"Hannah! Please. You're good for me. & I adore you. I'm telling you I want to change."

Her body seems to retract. She crosses her arms

defensively but her voice is sad: "Why don't you ask me what I want, Isabel?"

I stare at her, afraid; she looks like a sphinx, regal & closed. "Tell me what you want," I whisper.

Her voice almost dreamy. "I don't think you have any idea. I don't think you know how to ask. You're too used to telling others what you want. & too used to getting it. You don't have enough experience at failure to know the risks of opening your heart."

I grip my cup. I want to hurl it across the room, through the window. "I'm only thinking of you. Right now. I'm proposing to you, goddamn it."

She gnaws at her lip, then gets up & comes over to me & sits on the chair arm, one arm around my shoulders. She traces my mouth with her finger. "I wish I could believe you."

I grab her face with both of my hands. "Believe me," I whisper.

She leans down & looks into my eyes. "I want to."

"Kiss me," I say, my voice harsh in my ear, my breath caught in my throat. "Please."

October 7

I plan my campaign carefully. First, I cancel the Executive Committee meeting to delay the vote on Paula. I need time to plan my strategy with Hansen. In addition to hiring Hannah, I'll promise to deliver Paula next year. I even know where I can find the line: Collin Freed is up for tenure this fall & his case is weak. Or weak enough for my purposes. Unless everything is perfect in his dossier, he won't make it. &, I recall a lukewarm letter of review which I'll be forced to comment on in my summary of his file as Chair—it's my responsibility to be fair, after all. I make an appointment with Dennis, who chairs the search, for Friday afternoon. *I must have Hannah.*

When she leaves on Sunday, H. tries to persuade me once more: "Bella, this isn't worth it. Leave this place. Come live with me in Virginia. You'll find something in D.C. There are ten institutions that would fall on their knees to have you. Or you could consult. Change your life. This place is sucking the life out of you. It's a cesspool. Don't try to get me here."

"No, I can do it. You'll be happy here, you'll see." I begin to see a new life. & I'll show Miriam & Lester who really holds the power. I can still get what I want; it's just within reach. I ignore that little carping voice in my ear, that whisper of *Forget politics. It's crap; it never ends; it's an endless loop of illusion—false power, false hopes, empty nights & loveless days. Change your life & do it now* . . . As soon as I achieve this one coup, then I'll change. I'll make a clean sweep.

H. seems apprehensive. "I don't know. Something's just not right. Look, you remember your old student, Donna Farraday? She teaches in my department. She adores you. You could probably come to Maryland."

Donna Farraday. Oh, God, not her. I've forgotten. "That woman who was in love with Sig? Hannah, you've got to be kidding. I think she hates me."

Hannah cocks her head to one side, puzzled. "No. She told me once that she actually was quite infatuated with you at one time. I think she did have an affair with Sigmund, but who didn't in those days?" Hannah giggles. "She supports you, believe me."

The mention of Farraday unnerves me. She had a crush on me back then. But I knew she was baiting me at the time. She was straight. I was to be her experiment.

I burn at the memory. I remember her following me into the bathroom at a party at Darryl Hansen's house. The nerve. I'm washing my hands at the sink when she comes in without knocking . . . She leans against the door.

Pretty. Athletic, good figure, etc. At the time, I'm still in the closet, lying low after the affair with Miriam.

"You're not only interested in men, are you?" she says, her eyes at half-mast. She's wearing a low-cut top. She rests her hand between her perky little breasts & plays with a heart-shaped locket. The worst of it is that I'm tempted. She takes a step toward me, pushes the lower part of her body forward. She wants me to kiss her, or . . . My body flushes all over. Thank God I resist. I dry my hands & push past her; I don't answer her fucking question.

"Donna Farraday's a bitch," I tell Hannah. & *a fake* & *a fucking tease*. "I don't trust her."

"All right," H. says wearily. "But you won't get the committee to change its mind. So go ahead, follow your plan. It'll fail. & then we'll talk about your leaving here."

When we kiss goodbye, her lips, yielding & full, linger on my mouth & then graze my ear. "Take care of yourself." Voice soft in my ear. "Stay away from that girl."

I won't let her go. I kiss her again. I love the taste of her & the feel of her mouth. She's divine. "Stay," I say. "I don't care about that girl, any girl. Stay with me. Come back to bed."

"I'll be back next weekend," she says. Her breath a sigh on my neck. "I have to get back."

October 11
I court Mary Morton, even though it's almost more than I can stand. She fairly purrs in my office. I can tell she loves feeling like she has the ear of power. Of course, now that she's sleeping with that prick of power, Lester, you'd think she'd have her fill in that department.

Lester. I wonder about Mary's reaction if I tell her how her precious boyfriend makes a habit of coming on to every reasonably attractive woman he encounters. Maybe age is curing him of that. But I doubt it. Only last year when we were in the office after a late committee meeting, he asked me to have a drink with him. "To talk about old times," he says, a crooked smile on his little face.

After all these years, I feel short of breath just thinking back to Indiana. & Paula. "Not for me, thank you. 'Old times' don't make good times in my book."

He half-laughs & grabs my elbow & squeezes it & he keeps his hand there, his fingers massaging my skin. "Isabel . . . " He says my name slowly, like he's tasting it. "I've always felt we have things in common we've never explored. We're not so very different, you & I."

Horrors. I stare at his face, notice every pore in the flesh around his slit-eyes. How can he link the two of us, even in his dreams?! I'm proud of my writing & research, I have ethical standards toward students, I'm proud of my career. All of it is *mine.* Nothing borrowed or stolen! I'd earned my way, by myself, for myself. We have nothing in common! Was the man, this thief, this exploiter, mad? Sweat begins to drip down between my breasts. I can't think or speak. "I have to go," I say, my voice a rasp. "I'm not feeling very well."

He lets my arm go then. He smiles again. His lips curve at the corners but his eyes are dead & flat. "Some other time. We should get to know each other better. Or maybe differently."

I sit in front of Mary Morton & I force that memory away. Oh the nausea, the wash of acid in the throat . . . it all comes back. Of course I'll say nothing. Lester's interest in me makes me feel ashamed. In a way I've almost forgotten. As if it's my fault I attracted his attention in the first place. In a way, I owe it to Mary to warn her. *Save yourself* . . . As a female colleague, if nothing else. Yet I don't know how without making her question my motives. It's all too complicated. I struggle to concentrate. She's beaming at me with her open, Midwestern face. I take a swallow of water from the bottle on my desk.

"You were saying?" I say, feeling myself again. She looks at me so expectantly, so respectfully, it settles me down. I take a breath. I'm fine, just fine.

"I know there are people who would be very grateful to you if you can keep Paula Fabian off this campus," she says, her chunky legs crossed. Her cockiness puts me off, releases me from the woman-to-woman solidarity I've been imagining. She's callow, an opportunist. Keep Paula off the campus—as if Mary Morton is even fit to shine the boots of a brilliant woman like Paula Fabian! & she really better lose some weight before she turns forty. She'll see, those chubby cheeks of hers are cute now, but when they sag into her neck it'll be another story: from appealing chipmunk to appalling bulldog. I've seen it happen overnight.

I want to vomit. *People who will be grateful . . .* As if I'm doing this for the likes of Sigmund Froelich or Richard Lester or Collin Freed, the toady. It's almost enough to make me want to call the whole thing off, phone Miriam, beg for forgiveness. What a stupid blunder it all seems to be.

"What about Carlos Lambros?" I say, casual as a cat licking her paw. Carlos, a key member of the search committee, is Latino & desperately vocal in support of Paula.

"Well, there's a certain cachet in being one of the only minorities in the department," Mary says.

Cachet—I wonder if she knows that the word once referred to the packaging of a bitter pill. How appropriate. "I think he is heartily tired of that distinction," I say. "Carlos is very popular with students, a good scholar. We can't afford to lose him."

"I'll take care of Carlos," she says, all eager.

God forbid. "No, let me worry about him. He & Dennis are close. Let's go at it that way."

She leaves my office, not a moment too soon. If only I could, I'd fire her. But she's not even in my department. I shut the door behind her & then fume for a half hour. My problem is Hansen. He wants his new star black academic. But he'll get her. Instead of midyear, it'll just be fall. What's a few months? Oh, well, committee first, then the department, then the Dean. I must *not* get ahead of myself.

Then the wretched appointment with Dennis. Who shocks the hell out of me. He's so adamant, so pissed off, so obdurate about Paula. Gutsy move—never knew he had the balls. & so prickly about his precious boyfriend.

"Dennis, let's just wait a few days, till we both simmer down, & then talk again."

"Not on your life," he storms. I forget he's an actor. Maybe Captain Bligh is his idea of heaven. & then the bastard walks out on me with a pretty good line, I must admit: "Just be a bitch," he says, "& see where it gets you." It occurs to me later I could have—*should have*—said the same to him.

October 12

A misery of a day. First, Bettina storms into my office & berates me for how I'm treating her beloved Miriam. As if I'm responsible for everything that happens around here. She accuses me of trying to discredit Miriam's opportunity hire initiative.

"I'm all in favor of it." I go for blandest tone possible.

Bettina raps her knuckles on my desk. "Then put your mouth where your money is. Fill some lines with new faculty that support it. & stop bad-mouthing Miriam."

I have to admire her balls. There she stands, her glorious red hair standing around her head like Medusa's crown of snakes, chest heaving, telling me how to be Chair of the department. Perfect model for Donatello's Judith. That gorgeous torso curving forever. I can just see her with a sword in her hand.

"Look. The faculty voted me Chair, not Miriam, & that's what's really got you in a huff. Admit it. It's not diversity or initiatives or the Dean's favor or your admiration for Paula. Pick your favorite flavor—it's all just bullshit. A smokescreen. You're pissed because your pal isn't running things anymore."

She puts her face about three inches from mine & hisses: "Damn right I'm pissed. I'm just waiting for you to fuck up. Which you will. & then we'll see how long you stay as Chair."

Then she stomps out, the snaky hair rippling down her back. God, the woman is good-looking. What a waste that she only makes it with men. But maybe no woman has ever had the guts to try?

Then, on the stroke of the next hour, as if they'd timed it, Miriam waltzes in. The one-two punch of Graf & Held. God knows I've seen it enough times, but how do they manage it?

Miriam is polite & straightforward, as always. & brief. "Paula Fabian will be joining our department, hopefully as early as January," she says. Voice dry-as-dust.

"That's not quite settled yet," I demur.

"Oh, yes, I think it is," she goes on in that dogged, stubborn way of hers, like a border collie herding sheep. "You can't postpone the EC vote forever. & you can't buck the tide for much longer either." Her shrewd little eyes glitter at me like mica pebbles. "You know that, Isabel. Don't hitch yourself to a falling star."

"Are you calling my partner, your old saddle-buddy Hannah, a falling star?" I'm ready to pick an even bigger fight.

"No. I mean don't get in the way of progress. &, right now, Paula Fabian is progress. We need her, Isabel."

I feel the hum of blood in my ears & know I have maybe

thirty seconds before I completely lose my temper. Plus, my back is killing me. Like a knife digging into my spine. I breathe into the pain. "You may need her, Professor Held. But don't ever presume to tell me what I need." I look at my watch. "This is what I get for coming into the office on a Saturday. I had hoped to get some work done."

Miriam holds her ground, a superior smile on her face. "Work away. There will be a vote next week on this hire—whether you call a meeting or not." & she walks out the door, the thick soles of her black slides quiet. She's small but lethal. *Mighty mouse.*

Soon after, more definite footsteps sound in the hallway. I look up hopefully. & yes, finally, the one person, the only person, I plan to see today—the only one I *want* to see—comes through the door, my beloved, my Hannah—

$\mathcal{T}$hat's it? That's all we're going to get?" After reading the final page of the diary, Bettina's voice reflected disbelief. She rubbed at the table's surface as if to summon a genie who would magically materialize more pages out of the very ether. Her face, a study in frustration, slowly moved around Daphne's table, appealing to each of her friends in turn.

"Well, yes," Miriam said, looking entranced. She scrubbed her face with her hands as if to erase the grogginess of a long nap. "I imagine that when Hannah came she stopped writing."

"But God, it's so tantalizing," Bettina groaned. She rose out of her chair and stretched her back, her arms arching over her head. Then she flopped over, her fingertips touching the floor. From this position, she continued, her voice muffled: "We have everything except, what, the last hour of her life?"

"We have everything," Fiona said, her face white. The glimpse of the private Isabel in the diary—jarring, unfamiliar—left her feeling uncomfortably voyeuristic. Isabel had always stood for such authority. For her, reading the diary felt like eavesdropping on her parents' intimate life, only worse.

Bettina uncoiled from the floor. "What did Crane tell you was the estimated time of death?"

"Between one and three that day," Miriam said. "I think I left her office by one something, maybe one twenty."

"Well, it just can't be Hannah," Vivian said. "I don't believe she killed Isabel."

"No," Daphne said slowly. "Why would she? And yet, she's in a damning position. She came in that door after you left. At the very least, she must know something. And her continuing silence is suspicious. She can't be overlooked."

Miriam continued to pore over the last pages of the diary, her stubby fingers underscoring sentences as if attempting to feel out the subtext of what was written there. "This explains why Isabel changed her support to Hannah at least," she said. "And she really was, at different times, promising the job to both Paula and Hannah. Just as we suspected." She directed this last to Bettina.

"The student," Vivian said. "This Reggie. Isabel sounds genuinely afraid of her."

"Ahhh," Miriam clasped both hands beneath her chin and rested her elbows on the table. "This is a cumulative effect, I think. Remember, she says she's tired of the Reggie Bradleys as well as a host of other things, much of it generated by her own modus operandi. She's exhausted from the very suspicion and cynicism that resulted from her political striving."

"I know this is beside the point," Vivian said. "And I don't mean to sound like I'm being callous about what happened to Isabel. But her diary . . . well, she writes about herself almost as if she's a character in a story. Do you think she meant to publish it?"

Fiona spoke quickly. "I can't imagine."

"Well, we always used to joke that Isabel published so much she must have turned every scrap of prose into fodder for books and articles, down to her grocery lists and telephone messages," Bettina offered. "But . . ."

Miriam glanced at her sharply. "Isn't it possible that she simply enjoyed writing this? That, for once, she had a place to express her feelings, fully, where she would not be judged? Isabel was exceedingly private, perhaps too private for her own good. And, I can see now, very lonely."

"It's all horribly sad," Fiona said. "I wish we had known she was in such distress. She must have had someone to confide in—?"

There was a long silence. Vivian and Daphne curiously studied the faces of the three colleagues: Fiona registered helplessness, Miriam embarrassment, Bettina avoidance.

Bettina stared down at the diary pages. "Well, I don't think we came across too well, Miriam," she muttered.

Miriam laughed giddily, a tinkling trill that released some of the strain in the room. "She thought you were beautiful."

"Yes, well," Bettina said, with an eloquent shake of her head. "Beautiful maybe, but bitchy definitely."

"So," Daphne steered their focus back. "Who put the diary in your office, Miriam?"

"It was on Isabel's desk, lying open perhaps. Whoever killed her took the diary with them," Miriam said mechanically. "And that someone sought to implicate me by stashing it in my office. That much is clear."

"But why you?" Bettina said intensely. "Why point the finger at you when so many others had reasons to hate Isabel Vittorio?"

Vivian's frown magnified the deep ridges around her elegant mouth. "Because they thought her the easiest target."

Bettina nodded. "Yes. Miriam had the affair with Isabel, she lost the chair position, she led the diversity initiative. She represented the public face of resistance to Isabel."

"Not only the easiest target but the most tempting one to shoot down. By discrediting you, Miriam, he—or she—could take away your considerable influence as well," Vivian said.

Daphne tapped the table with a blunt finger. "Politics aside, this person has personal, even intimate motives. Your past history with Isabel, Reggie's love for her, Hannah and Isabel, the mysterious other younger woman—sexuality is paramount in this case. Susan Crane was correct when she told you that, Miriam."

"Do you mean the murderer has to be a woman, then?" Fiona asked, breaking her silence. Her nervous system, overloaded, had retreated into numbness.

"Oh no," Daphne said shrewdly, "but that is what the killer wants us all to think."

Bettina agreed: "This case is about sexuality, yes, but influence too. They are intertwined like a double helix. If Isabel had not been powerful, she would not have died. I'm sure of it."

"Power, sex, and let us not forget reputation," Miriam said, twirling her reading glasses absently. "That about covers most human motives."

"Except money," Bettina said and then laughed. "That's a word guaranteed to stop most academics in their tracks. Aren't we supposed to have higher things on our minds? Ha."

Daphne gave her a sharp look. "Reputation translates into money, not just prestige. Perhaps we've overlooked something." She left the table and plopped down in an overstuffed green chair at the edge of the room. Mounted on the wall above her was a piece of cloth, a Chinese stone rubbing, depicting butterflies in flight. She closed her eyes, took several deep breaths, and withdrew into what looked like a deep meditative state.

Vivian watched her expectantly, as if waiting for a message from an oracle, but when Daphne said nothing further, she turned to the others. "Back to sex. Has Crane learned anything from Reggie Bradley, do we know?" She added: "There have always been troubled students, even dangerous ones. But does it seem to the rest of you that the problem is on the increase?"

Miriam nodded. "The stress on these young men and women is immense. The competition—for grades, awards, financial rewards—gets more hardscrabble every year. All this in a population with few emotional resources. And Reggie was not in good health, mentally or physically."

"A loose cannon," Bettina said softly. "Whatever she set her sights on could have become a target."

No one spoke as the four women looked at each other, their faces registering sudden tiredness. It was as if the rising adrenaline of the afternoon, like the cresting of a high fever, had peaked and evaporated, leaving only lethargy.

Fiona broke the silence. "I haven't heard anything about Reggie. But Hannah is still here, staying at Isabel's house. Will she talk to you, Miriam?"

"I don't know. I assume she's told Susan Crane everything already." Miriam sounded reluctant.

Daphne stirred back to attention with Miriam's words. She said in an alert voice, as if refreshed by a nap: "I wouldn't assume that," she said. "Do you want me to go with you?"

"As a witness or to protect me?" Miriam said, trying to laugh lightly as she had before, but instead managing only a nervous croak.

"Whatever you need most." Daphne picked up her bag. "Let's go. We can't afford to waste a moment."

Fiona watched them march out the door. "The avengers," she said involuntarily.

Bettina pursed her lips. "I hope Hannah has a strong heart and a strong stomach. With a brain to match."

Vivian tidied up the diary pages into a neat stack and anchored them with a granite paperweight in the shape of a heart. "She survived Isabel, didn't she? I trust she can take care of herself."

13

Death is most frightening to those who fear the inevitability of change.

Daphne Arbor

Death is terrifying because it means the end. Period. No wake-up call possible.

Susan Crane

Those eminent Victorians loved their wordplay, cloaking death as a gentleman caller and orgasm as the little death. Some people need a little eros with their thanatos.

Bettina Graf

Exhibit C: Transcript from Susan Crane's interview with Reggie Bradley, recorded October 27, 2002

(Subject sits at the table in a black crop top, blue jeans, and flip-flops. She is noticeably nervous—chewing on the skin around her nails [already torn and red], scratching her head, drumming her fingers on the table—but coherent. Her posture is poor and her hair unwashed. The interview begins at 2:30 p.m. CST, Sunday, October 27, 2002.)

I didn't . . . I wasn't spying on Dr. Vittorio . . . Well, sometimes we just happened to be in the same place. Yeah, we'd had kind of a rocky time of it. We used to be really tight, you know? I felt like I could talk to her. And she was really smart. And sharp. I liked how she dressed and the way she walked and stood—she was just so strong and so, well . . . tall. She was just, like, the most together person I'd ever met. She made other people just look pathetic, she was so together. She knew what she wanted. She took no shit, she was a baaad girl, if you know what I mean. Nobody messed with her, ever. You just knew you couldn't fuck with Vittorio, you know? I really grooved to that.

Things changed in the fall. I don't have a clue why either. Zip, nada. She turned on me, it seemed to me. It was like I had pissed her off or something. I dunno. She was sure different than she had been. I mean, I'd been her special assistant for two semesters. I did everything for her. Well, not everything . . .

Here's what I think. She was seeing someone. And keeping it secret. That person, no, I didn't know her. I didn't meet her either. Well, just that day, the day I guess Dr. V. died. But I think that woman was like a really bad influence on Dr. V. She changed: all of a sudden she seemed moody and upset, off somehow, not so sure of herself anymore. She always had kind of a quick temper, but not like she did later, like in August, then she went kind of ballistic. That was new.

Saturday October 12. Let's see. Well, yeah, I was on campus. I was in Helmsley Hall. Well, I work there. No, not for Dr. V., not anymore. But a friend of mine, a grad student in film, she lets me use her lab space sometimes. It just happens to be by the elevators, which is around the corner from the main office from Lit. & Rhetoric where Dr. V's office is . . . was. Well, what happened was I went down the hall to the bathroom. The women's room is on the same corridor as the elevator and around the corner is Dr. Graf's office and across from hers is Dr. Held's. So that's how I know both of them were there on Saturday. I came out of the women's room and I saw Dr. Graf kind of pounding down the hallway. She had on sneakers, but she was walking fast and hard, like she was pissed off, you know? I kind of flattened myself against the wall by the bathroom because she didn't look like she wanted to see anybody.

Then I went back to my lab space which is directly across from the elevator. I don't know, maybe sometime after one

188

o'clock I saw Dr. Held take the elevator down. She looked kind of mad too, but she's quiet, you know the way she is, kind of in control. She doesn't throw her body around like Graf.

So, yeah, I can't remember why I decided to go see if Dr. V. was in. I thought she probably was. *(laughs)* Cuz Dr. Graf and Dr. Held weren't her favorite people and if they were all pissed off . . . well, I don't know, I just thought they might have been talking to Dr. V. Noooo, I didn't have an appointment or anything. I didn't have any big *reason* or anything. I was just curious. And . . . I hadn't had a chance to talk to Dr. V. for a long time. *(ducks head)* I don't know if I'd have really had the guts to say anything, though, she didn't want to see me anymore.

The main office door wasn't locked. Of course not, cuz otherwise I couldn't have gotten in. I waited a while after Dr. Held left. I heard the elevator again. I saw the woman coming out. Yeah, the woman who was Dr. V's friend. No, I hadn't met her, like I said before. But . . . but I happened to see her at Dr. V.'s house one day. I just happened to be walking by and I saw her. I don't know, maybe a week before. No, I don't live in Tarrytown where Dr. V.'s house is . . . I live near campus . . . but I have a friend nearby. Yeah, sometimes I walk my friend's dog and we go by Dr. V.'s house—it's a nice street, you know, lots of trees and quiet and everything.

Yeah, Hannah Weinstein, the woman who fainted at Dr. V.'s memorial. She came off the elevator. Well, the offices where I work are tiny, so basically if you stick your head out the door, you'll see who comes off the elevator . . . it's not like you even have to try or anything. So she went down the hall and about two minutes later I went down there too and kind of crept into the main office, real quiet, and then well, Dr. V.'s office door was open. That kind of surprised me. Cuz usually all the profs, if it's the weekend, keep their doors closed. At least that's what I've found. Cuz, you know, I'm there on the weekends a lot.

(subject suddenly agitated, flinging her arms about, face reddening) Yeah, they were in Dr. V.'s office. Dr. V. was sitting down, kind of leaning back in her chair . . . and this Weinstein person was sitting on her lap. *(subject begins blinking rapidly)* They were kissing. I don't mean just a little kiss either, I mean like all-out open-mouthed kissing, like hot. She had her hand inside Dr. V.'s shirt. It was *disgusting.* Why? *(starts to cry)* This woman, this Weinstein person, wasn't good for her, that's why. You have to know that. That's really important. I just hated it . . . I hated her . . . She was the reason Dr. V. was all upset and making bad decisions, why she didn't talk to me anymore.

So I just stood there for a second . . . I didn't know what to do. Then I guess I took kind of a step forward into the doorway and the other woman saw me. Her eyes got really big and angry, so I took a step back. She scared me. She said something like "Get out!" I think she started swearing at me . . . yeah, she called me a bitch I think . . . I don't remember. Then Dr. V. gave me this unbelievable look, like I was the last person she ever wanted to see in her life. It was terrible. Her face turned all white and then kind of blotchy red. And then Weinstein looked like she was going to get up. I was sure she was going to come for me.

(subject is wringing her t-shirt in her hands, almost doubled up in her chair) So I don't know what happened. I can't. . . . I was scared. I didn't have anything in my hands, no belt, nothing. But when you walk into Dr. V.'s office there are these bookshelves, kind of low ones, you know? On the top shelf are these cool bookends, white marble horses or something. I reached my hand out and picked one up. I didn't even think about it. I didn't mean to. It's like it jumped into my hand . . . and I . . . I don't know how I did this cuz my legs were shaking so bad . . . but I kind of took a

few steps closer to where they were sitting and I threw this . . . this rock right at Weinstein. I hit Dr. V. in the head, I didn't mean to. . . .

(subject falls into a kind of trance) And then she starts bleeding. There's all this blood. And her . . . her friend starts screaming so I go back and I get the other one, yeah the other marble thing, and I throw it at her . . . anything to shut her up. It hits her and she stops all right. It's real quiet then. And there they both are, kind of slumping over on the desk. *(subject, breathing hard, stops speaking)*

(subject drinks water, seems calmer) They might have been knocked out. They weren't dead, though. They were breathing. I knew they'd come to in a minute. I couldn't be there when they did, could I? For sure, I didn't know what to do. And I ran. I just ran.

You believe me don't you? *(subject pushes her chair back from the table; she falls on her knees, her hands covering her face)* I would have done anything for Dr. V., anything. I didn't mean to hurt her. I didn't. I don't know . . . What happened after that. . . . I don't know . . . I don't remember . . . I ran out into the street . . . and I . . . uh . . . uh . . . *(unintelligible sound)* . . . I kept running. The next day I woke up in the park by my apartment. It was so cold on the ground. Freezing cold. I had leaves in my mouth. . . .

(subject looks up, as if in appeal) What can I do now? Tell me. Please. What is there for me to do? . . . What? . . .

(the interview is terminated at 3 p.m. CST)

At five-thirty on the Monday afternoon after the gathering at Daphne's, Miriam sat in her study, listening to a CD of Alicia de Larrocha playing Mozart sonatas. The pianist coaxed the keys to sing with a sure and subtle touch. It was October 28, only two weeks after the discovery of Isabel's body. Miriam felt like she was living in an alternate galaxy, one that pulsed to a different rhythm, where the planet had tilted off its axis into a fifth dimension, out of space and time. But the music reoriented her. She smiled as she recalled having read somewhere that de Larrocha was very short, barely five feet tall, yet the psychological reach of her hands seemed infinite.

Outside, Vivian threw yarn balls in the backyard to their cat, Alice, who twirled and leaped and batted the air. Poirot ran frantic circles around Vivian and Alice; periodically he snatched a ball away from the cat and sprinted away to bury it. Miriam sighed, watching this ballet accompanied by the strains of the Mozart; she could only hope that soon life might return, if not to normal, to some acceptable balance. Yesterday she and Vivian had gotten up at dawn and driven to the waste treatment plant at Hornsby Bend to check out the fall bird migration. Ducks of all kinds paddled in the ponds—ruddy ducks and scaups and redheads—and a black-crowned night heron lurked in the reeds. As she zoomed her binoculars in on an osprey cruising above the water for prey, Miriam felt happily outside herself for the first time in weeks.

The doorbell rang. Stifling a yawn, she got up to answer it. She reached the door, cup of tea in hand, and turned the knob to greet Sergeant Crane's stolid frame in front of her. She shuddered slightly, but said in as pleasant a voice as she could muster: "Hallo, Susan. You'll want to come in, I imagine."

Miriam gestured to a chair in the living room in front of the unlit fireplace; temperatures outside were pleasantly situated in the seventies. Sitting opposite the detective, Miriam offered, "A cup of tea? I can offer only that—there are no mysterious notebooks in the house this time, I'm afraid."

Crane showed her teeth in a slight, strained smile. "No, thanks. I have some disturbing news for you. About a student in your department. I thought I should tell you at once."

Miriam set her cup down on a small hinged-leaf table. "Oh?" She regretted her foolish attempt at a joke about her jottings and Isabel's diary.

"Reggie Bradley. Do you know her?"

"Oh, yes, a student of Isabel's."

Susan Crane took off her glasses and rested them on one knee of her khaki slacks. "She killed herself this morning. Or, rather, we found her body this morning."

Frozen in place, Miriam sat quietly. Swamped by a wave of regret (hadn't she known this girl was drowning?), she breathed shallowly. Unconsciously, she'd been expecting—no, dreading—another disaster. But this possibility had never occurred to her. An ache spread through her chest as she registered the loss of the young woman's life. "How terrible," she said, her voice hoarse. "This is a bitter blow."

"You knew her well?" Crane asked, leaning forward slightly.

"No, no, I didn't. But I had talked with her since Isabel's death. I . . . well, I had suggested counseling and tried to take her to the counseling center one day myself. But I hadn't followed up . . ." Miriam's eyes smarted with tears. "I should have, but I didn't."

"I see." Crane nodded and bit her bottom lip. "So she appeared distressed to you at the time?"

"Very. She seemed, well, she told me she was in love with Isabel. I guess I can tell you that."

"Yes, it was apparent that she was either in love or obsessed, I'm not really sure which. I interviewed her only yesterday."

"How did she do this terrible thing?" Miriam said and shut her eyes, not certain she wanted to know the details.

"An overdose of Percodan."

Pain pills. To dull a pain so terrible that no amount of medication could assuage it. Miriam hung her head. "The poor child. Was it her prescription?"

Crane shook her head. "The bottle in her house bore her grandmother's name. Who died two months ago. Her parents don't know how Reggie came to have the pills."

Miriam, sunk in her chair, stared at the dark fireplace, feeling an urge to light a flame. To warm herself, and to honor Reggie's spirit. "I'm afraid I should have seen this coming."

Crane, her eyes shadowed, said, "The fault is entirely mine. She was utterly distraught yesterday and I . . . well, I let her just leave the station. Not alone but in the company of her father, who was also acting as her legal adviser. He promised to supervise her. I assumed, with his help, she could cope. I should have guessed that something was wrong there."

"What do you mean? Abuse?" Miriam asked, suddenly alert.

"I don't know, of course . . . but something in the way she held herself away from him, pulling back from his touch. The defensive posture, head hanging, the avoiding of direct contact. I can see now that the girl was afraid of him. She felt ashamed." Crane lifted her hands wearily. "In retrospect, I should have inquired more deeply. I let myself be distracted by what I had learned from the interview."

Miriam massaged her forehead. "An abusive parent. This makes sense. Her symptoms are almost classic. Her nerviness, her lack of care for herself, her secrecy. And I don't think she was sleeping. How could I not have seen it?"

"She's a student," Crane said reasonably. "I imagine they often don't sleep or eat properly and are anxious. I'm sure you see some of those symptoms all of the time."

"But this young woman was unusually desperate. And now it's too late." Miriam's voice was shadowed with gloom. Reggie had been the priority of no one. "She has committed the ultimate act of desperation. I wonder if she couldn't face that she would never see Isabel again."

"She couldn't face her own responsibility in Isabel's death," Crane said, patting the pocket of an oversized, waffle-weave vest. She pulled out a package of cigarettes. "I don't suppose you smoke?"

Miriam shook her head.

Crane put the cigarettes back longingly. "I can't tell you exactly the details just yet. But she was in Isabel's office Saturday after you left. I think we know now how Isabel's head got bruised so badly and her collarbone broken."

Miriam sat up; a muscle twinged in her mid-back and for a moment, it hurt to breathe. "Are you saying Reggie Bradley murdered Isabel Vittorio?"

"She had a pivotal role in her death, let's say that. If Hannah Weinstein were not alive, I might think we had our murderer. Do you know why I say this about Hannah?" she added sharply.

"Sergeant, Sergeant," Miriam rubbed her eyes. The inside of her lids felt raw. It occurred to her that she hadn't let herself cry for Isabel. "I don't know what you're talking about. Why wouldn't Hannah be alive? I tried to talk to her over the weekend but she didn't answer the door at Isabel's. I'm certain she's living there."

Susan adjusted the collar of her crisp white blouse. "I came here to tell you about Reggie. But also because I need your help. I have, of course, interviewed Hannah Weinstein. She was with Isabel in her office after you left on the Saturday as well. I imagine this is not news to you." She focused her light blue eyes on Miriam who flushed slightly. "The diary . . ." Susan added.

"Yes, I have read the diary," Miriam said. "Only recently. I don't know how the original came to be in my office, however. I never saw it. I read a copy only yesterday."

Susan held up her hand. "Don't tell me how you obtained the copy. I told you before I'm deluged with paper in this case. Everywhere I turn there's another pile of scribble. You'd think we weren't living in an electronic age, after all," she said irritably.

Miriam kept silent. Like a farmer in a drought scanning the horizon for the tiniest sign of impending rain, she studied Susan Crane's face, feeling the barest hope that at last the detective might be turning her suspicions elsewhere.

"I would like you to have a conversation with Hannah Weinstein. In a place where I can overhear the conversation. It's most important," Susan said.

"If there's anything I can do . . ." Miriam said. "I don't know if she'll tell me anything. But Susan, when you say 'since she's still alive' . . . she must be terrified for her life. Are you saying she is the final witness?"

"I don't know." The detective cleared her throat. "You might be interested to know, however, that Reggie Bradley did tell me that she saw you after your conversation with Isabel on that Saturday. She concluded that you were leaving the building."

"I did leave the building!" Miriam said. "You must believe that."

"You could have come back again, however," Susan said, and

rested back in her chair, ankles crossed and fingertips together, as if carefully weighing this possibility.

Miriam shut her eyes once more. Susan Crane had no intention of believing her. All this time she had only been toying with her. Her life, her reputation would never be restored. The back of her throat, dry and raw, ached every time she took a breath. Everything—the worrying, the endless conversations chewing over details, the constant thinking and research to ferret out the truth, the giving of every ounce of her energy to find out what had happened to Isabel— had been futile. Isabel's killer had won. She was finished. Tears came into her eyes and she stood up clumsily. "I'm sorry, I need to excuse myself." She held her hands out in front of her blindly.

"Miriam," a steady voice said.

When Miriam opened her eyes again, Susan Crane was looking at her in a kindly way. "I don't believe you did come back into Helmsley Hall that day," she said simply.

To Miriam, those few words seemed like a huge concession. "Thank you," she said. Almost immediately, relief lifted ever so slightly the cloak of worry that had pressured her shoulders since Isabel's death. Briefly, she imagined a hawk taking wing in joyful flight across a broad prairie. She wanted to rush outside and tell Vivian. Not just tell her but lift her in the air; her feet practically twitched, so great was the urge. Instead she smiled, a little uncertainly. She wasn't convinced, yet, that she was entirely clear of the noxious cloud that had enshrouded her for weeks.

Resuming her seat, Miriam attempted to clap her hands together smartly. She managed only a weak tap, but said gamely: "Well. Shall I call Hannah and see if she will come here?"

Susan Crane considered. "Are there plans to move someone into Isabel's old office?"

"We were waiting for police clearance. I assume it's a crime scene?" Miriam spoke eagerly, visions of *Law & Order* and *NYPD Blue* flashing through her head. Like most of the American public, she felt television had given her inside knowledge of police procedure.

Crane shook her head lazily as if a disturbed crime scene was of little importance in the grand scheme of things. "Everything down to the last mote of dust in that room has been photographed and analyzed and finger-printed. I don't think there's more to learn on that score. No, I think it might be of much more use for you to move into that office."

Miriam abruptly rose. "I'm going to have a single malt. Would you care to join me?" At Susan's nod, she walked to a cabinet at the far end of the room and pulled out a bottle of Glenmorangie from one shelf; from another she took two glasses. As she poured, she said: "I don't know if anyone has told you. I stepped down as chair temporarily in light of my suspect position in this investigation. I did not do it by choice."

She returned to her seat and handed Susan a glass with two inches of liquid in it. "I'm sorry to hear that," Susan said. "Um, could I have some ice?"

"Of course," Miriam said. She walked to the far side of the room once more, into the hallway and turned into the kitchen. There was the crush of an ice machine. She returned with a small bowl containing three ice cubes. "I forgot to ask if you also like soda?"

"This looks too good for soda."

Miriam nodded approvingly. "Good decision. In the old days, we were told that the cardinal rule of imbibing single malt was to drink it neat. Now, there is some debate about whether drinking it with a single cube of ice releases more flavor. As you can see, I'm old fashioned." She held up her iceless glass and took a hearty swallow.

Obligingly, Susan dropped just one cube into her glass. She sampled it and pronounced: "Delicious." Her lips curved happily, and a crinkle appeared around the extraordinary blue eyes. Miriam cursed herself for not having discovered the sergeant's weakness much sooner. They sat for a moment and sipped companionably. Then, Susan crossed her legs and asked, in a voice alive with interest: "So, who is the temporary chair?"

"Richard Lester," Miriam responded, controlling her face rigidly; of late, the very sound of the name pained her.

"I don't suppose he's any relation to the Richard Lester who directed the Beatles film way back when?" Crane asked unexpectedly, her expression keen. At Miriam's negative head shake, Crane took another drink and tipped a satisfied face upward, where she appeared to study the pressed-tin ceiling. She seemed to have dismissed her sudden interest in Lester's familial history. Miriam shivered. Lester had always appeared to her as so singular, and so unpleasant, that she couldn't bear to imagine what combination of earthly creatures might have produced him. Perhaps he had simply appeared on the earth, a perverse display of *deus ex machina.*

"Oh, I think this will suit us very well," Susan said quietly. Miriam focused her attention back to the detective, wondering if she had missed a vital connection in the conversation. But Crane appeared lost in her own thoughts. "Fabulous ceiling, by the way," she said. "Now, look, you said Isabel's office is empty, but what about Richard Lester. Does he plan to move in?"

"I doubt it." Her throat thickening with outrage at the mere thought, Miriam swallowed painfully, and half-choked in the process. "Excuse me." She cleared her irritated throat with a cough. "Lester is, shall we say, a very assertive person. Yet even he would know that others would view such a move by an interim chair as extreme hubris." But even as she said this, Miriam wondered if she were giving Lester more credit than he was due. The mantle of hubris was one Lester wore very well.

"All right," Susan said evenly, her mild tone signaling no opinion whatsoever of Lester. "But I'm assuming you still have the master key to all the offices?"

At Miriam's assent, she continued: "I'd like for you to arrange to meet Doctor Weinstein in that office." And Crane, very concisely, outlined her plan and the role she wished Miriam to play in it.

---

editor's note:
Given the fate of Reggie Bradley and the precarious position of my friend Hannah, the reader might think it imprudent of me to allow myself to be used in this way. Almost as a decoy. But so relieved was I to

feel the guillotine of suspicion lifted ever so slightly from my neck, I would have done anything Susan Crane asked of me. That is, anything short of murder.

14

Life imitates art, art translates imagination into life. People talk all the time about the border between reality and fantasy. There is no border. If you feel it, it's true. If it affects you, it happened somewhere, sometime, in some realm of consciousness or unconsciousness. Sound dangerous? Living is dangerous: it will kill you.

Daphne Arbor, notes from "A Meditative Life"

After repeated calls to Isabel's house failed to roust Hannah, Miriam drove on Tuesday morning across town to Tarrytown, an affluent west Austin enclave. Property values had risen astronomically in central Austin neighborhoods like this one and Hemphill Park, where Miriam lived, pricing such areas out of the reach of most professors unless they had managed to slide in under the wire of the mid-nineties market mania.

Dormarion, Isabel's street, was manicured and private. Miriam imagined Isabel had felt relatively hidden away here, which would have perfectly suited a person like the former chair, high profile professionally but personally inclined to the reclusive. Miriam parked in the driveway. From her car, she reviewed the property, immediately noticing a look of laxity that pervaded the landscaping. Isabel's service had kept the Japanese boxwoods along the drive neatly clipped, the Saint Augustine lawn to three-quarters of an inch, and flowers, like petunias, impatiens, pansies, and johnny jump-ups—whatever was in season—blooming and weed-free in beds around the front door and side of the house. Now the plants looked scraggly and yellow from either lack of water or minerals or both. Things looked too run-down to be the result of only two weeks of neglect. Perhaps Isabel had been too distracted to bother with maintaining the landscaping before her death. Given the almost slavish regimen of discipline Isabel had followed in her life, Miriam found the disrepair notable.

Miriam left the car, walked around to the side of the garage, and peered through the back fence. The back deck showed no signs of recent habitation, and Isabel's pool looked scummy and leaf-infested. Perhaps Hannah wasn't here after all?

She knocked on the front door. The lack of an answer only confirmed the feeling of emptiness pervading the place. Miriam skulked from window to window (fortunately the house included only one story), finding each either securely shaded or revealing an unoccupied room. She went back to her car, wrote on a sticky-note: "Hannah, call me. IT'S URGENT!! Desperately, Miriam" and went through the back gate and stuck it on the back door. Dispirited, she drove away. She had little faith that Hannah would contact her, given her virtual disappearance since Miriam had last seen her at the hospital following the memorial service.

She taught her morning class, a survey of feminist criticism post-1970, and retired to her office. In class, her students responded contentiously to an essay by Hannah Weinstein on readers as performers in postmodern fiction. When she checked her email, she was heartened by the synchrony of finding a message from Hannah waiting in her in-box. In the email, Hannah said she was in Maryland, touching base with her classes and her house, and would return to Austin on Friday. She could meet Miriam anytime after three that day. Miriam, after a confirming call to Susan Crane, replied that she would meet her friend at four in Isabel's old office and suggested that the two of them, plus Vivian, have dinner later on that evening.

"Now, when you meet with Hannah, try to forget about me. I don't want you to be self-conscious," Susan had coached her. "As luck would have it, a former occupant has installed a wardrobe in Anna's space, in the anteroom. I've discovered I can stand in it quite comfortably. If I hold down consumption of pasta and wine the day before," she added wryly.

"Wasn't Anna alerted when you asked her to empty the wardrobe?" Miriam asked. Anna was tediously prickly about any organizational changes. "Actually, I put that wardrobe in there," she said almost apologetically. "I got tired of hanging my things in plain view; you know, an extra jacket or blouse, my gym bag. Not that I've been making much use of that these days." Miriam patted her stomach with dismay. Instead of snacking, drinking, and otherwise ingesting instead of expending, she needed to resume her walking program to alleviate stress.

Susan responded knowingly: "For short people like us, a few ounces are enough to affect the waistline."

"Oh, yes," Miriam agreed and confided: "Tell that to Vivian, who at five ten wouldn't notice a pound or two. But of course she isn't prone to gaining so much as a gram."

"Disgusting," Susan said. "But back to business. I didn't ask Anna for permission. I told her she can't be in her space on Friday, that's all. Since she's no longer speaking to me, I haven't noticed how annoyed she is." After a chuckle, her light tone evaporated and she spoke crisply: "Don't forget to leave the door to the chair's suite unlocked after you enter. I believe the connecting door between Anna's anteroom and the chair's office has no lock?"

"That's right," Miriam assented.

"Good. Now, it's imperative that you speak in a normal voice when Hannah arrives. Don't worry about my ability to hear you. What's important is—"

"But what if Hannah doesn't get back from Maryland in time? Surely, it's not wise that she's left Austin." Miriam interrupted.

"Leave that to me." Crane's voice was so confident that Miriam wondered if Hannah was secreted away in the city after all. The detective continued pointedly: "What's important is that you tell Hannah you are looking for the last diary entry that Isabel wrote. Tell her that when the diary was recovered, it was missing."

202

"But the entry wasn't missing, was it?" Miriam felt on unsteady ground.

"It doesn't matter," Susan said firmly. "It just matters that she thinks it missing. It's what she does or says when she digests this information that will be useful."

"But I need to know to be convincing . . ." Miriam began.

"No!" Crane's disapproval cracked through the receiver. "The more uncertain you are yourself, the better."

"But . . ." A creeping foreboding assailed Miriam. She was uncomfortably aware that Crane, the professional, held all of the cards, yet she, the novice, was expected to play the hand.

"Miriam, please. I'll explain all of this later. Trust me."

Trust me. Such simple words. Isabel had said them to Hannah in the diary. How many times had Miriam herself uttered them? And how many times had the speaker of that phrase disappointed someone, failed to live up to her promise, or, in Isabel's case, failed to live at all? Usually it didn't matter—the stakes weren't high enough. But this time, in this situation, Miriam felt it mattered a great deal.

*M*iriam occupied the days until Friday in a stoic blaze of work and activity. She managed to rough out a thirty-page draft of an overdue chapter on Gertrude Stein's American tour in the thirties, one she had promised to complete a month earlier for an anthology on expatriate Americans. Miriam feared that when she reviewed it in the cold light of later sanity, it would read like pure drivel. Nonetheless, she marked the task off her list. She cleaned out a large landscaping bed that bordered the street in her front yard, pulling straggles of grass from around lantana plants, still loaded with their yellow and orange popcorn-like blooms, weeding around the purple fountain grass and fragrant salvia. To Vivian's amazement, Miriam mowed the lawn one last time, drained the oil out of the lawnmower, and flushed the air filter. These activities, plus teaching two classes, attending four committee meetings and two thesis advising sessions, and preparing dinner on Wednesday, consumed the hours until Thursday afternoon. At which time she accepted an invitation from Fiona to join her in a doubles match with Darryl and Dennis.

On the scale of trepidation, the tennis rated right up there with her nerves about Friday's rendezvous with Hannah. Not only was Miriam barely five feet two inches tall—and competing with three people all over five feet nine—but she hadn't played tennis in five years and had at least five years on the oldest member of that trio, Darryl, who at fifty was a former tennis coach and still competed in masters' triathlons. Compared to her companions, Miriam felt like an out-of-shape Lilliputian on a playing field of power-lifting Brobdingnagians. As she miserably searched her bureau for a pair of tennis shorts that fit, she decided that, given her developing empathy for the hapless Gulliver, whose physical stature was always out of sync with each landscape he visited, she would teach *Gulliver's Travels* in the near future.

She reached the courts ten minutes early and, with a sense of impending humiliation, filled two quart bottles with water. Given the warm weather and her level of conditioning, she'd be certain to be gasping and sucking down fluids within two games.

"Miriam!" Fiona bounded toward her on tanned and shapely legs, carrying a tennis bag with two rackets. She kissed Miriam's cheek in greeting and smiled. "You are a peach to come and play. Marvin cancelled on us, and we were at wits' end until I thought of you."

Miriam studied Fiona for any signs of irony before replying: "You are aware it is Halloween today. Maybe I should have dressed in costume?"

"You mean, like, as Martina Navratilova?" Fiona asked, amid the hiss of releasing air as she popped a fresh can of tennis balls.

"Ha," Miriam said. "So do we take on the men?"

"We'll trade off," Fiona said. "Why don't we begin with you and Dennis against me and Darryl?"

"Okay." Miriam doubted that she would last beyond this first pairing.

"I brought you a racket in case you discovered that your strings were out of shape," Fiona said. "You said you hadn't played in awhile."

Miriam, who had purchased her racket at K-Mart fifteen years before and never had it restrung, accepted the racket with humility. These people were serious. If only merely her strings were out of shape . . .

"Um, Fiona," Miriam called as her friend jogged over to the other side of the court and began tossing up balls and cranking her shoulder and racket into a practiced motion. Miriam dodged and ducked the resulting series of sizzling practice serves. "I don't think I'm in the same league as the rest of you. Perhaps I should . . ."

"Don't worry about it." Fiona ratcheted four more balls inside the "T" on Miriam's side in rapid succession.

As she scanned the sky hoping for an idea to drop from the heavens providing her a dignified way out, Miriam noticed that in the court next to them, Mary Morton rallied with enviable leisure with Richard Lester. Miriam gazed at their play longingly, at the slow, moon balls favored by Mary and the two-step method of Lester—if he had to move more than one step in any direction away from where he was planted, he let the ball pass him by. Their looping strokes and relaxed strolling about the court was soothing; they didn't appear to bother with actual games or scoring.

"Miriam—heads up!" Fiona chirped as she whacked a backhand down the line. "Want to take a few at net?"

Just then Dennis and Darryl arrived to give Miriam a two-minute respite. Darryl planted a light kiss on Fiona's lips while Dennis hugged Miriam and laughed when she said: "Since you're ten inches taller, how about I just stand at net and direct traffic?"

Their noisy greetings attracted the attention of Lester, who waved and then scurried over to them. "Miriam! Think of it—we've been colleagues all these years and I never knew you played."

"I have my secrets, Richard, even from you," Miriam bantered, thinking *a reprieve is a reprieve is a reprieve* . . .

Out of the corner of her eye, Miriam saw Darryl rapidly executing a series of stretches. She turned back to Lester when a yell and the clatter of a racket striking pavement sounded from the other side of the court. Darryl had fallen to the pavement clutching his ankle. "Aaargh!" he said. "I think I've torn something."

Fiona dropped to his side and took charge at once. "Your Achilles?" In short order, she placed exploratory fingers on the offending left calf and ankle before helping Darryl to stand on one leg. She grabbed his waist, and they proceeded to hobble together toward the parking lot. "I'm taking him to the clinic. Sorry about the game!"

Miriam stood on one leg and wiggled the ankle of the other apprehensively. She said to Dennis. "My enthusiasm has somewhat faded. How about you?"

Dennis gave her arm a friendly squeeze. "If you want to go, that's okay. I'm sure I can find a pickup game. Or, I'll hit the gym. Poor Darryl."

"I'll bet he's vicious on the court," Miriam said. "In the normal course of things."

Dennis grinned. "Lethal. Maybe this will slow him down so I'll have a chance to win once in a while."

"Sounds only fair," Miriam said. Then, her mind snapping back to her upcoming rendezvous with Hannah: "By the way, your advice to call Blake that night was excellent. He was very forthcoming about Paula's history."

Dennis nodded. "Yes, I've spoken to him since." Dennis looked down at her, his face uncharacteristically somber. "You know, in hindsight it seems clear that the events in Indiana all those years ago set up the train wreck that crashed into Isabel. In fact, if I leaned toward conspiracy theories . . ." He glanced over his shoulder to see Richard Lester coming their way from the adjacent court, and he lowered his voice: "For God's sakes, Miriam, watch your back."

Miriam received Dennis's bear hug gratefully. "Thank you, dear friend. You too."

"Miriam, we were just finishing up. Might I have a word with you?" Lester called as he approached.

Dennis, with a last worried look at Miriam, retrieved his tennis bag and loped off. Miriam looked over to the next court, but Mary Morton had vanished. "All right, but I just have a minute," she said, to give herself an out. Who would have thought a tennis court could be a place fraught with so many hazards?

They sat on a bench outside of the metal court surround. Lester said nothing for a moment. In the silence, Miriam said: "I'm amazed at Fiona—such confidence and fearlessness! She's normally so diplomatic and conciliatory. I seldom get to see this side of her."

"Yes. Obviously a natural athlete. Unlike me, I'm afraid." Lester said, crossing one thin, veiny thigh over the other.

She nodded companionably. "Ditto me on that score."

Lester looked at her narrowly. "You don't think Fiona is ruthless enough to have done away with Isabel, do you? She certainly looks strong enough."

"Richard, you're not serious?" Miriam laughed uneasily and wondered how he knew that Isabel's murderer needed strength. The police had never revealed the state of Isabel's body in any detail—or the cause of death—which had provoked endless conjecture throughout Helmsley Hall.

"Just a thought," he said and then edged closer to Miriam on the bench. "Look, I received a rather curt note from the dean a few days ago. He reminded me that my assuming the chair was strictly provisional and, in fact, illegal as any change in chair required his approval. It was rather nasty. I'm wondering if you know anything about it."

The good will she had been feeling toward Lester over their shared, and lowly, athletic status seeped away as she noted the critical set of his mouth. "No," she said simply. "I have not communicated with the dean about this."

"That's hard to believe. You're such pals," Lester said with a mix of envy and annoyance.

"Believe it or don't. I assumed our department made this . . . informal arrangement . . . out of channels, so to speak. I didn't think Darryl really needed to know about it."

"How naïve," Lester sniffed. "'Out-of-channels' as you call it is just another channel."

Miriam noticed she still gripped Fiona's racket in one hand. She bounced the racket face against her other palm. "I have to go. I assume you told Darryl yourself. Here's a tip from an old hand: talk about yourself less if you don't want people to talk about you. Bye."

*F*riday morning, after a night of broken sleep and staccato dreams, Miriam woke at four a.m. The street outside their bedroom window the night before had been raucous, with trick-or-treaters shrieking and even some fireworks going off long into the evening. Miriam had felt agitated before bed, as if her nerves were inflamed. Every sound, each sweep of headlights from the street streaking across her bedroom windows, had provoked an answering twitch or start in some muscle or limb. Before dawn, she wallowed in the bed, her head achy, her eyes gritty. Beside her, Vivian slept on, the high dome of her forehead smooth and relaxed.

Suppressing a grumble, Miriam hauled herself out of bed and quietly descended the stairs into the kitchen. She made herself a very strong pot of Earl Grey and glumly ate a bowl of cereal without even the solace of her addiction, the morning newspaper; neither *The New York Times* nor the *Austin Journal Observer* arrived before six.

As she drove to the university, Miriam wished, as she had so many times in her life, that she still had her father to talk to. Paul Held had run a small publishing house in Chicago, specializing in serious theological and spiritual titles. He had died before new-age literature achieved mass popularity, but Miriam doubted he would have given way to the commercial sway of this tide in his business. With a master's degree in philosophy, he considered himself something of a scholar and occasionally taught a course in the religion department at the U. of Illinois's Chicago campus. Raised in a Jewish family, he had lived life as a pantheist, fascinated by an eclectic array of doctrines and denominations. Miriam's predicament, she knew, would have intrigued him intellectually, even while it would have emotionally caused him distress. She imagined him sending her clippings from treatises on good and evil, avidly lecturing her from the teachings of favorites such as Martin Buber and Emanuel Swedenborg.

Human motive in the abstract had stimulated his capacious mind. As a girl first discovering the adventures of Sherlock Holmes, Miriam had been almost certain that her own father must have been Arthur Conan Doyle's catalyst in creating his logically brilliant detective. However, Paul Held, born in 1920, arrived in the world much too late to have served as an inspiration for the Victorian Doyle. Nor had he been a doctor like the famous Joseph Bell, who had apparently served as model for the Edinburgh physician's colorful creation.

Fatigue and uncertainty blocked her intuitive self, however, and try as she might, she couldn't find inside herself a place quiet enough to summon her father's patient and dispassionate energies. So unnerved was she by her coming mission, she couldn't even recall the sound of his voice or the steady touch of his hand on her head. These sensory remnants from her early life with her father had reassured her at trying moments her entire life. On this day, she deeply missed their comfort.

The day advanced slowly with routine tasks—checking email, reviewing the coming week's course plans, returning phone calls. Concentration was impossible. Anything that required an ounce of creativity or mental focus outstripped her abilities. She called Vivian three times and Daphne once for moral support. Even though she hungrily absorbed the outpourings of Vivian's love ("You know you can do anything, my darling!") and Daphne's affection ("Quel courage!") during these conversations, as soon as she hung up, Miriam felt horribly alone. The coming meeting with Hannah increasingly disquieted her. Although she had known Hannah very well when they were younger, she felt the gulf of the years. The barriers of guilt and suspicion dividing them over Isabel's death seemed insurmountable. A feasible scenario for encouraging her friend to talk eluded her, considering the circumstances. How could she comfort Hannah about her loss and carry out Crane's wishes at the same time? Miriam felt herself drifting onto the shoals of very deceptive waters.

By two that afternoon, the torture of obsessively waiting for the minutes to creep by drove her to action. Given Anna's banishment for the day from the small office adjacent to Isabel's, ensuring a degree of privacy, Miriam decided to arrive early and prepare herself. She thanked the powers that be that it was a Friday and, even better, the day after Halloween. A number of people had apparently headed for an early weekend or were otherwise indisposed or absent. The corridor was quiet, and the main office receptionist busy in the mailroom around the corner when Miriam slipped in and used her master key to access the door to the chair's suite. First taking care to release the doorknob's self-locking device and so prevent the door from bolting behind her, she passed through Anna's small office, and stepped, she hoped soundlessly, through the connecting door into Isabel's old office.

Miriam was startled to see the office so little changed. She tried to remember when she had last been in it; for a moment, the fact that she had confronted Isabel there on the fateful Saturday fled her brain. She closed her eyes and tried to visualize what she'd seen: on that Saturday, a short knit blue jacket had been resting on the back of Isabel's chair. Isabel was sensitive to the Texas style of chill-to-the-bone climate control used in the building and was frequently cold. That jacket was no longer there. The desk had been unusually cluttered, Miriam remembered. Now it was bare except for a desk calendar, a blotter, and—she recoiled at the sight—Isabel's diary, open in the center of the desk, as if waiting for its owner to resume an interrupted entry. The diary lured her as powerfully as a Siren's song, and before she thought about it, Miriam found herself settled firmly into the high-backed chair, staring down at the paper.

The pages displayed the penultimate diary excerpt, the Friday before Isabel died, October 11. Miriam turned the last page: the Saturday entry was indeed missing. Susan Crane must have placed the diary in this way, removing that last entry, but why? Miriam lifted the pen that lay beside the notebook. It was a silver Cross roller ball pen, with a fine blue point, the pen that Isabel always wielded at meetings. And, Miriam glanced at the last page, she had used this same pen—or a felt tip of the same color and slimness—to keep her record.

From the desk which occupied the rear third of the space, Miriam's eyes swept over the room. As she sat in Isabel's chair, she faced the door to Anna's office; anyone could see her at the desk from the doorway. A small table and two chairs were placed in front and slightly to the left of the desk. A blue-and-green rag rug rested under this small conversation area. The remainder of the wall space on that side of the room was taken up by built-in bookcases and metal file cabinets. Books, journals, piles of student papers, a few framed photos and two small vases filled the built-ins.

Near the door on the right wall stood a small hardwood bookcase, containing only four shelves, where Isabel stored the books used in her current teaching. On its top surface stood the twin horse head bookends Isabel had owned and packed from office to office all the years Miriam had known her. But they were placed differently than usual. Miriam blinked, the inside of her lids sandy from lack of sleep. No, that wasn't it, was it? These bookends were grayish-white and Miriam was certain that Isabel's had been yellowy-white. Recalling darker strands striating the ivory marble of the originals, she stared at this pair stupidly, until the horses' curving necks blurred into blobs of stone. Above the small bookcase was a framed poster announcing a Tanglewood concert three years before; a large cello rested in the foreground against the backdrop of the green Berkshire mountains.

The mechanical clicking of a round clock on the wall behind her registered on Miriam's consciousness. She swiveled her torso to note that the clock hands registered two-thirty. Watching the second hand, Miriam felt a flutter of panic and a wave of claustrophobia. She couldn't imagine sitting in this office until four o'clock. She looked down at the diary, at her right hand gripping Isabel's pen. Why had she picked it up? The hand trembled. Aware that her palm was sweating, Miriam dropped the pen, which thudded against the blotter and clattered as it rolled to the edge of the wooden desk.

Miriam's hand blocked the pen from falling to the floor; then, her fingers slid down the side of the desk. She aimlessly opened the third drawer on the right side. It was a file drawer, yet it contained only one file. She touched it with the tip of her index finger, the tab sharp against her skin. As she removed the file from the drawer, she glanced at its label: "Hannah Weinstein." Had Susan Crane left this here as well? Why?

Aware that her neck inside the round collar of her blouse was damp with perspiration in the chilly room, and overcome with certainty that her presence in the room was a mistake, Miriam's mind skittered to a favorite expression of Dennis's: *flop-sweat.* Drawing a deep breath—she must concentrate—she opened the manila folder and laid it on top of the diary. Inside was a letter from Hannah to Isabel, hand-written. It was clearly a personal letter, but Miriam couldn't tear her eyes away.

Dear Bella,

When I come to meet you on Saturday, it will be for the last time. I don't see a future for us anymore. When we first met, I felt such unlimited possibility. And such joy. Now, instead, I feel that our lives are filled with unanswered questions. This student of yours, Reggie, for example. I'm not sure you're being honest with me about her. I'm not sure that you haven't encouraged her. I doubt that her obsession with you is unprovoked. And how would I know, seeing you as I do only twice a month? And then there is my interview for a job at the university. . . . I deplore how you've handled this. I feel humiliated . . . and betrayed. What are your ties to Paula Fabian? What is your relationship to Miriam and what has it been? Why do you suddenly want me to commit myself to you when you have never mentioned anything permanent before? You have not been honest with me. I find there is so much that I don't understand.

Isabel, I doubt your commitment to me. I doubt your affection. And I doubt your motives. I love you but I no longer trust you. I gave you my love. I put my life in your

hand. The hand is closing, not opening. You are breaking my
heart . . .

Hannah

The letter was dated October 9. Miriam paged through the calendar
on the desk, still open to the week of October 6 through 12. The
ninth had been a Wednesday.

After paging through the folder to find copies of Hannah's application letter and c.v.—documents she had seen before—Miriam
closed the file. Was Hannah really prepared to say goodbye to Isabel
or was the letter a last-ditch attempt to get Isabel to pledge herself
more strongly to her? Most of all, Miriam wondered how this letter
had affected Isabel's actions in those last days. Perhaps her adamant
reversal in favor of Hannah resulted from her reaction to it. Miriam
knew Isabel well enough to imagine how she would have been
jolted by the words Hannah had written, for when Isabel had ended
an affair of hers in the past, it had been because she decided it was
over—Isabel always left a relationship first. For someone to say no
to Isabel . . . well, Miriam doubted that Isabel's sense of self could
tolerate it.

Hannah had used the word "betrayal." It struck Miriam how
many betrayals lay at the core of Isabel's death: Reggie had felt her
affection and loyalty betrayed; for Dennis and Bettina, their sense
of fairness; for Hannah, love; for Lester, his secret; for Paula, her integrity; and for herself, for Miriam, her sense of fair play, of colle-
giality, of justice. How could a person endure when she had robbed
so many people of what they held dear? In a sense, the way Isabel
had lived her life, the disregard she'd shown other people, had killed
her. Miriam chided herself for being self-righteous, for hadn't everyone put actions into motion that could destroy him or her? Hadn't
she bruised egos, repudiated desire, put her own interests before
others? She had read somewhere that to live at all was to betray
other human beings no matter how good one's intentions. In the
course of any life, someone along the way must be wounded or left

behind; for one person to move ahead, someone else inevitably lost ground.

Miriam put her hands on the arms of the chair and prepared to force her weary body, further drained by the murk of her thoughts, into a standing position when the door opened. She froze, fearful that someone might view her occupation of the dead woman's chair and office as a macabre act of voyeurism.

"Miriam!" Hannah teetered in the doorway, one hand still on the knob, an arm raised in front of her face. "I didn't expect you to be here yet." She lowered her hand and Miriam saw a long narrow scab above her left eye where she had noticed a bandage the day of the memorial. Except for the angry line of red circled by a yellowish bruise, her face was pale.

"I . . . I couldn't stay away," Miriam blurted out.

Hannah's lips moved slightly into a lopsided ghost of a smile. Her eyes, threaded with broken vessels, narrowed in the bright fluorescence of the overhead light. Her voice was shaky but composed. "Yes. I often found I couldn't stay away from Isabel. I understand this is something else that we have shared."

"Oh, that was a very long time ago now," Miriam said.

"Maybe. But Isabel never told me about the two of you. And neither did you. Why is that, I wonder." It was a flat statement, with no inflection in her tone.

"Hannah, I'm so sorry . . ."

There was no softness in Hannah's face. Her brown eyes, cloudy and strained, looked accusingly at Miriam. "About you and Isabel? Or about what I have suffered? Or are you sorry that Isabel has died so . . . so terribly? Which is it?" She looked thinner, and her wiry hair looked dull and uncombed. Instead of her usual flowing, co-ordinated fabrics, she wore a black sweat suit. Unsteadily, she took a couple of heavy steps into the room. Miriam saw both fear and rage in the tight compression of her lips.

Miriam hastily abandoned the chair and moved out from behind the desk. "What is it? I *am* sorry for what you have lost, what you

214

have gone through. You must know I had no part in what happened to Isabel."

Hannah's voice was bitter. "Not you. Not Saint Miriam! Of course you are blameless. But what were you doing to help Isabel while she was being destroyed? Being ground to bits by the people around her. What did you do to help her?"

Miriam gripped a chair at the small table to the side of Isabel's desk. "Please, sit down."

Hannah stayed upright but she came closer. "I have not been feeling well," she said unexpectedly.

This admission released some of Miriam's uneasiness—Hannah didn't seem as volatile as she had feared. Miriam approached her and touched her shoulder very lightly. "Please. Won't you sit down?"

With a sharp glance at the door, Hannah allowed Miriam to lead her into a chair. Hannah looked fearfully back at the door and whispered: "Miriam, I was here with Isabel in this room when she was attacked."

Miriam stiffened. "Attacked? How?"

Hannah pointed to the cut above her eye. "That crazy girl came in here. She found us. She threw the bookends at us. Our heads were together. I was knocked out."

"And Isabel?"

Hannah's eyes were huge and unfocused. "Both of us."

"So what happened?" Imagining Reggie striking out in a rage, Miriam felt her own body vibrating; she wanted nothing more than to flee herself. The room felt charged and unsafe.

"I don't know!" Tears filled Hannah's eyes. "I honestly don't know," she whispered. "I'm afraid Isabel killed herself."

"What?" Miriam felt the blood draining from her head; she hastily sat down herself.

Hannah grabbed Miriam's arm and dug into it with her nails. "I came to and I left this building. I must have because I woke up the next day in Isabel's house. But I have no idea how I got there. None."

"Was Isabel alive when you left?"

"I think so. But I don't know. Miriam, I did nothing! I didn't call an ambulance, I didn't help her. And I don't know why. I don't remember anything . . ." Her voice quavered, high and thin. "Oh, God, I can't live with myself."

Miriam broke in: "How can you be sure you didn't call anyone? You said you were in bad shape . . ."

Shaking her head from side to side with ragged energy, Hannah grimaced. "Because the police told me that there was no call recorded: not to emergency, not to any of the hospitals. Oh, God . . ." Before Miriam could offer any words of comfort, she said: "I saw that girl come into the office. I saw the look on her face when she saw Isabel and me together. We were kissing." A wash of color tinged her pallid cheekbones. "Isabel's blouse was partly unbuttoned. The girl just froze. Her face was terrible. Such shock. Such hate . . ." Hannah's mouth twisted as she muttered so softly Miriam wasn't sure she deciphered the words correctly: ". . . but, worst of all, so very much disgust . . ."

Speaking deliberately, and loudly, Miriam sought to penetrate Hannah's morbid recollection. "Listen to me. You didn't kill Isabel. You couldn't have. You were injured horribly, and unconscious yourself. You're not responsible."

"Kill Isabel?" Hannah's voice broke into a muffled, sobbing laugh. "I would sooner kill myself. Of course I didn't kill her! But I had written her a letter saying I never wanted to see her again. And then I left. I didn't save her. I abandoned her. Don't you see?"

Bewildered, sweating, Miriam shook her head. She felt light-headed and nauseated. "No."

"That girl ran out of here. Ran out to spread terrible stories about Isabel. Isabel thought I would leave her. And I did—I walked out of here with her lying in a pool of blood! I'm trying to tell you I did nothing."

"But why do you think Isabel killed herself?"

"Waking up in this room, alone and bloody, deranged, frightened? She was taking a narcotic, something for her back, which bothered her on and off. She had those pills with her. I'm afraid, in the state she was in, she took them. What if her head pounded and she didn't realize what she was doing? As I didn't? Oh, God . . ." a low, guttural moan escaped her lips.

Miriam immediately thought of the Percodan that Reggie Bradley had swallowed. Had they been Isabel's pills? "Did the police tell you this?"

"No. They've told me nothing. They don't believe what I've told them. I think they believe I killed her."

Miriam grasped the terrified woman's hands, which were cold and clammy, and chafed the skin, trying to warm it. "No one thinks that about you," she murmured, attempting to be soothing in spite of the tide of jitters inexorably swamping her own nervous system.

Hannah jerked her hand away. "Then what happened? I was all right, except for a concussion. She would've been too. Something else happened to her after I left. What?"

Barely able to think, Miriam blurted: "The diary. Isabel's diary. Did you see it when you arrived?"

"I don't know. She was writing something. Why?"

"The last entry, from that Saturday, is missing. Did you see it?"

Flecks of saliva dotted Hannah's dry, cracked lips. "You don't understand. One minute I was kissing Isabel—getting ready to tell her to disregard my letter, that I loved her, that I would stay—and the next I was being smashed in the head! I didn't pay attention to anything else."

"Hannah, this is very important: you said Isabel's blouse was unbuttoned. But when you left, were Isabel's clothes on? Because Susan Crane told me that Isabel's body was naked when it was found."

There was a footstep, a sharp click of a doorknob turning, and then a low, slurred voice from the doorway: "I felt naked in front of her once. She stripped me of everything. I thought she should feel what it was like." Richard Lester walked into the room, his gray hair glittering under the fluorescent lights. In the harsh light, the skin of his face looked stretched tight across the bones, every plane of his skull visible.

217

He stopped by the small bookcase, held on to it a moment as if to steady himself, and then grabbed both of the bookends from the top shelf. He unsteadily hefted one in each hand and grinned lopsidedly. *He's drunk,* Miriam thought at the same time that she noticed how small his hands were, how thin his wrists, and yet his forearms were corded with muscle. Released from their constraints, several books slid from the top shelf and clattered to the floor.

"Do either of you have any idea what it's like to be humiliated by a woman like Isabel?" His eyelids fluttered like thin membranes over his small gray eyes. For a moment, with his head hunched on his shoulders, he resembled a blind, nocturnal mammal as he peered seemingly inside his own brain. "You may think you do, but you don't."

He stood over them, his biceps straining against the thin cloth of his blue sport shirt as he held the bookends, like barbells, curled against his chest. "You don't know what it means to be a man," he said dreamily, a sliver of saliva in the corner of his mouth. "A man with pride and a sense of purpose. With a *career,*" he spat out the last word. "And children and a wife to support. You can't imagine the burden of being a husband, having to provide for his family, the pressure of it. The demands. And then to have a woman, a beautiful, unattainable woman like Isabel, tether you like you were a pony she keeps tied to her porch railing." He lifted one of the bookends higher and tilted his head toward it. "You knew that Isabel was a great rider once? That's why she had these." He laughed, his voice excited and hoarse. "Don't you think it's perfect that she was killed by a stone version of the flesh-and-blood beauties she once loved? The beauty destroyed by gorgeous creatures more haughty and merciless than she."

He staggered and took another step toward them. "She thought even of her beloved horses as creatures to master. They were just another extension of her fiefdom. We were all her creatures in her mind, subject to her control, don't you think? We weren't people at all."

"Richard, you've been drinking." Miriam finally managed. "What are you doing here? You have no business in this office."

Hannah sat rigid beside her as if she were paralyzed, staring at the statuettes he held. Lester looked at Hannah with pity. Miriam saw his eyes take in her disheveled hair, her slack face, her small shoulders. She saw his tight, derisive smile as he regarded them both. Miriam saw starkly at that moment that Richard Lester, who had had two marriages, many affairs, and pursued female faculty and graduate students compulsively, despised women. As he sneered down at her, Miriam felt that as clearly as if he were spitting in her face. Which was what he was doing, what he had always done, in his way. His dismissal enraged Miriam and made her feel fearless and clear-headed.

"What am I doing here?" he asked. "I could ask the same of you. This will be my office. Is my office now. Not yours. I need to look at my space." He laughed. "I need to decide what to do with these." He looked down at the horse heads.

Miriam thought if she lunged at him when he was focused on Hannah, she might be able to knock him off balance. "Richard, put those down. You're frightening Hannah."

"Oh, I'm soooo sorry," he mocked, his voice getting higher. "Are you afraid, poor dear?" he said to Hannah and laughed. "You're not the man you thought you were, after all? Is that what you thought you were when you seduced the proud and lovely Isabel Vittorio?" His lips twisted to one side.

He's jealous. When had Lester tried to sleep with Isabel? Miriam wondered fleetingly. But then he took a step closer and she tensed, preparing herself to push out of her chair. "What did you do after you took Isabel's clothes off, Richard?" Miriam spoke loudly and firmly.

Lester glowered at Miriam as if she were a particularly stupid student. "I left her the way she had left me many times. Completely exposed. It wasn't easy. She was bleeding a lot." He gestured clumsily at his head. "Scalp wounds. Very messy. She hadn't come to yet. I wanted to wait 'til she did so she could see me. I wanted her to look at me and feel afraid. Know that she was in my hands." His lips lifted crookedly. "But I was afraid you would come back, Hannah. I'd watched you stumble from the room. I thought you'd gone to get help."

Hannah finally stirred from her stupor. "But you . . ." She peered at Lester as if she had never seen him before. "You were here," she whispered. "Yes, you were!" She pressed her petite and plump hands into her forehead. "I was standing by the door, holding on to the molding, my head . . . I thought I was going to faint. You said something to me." She looked up at Lester again, who inclined his body away from her as if her physical presence was distasteful to him. "Yes, yes, you did."

Excited now, Hannah turned to Miriam. "He told me he would call 911. He told me to go and take care of myself. He would take care of everything, he said."

Lester shook his head. He rolled his eyes at Miriam. "That's ridiculous. She's raving."

"So you took care of everything, just like you told her you would, Richard. Yes? After Hannah left, you smashed Isabel again with the bookend and then you removed her clothes and you ran?" Miriam braced herself on the edge of her seat.

Lester smiled at her. He raised the bookends. "Maybe I'll do that again. Just exactly the same way. A neck is a very vulnerable thing, I found out. And so is a skull. Easy to crack. Just one well-placed blow . . ." He gestured with his right hand and then appeared to pull himself together. He said succinctly: "Yes. And that will complete it. Ridding the world of a menace—a ménage à trois everyone will think, three pathetic lesbians who couldn't share, who . . ."

Miriam shot out of her seat and butted her head into Lester's stomach with all of her strength. He grunted in surprise and pain and doubled over, falling against Miriam and smashing both women down onto the floor in a tumble. Hannah screamed but grabbed one of his arms and twisted it. The bookend fell out of his hand and crashed into a table leg. Hannah hoisted it high in the air and was about to bring it down on his head when there was a sound of splitting wood and Susan Crane ran into the room holding a handgun. "It's all right, Hannah. You can put that down now."

Crane was drenched in sweat, breathing hard. "The cabinet . . .

the door was stuck," she panted. She gave Miriam a hand and hauled her to her feet. "Doctor Lester, stay where you are."

"Were you locked in?" Miriam asked her. Adrenaline coursed through her body; she felt wired and powerful.

"I'm not sure. There was resistance from the other side." Crane glanced at Lester.

"There's a latch on the outside of that cabinet. I imagine someone secured it to make it difficult for you." Miriam gestured at Lester and then placed one foot lightly on his wrist, the one that held the other bookend. "These aren't Isabel's," she told Crane.

"No," Susan said. "The other two are badly damaged. One is broken." She turned to Lester. "The one that you used to smash Isabel's cervical spine."

"Are you sure I killed Isabel?" Lester said, his face pale and lined. Against the floor he looked small and inconsequential. "She was in bad shape when I found her. Maybe Reggie came back after Hannah left and finished the job. Reggie Bradley's dead, so how will you ever know? I may have just torn the clothes off a dead woman. Is that a crime? And maybe I didn't even do that. Hannah and Isabel might have been in this room making love, nude, when Reggie came in." He shrugged, his lips tight. "Your guess is as good as mine."

*A*fter backup had arrived from Susan's precinct in the form of two young men who firmly herded Richard Lester into a squad car, Miriam drove Susan and Hannah back to Isabel's house. They installed Hannah on the sofa in Isabel's living room and removed her shoes. Miriam covered her with a yellow mohair throw. She offered to prepare tea or food, but Hannah accepted only water; she drank a few sips and lay flat, her head sinking into the pillow like a dead weight.

As Miriam turned to go, Hannah drowsily clutched at her friend. "Miriam, it wasn't my fault, after all, was it? I did tell someone to get help." Tears leaked out of her swollen eyes. "It didn't help Isabel. But I tried." Miriam took her hand for a moment, encouragingly, but

221

Hannah said nothing more. Soon her eyelids twitched, her breathing slowed and deepened, and Miriam hoped she was asleep.

The women withdrew to the dining room. Miriam, her limbs suddenly loose with fatigue, lowered herself into a chair at the table. Taking a seat across from her, Susan drew from her briefcase a copy of the transcript of the interview with Reggie Bradley and slid it across the table. Miriam studied it as she would a first edition of a rare manuscript, searching the margins and between the lines for a more definitive explanation of Isabel's death. In spite of her scrutiny, the words remained too few and too bald in their import. No tantalizing alternate version lurked beneath the surface; no matter how Miriam angled the page, no palimpsest emerged like a shadow under the script to reward her with precious new details or insights.

Finally, Miriam asked, "Can we be sure Reggie's blow didn't kill Isabel?"

"Not absolutely. The autopsy indicated two blows. And Lester's fingerprints were on one of the ivory bookends, along with Reggie's."

"But we all touched those bookends at one time or another. They were so smooth, and they sat right by the door. I know I put my hands on them many times," Miriam said.

"There were a lot of old smudges, yes," Crane said. "But Reggie and Lester clearly and recently had handled them. We found Lester's fingerprints on the diary as well."

"He hid it in my office?" Miriam asked. "I thought he had. He was so smug when I stepped down as chair. In the meeting where he orchestrated his coup, he played so much the paterfamilias. Nodding his head at the faculty like a pleased conductor in front of an orchestra."

When Crane nodded, Miriam asked: "What about the narcotic Hannah mentioned? Had Isabel taken anything?"

"There was a quantity of Percodan in her system," Crane revealed. "A smaller amount than Reggie had taken. The medical examiner said not enough to kill her." Crane thoughtfully stroked the side of her neck. "But a strong sedative that induced unconsciousness after a severe concussion could have been the final blow."

"So we don't really know what happened?" Miriam said, feeling a rising frustration.

"We know that Reggie threw the bookends, we know that Hannah left the scene and did not visit a hospital—nor did she place a call for an ambulance for Isabel. We know that Isabel took Percodan in the last six hours of her life, we know that Richard Lester didn't go for help—as he promised Hannah he would—and we know that he handled one of the horses' heads. It also appears he removed Isabel's clothing. From what Hannah told us on the way here, Isabel's blouse gaped open when Reggie interrupted them. But, otherwise, she was clothed." Crane ticked each of these items off on the fingers of one hand.

She leaned back in her chair and raised the other hand: "Here's what we don't know: One: whether Isabel took those pills or someone jammed them down her throat. Two: whether Reggie alone killed Isabel or if the effects of her blow were compounded by Lester striking her again. And three, how much effect the drugs in Isabel's system had in the end. Reggie may have returned and thrown the bookend again. I sincerely doubt it, but we don't know absolutely."

"So at least two people killed Isabel, either directly or through negligence. Three, if we count the indirect role of Hannah—perhaps if she hadn't left, Isabel would still be alive."

"Four, if Isabel took the pills herself and they proved to be one too many assaults on her compromised system."

"But Isabel and Hannah don't really count," Miriam objected. "They were victims. Perhaps they chose a poor place to be sexual, but they did not choose to be attacked. When Reggie threw the bookends, she set all the rest in motion. Without that act, Isabel would most likely be here today."

"I agree, initial responsibility lies with Reggie. I don't believe Richard Lester would have had the courage to confront Isabel unless she was weakened. His contribution to the crime was an opportunistic one. Yet that excuses nothing. He made no efforts to summon the help that might have saved her life." Susan struck the tabletop with one fist. "One thing is certain: Richard Lester wanted Isabel dead.

Reggie had no such motive. She reacted—spontaneously, I believe— out of shock and jealousy. Lester, on the other hand, made a conscious decision to do nothing."

"Yet both of them acted from jealousy and rage, and a certain covetousness about Isabel." Miriam's eyes met Susan's hesitantly. To her surprise—her own memories of Isabel?—she felt embarrassed discussing the sexual aspects of the crime. "Two completely different people, both motivated by the same things. Isn't that strange?"

Susan Crane merely shook her head. "Don't forget love. It was there, too. Even though, in the case of Lester, perhaps perversely. Those things motivate all of us. There aren't really that many distinct human emotions, are there?" Her face was pensive but then she ducked her head as she removed her glasses and polished them. In a moment, she rose to check on Hannah, asleep in the next room. "Sawing logs," Crane said as she made her way to the bathroom off the kitchen.

Miriam's tired brain sifted through all of this information. Finally, when Crane reentered the room, Miriam sought to put into words something that had been nagging at her for some time. "But why did you want me to ask Hannah about the diary? She didn't seem to know anything about it—in fact, I don't think she even noticed it was on Isabel's desk that day."

"We know that now," Susan said. "I needed to know how she would react. If she had read it. And taken it. A final test to see if she was implicated in Isabel's murder." She paused and thought a moment. "I needed to know if she had any links to Richard Lester at all. I didn't think so, but . . ."

"But you removed that last entry?" Miriam asked.

"I did."

Miriam felt like a slow student during an exam review. "So if she had reacted to the missing last entry—I remember her name was the last thing Isabel recorded—it would have meant she had killed Isabel?"

"The entry established that Hannah arrived after you did." Crane's face suddenly showed signs of fatigue. "But I was fishing for bigger bait."

"You couldn't have known Lester would come in." Miriam still struggled to keep the detective's methods in focus.

"I knew the person I sought wouldn't be able to stay away from that office. For one thing, the horses' heads—he or she would want to know if they were still there. I had my eye on Richard Lester for a very long time. The chair's office was a magnet for him, for many reasons. During our examination of the room, for days, he kept turning up. He'd walk by Isabel's office—questions for Anna, mostly bogus, I imagine—and then duck into the mailroom. He must have checked his mail ten times a day." The detective paused, and licked her lips. "He envied everything about Isabel, not the least that she had occupied the position he most wanted. He lusted after it. It was an obsession."

"And that's why he put the diary in my office. I was the current chair. And, in his eyes, the latest usurper of what was rightfully his."

"And an easy target—he thought." A smile slowly ignited Crane's whole face. "He was very wrong about that. Underestimating you proved to be his biggest oversight. That and not realizing his precarious position as a suspect. He had motive. And opportunity."

"I want to say, 'poor Richard,' for some reason," Miriam said slowly. "Even though I deplore so much about him. Yet he has so many gifts. And he has squandered them. It's almost tragic."

Crane's voice sharpened. "I seem to remember that tragedy requires an heroic dimension. I see nothing heroic in Professor Lester. Maybe there was when he was younger."

Miriam chewed on her bottom lip. "Only his desires seem to have been outsized," was all she said. Miriam's eyes blearily regarded the prone form of Hannah, who was muttering softly in her sleep. "I knew it couldn't be Hannah."

"No, she loved Isabel. She wanted only to protect her." Susan Crane's lips turned down sadly. "You know, the only person who seemed genuinely moved by Isabel's death, outside of Hannah, was Sigmund Froelich. They were apparently great friends."

"Sigmund. A hard man."

"Perhaps a hard man to like, but very soft on Isabel," Crane said.

Miriam stirred, realizing she had been breathing shallowly and bracing her body in her chair for what seemed like hours. Like a mannequin frozen in a window, she thought, caught in an expression of perpetual surprise. She rose, joints protesting, crossed the room to the window, and stared out into Isabel's side yard. Hannah's accusation earlier stuck in her mind—what had she done to help Isabel? She watched a hummingbird's long beak grace the tightly furled red buds in a mass of Turk's cap and then dart away. The hummingbird needed the flower for food; the flower reproduced by means of the bird's attention. Miriam wished the give-and-take between people might always be so mutually satisfying and beneficial. She turned around and faced Sergeant Crane. "If only I had known how very precarious Isabel's position was becoming before it was too late."

"And what would you have done? What *could* you have done?" Crane asked, her pupils dark in her pale blue eyes.

Miriam was silent. There was no satisfactory answer. There was only speculation; she imagined she would torture herself with that for a very long time.

𝓂iriam arrived home at five in the afternoon. The November days were shortening, and the diminished light only added to her feeling that it was very late in the day.

"Vivi!" she called from the hallway, almost tripping over Poirot, whose short legs scrabbled across the floor in welcome as she entered.

Vivian's face and body were a study in relief as she hugged Miriam. "Is it over?" she asked breathlessly.

Miriam nodded, sinking into her lover's shoulder.

"I'm so glad," Vivian said.

"Me too." Miriam felt strangely numb, her nerves crackling with a kind of white noise. She felt insulated from sight, sound, and touch, until she looked up and saw Vivian regarding her as if she were a rare and infinitely precious being. Then, tears welled in her eyes as relief and delayed shock flooded her system. Protective dullness gave way as she finally felt the raw danger of two hours earlier. She held Vivian tightly and said in a hoarse voice: "I'm so glad to be home."

Vivian nodded and touched Miriam's hair. After some time, Vivian prodded, gently: "And Hannah? Is she safe?"

"Physically, yes. But I'm afraid she's in pretty bad shape," Miriam said, her voice muffled. "I'm not sure how she's going to come back from all of this."

"But she knows now that she's innocent?"

"Oh, yes. There's nothing she could have done. But she feels she should've saved Isabel. She's in hell."

"Darling, I know you're exhausted," Vivian said tentatively. "But do you think we could take Hannah something to eat in a couple of hours? I hate to think of her all alone after what the two of you have been through."

Miriam smiled. Among Vivian's many talents was being a warm and generous friend. "Yes, I think I can do that."

Vivian grabbed her hand and led her down the hallway. "Good. That gives us some time. I want to hear everything that happened, and you absolutely need to rest for a while."

Miriam allowed herself to be maneuvered into the bedroom, where Vivian insisted on removing Miriam's clothes, helping her into a robe, and situating her on the sofa with several pillows behind her head. For good measure, she placed an ice pack on Miriam's head and a single malt in her hand.

As Miriam closed her eyes, splintered images played across her eyelids: Hannah's and Isabel's bodies rigidly twisted together, blood seeping around the creases of skin, a broken slab of marble, its ivory edges jagged and stained. And the fractured faces of Reggie Bradley and Richard Lester merging—distorted mirror images—into one another, her bleached cropped hair giving way to his gray brush-cut, their mouths leaking fury.

She clamped the ice pack firmly to her neck. Opening her eyes, the hallucinatory fragments melted away to Vivian, sitting on the edge of the sofa with watchful eyes. "Miriam? Are you all right?"

"I will be, after a while."

Vivian reached out and stroked stray hairs away from Miriam's forehead. "I've been worried about you."

"I know."

Vivian caught her lower lip between her teeth. "I've watched you get so involved in what happened to Isabel. At times, I've been afraid . . ."

"What?" Miriam said, alarmed.

"Well, that you felt some old . . . *pull* toward Isabel. As you grew to know her more fully. Saw her vulnerability. And thought about her with Hannah. I remember the day at Daphne's when we read the diary. You seemed so wistful, so sad."

"Oh, no—"

But Vivian hadn't finished. "The dead have incredible power. Their actual lives fade to us as time passes and our minds fill in what we wish they had been. I've seen it so many times. I've felt it myself. The yearning to remake the past. Isabel . . . well, I can see how she would grow larger, and more compelling, in memory."

"No. Not for me." Miriam barely trusted her own voice, so intensely did she want to make herself understood. She couldn't bear for Vivian to be hurt by misperceptions about her feelings for Isabel. "It wasn't that I regretted anything. Or wished for anything that we didn't have together. It was . . . how can I explain? It was the incredible waste of it. The feeling that Isabel had somehow misplaced so much of her passion. She was such a magnificent spirit in so many ways."

"Ah," Vivian said with a sigh. "That was true, wasn't it? So much intensity given away. But not into her own life or happiness."

"Yes, that's it. She didn't know how to be happy." Miriam smiled up at Vivian. "I love that about you. Your joy. Your pleasure in what you have."

"I have so much," Vivian said, her fingers gracing Miriam's cheek. She leaned over and kissed Miriam on the lips. "I'll turn on some music."

"Yes," Miriam said. She stretched her legs, which ached, flexed her back, and settled her body more deeply into the sofa.

Vivian rose to turn on the CD player, but Miriam clasped her wrist and stopped her. "Is any woman more fortunate than I?" Miriam said, looking at her intensely. "You are the most perfect combination I can imagine: sweet, practical, and gorgeous. Have I forgotten anything?"

Vivian looked down at her with a frown. "You didn't say anything about being desirable, I don't think."

Miriam grabbed Vivian's hand and pulled her down on top of her on the couch. "Some things are better left unsaid once in a while," she said, kissing her, amazed to find a small reservoir of vitality left inside her body for just this moment.

15

When F. Scott Fitzgerald said that there were no second acts in American life, he would have been astonished by the obsession of a twenty-first-century America with dysfunction. Failure has become almost a qualification of contemporary success—the entrée to talk shows, book tours, and media celebrity.

Darryl Hansen, excerpt from a luncheon speech delivered
at the annual convocation of deans of liberal arts

On Saturday, Miriam helped Graciela Brown, Isabel's sister, box up the remainder of Isabel's effects from her old office. Miriam, on the faculty's insistence, planned to execute her occupation of the chair's suite the following day.

At the elevator, Graciela enfolded Miriam's hand in both of hers. "I want to thank you for your efforts in finding out what happened to Isabel."

"You're very welcome. I only wish things had turned out differently."

Graciela turned slowly to take in the spartan corridor, the gun-metal sheen of the elevator, the porous and streaked gray walls which seemed to absorb rather than reflect light. "It's hard for me to imagine that this building is where my sister died. She was so colorful, so dramatic."

"I'm afraid our building is very drab and utilitarian," Miriam said apologetically.

"It's not just that. It feels devoid of life," Graciela said simply. Her thin face crinkled in a sad smile. "In that sense I guess it is appropriate. Now. It's hard for me to accept that she is gone."

"Of course. Were you very close?"

Graciela's hazel eyes, with their gold flecks, so similar to Isabel's, searched Miriam's face. "Not really. I was six years older. I was already away at school when our mother died."

Miriam hesitated. "You know, Isabel never discussed your mother with me in all the years we knew one another. I hope you won't take this as prying . . . but I understand her death was the pivotal event of Isabel's young life."

"She was my mother's favorite," Graciela said, a tone of wonder underlying her words more than any indication of bitterness. "They were very attached to one another, perhaps overly so." She bowed her head, her midlength, fine silver hair partially obscuring her face. "I don't mean to suggest anything abnormal, but it's not good to love a living thing the way Isabel did our mother: so fiercely, so possessively. No one else ever really mattered to her in our family."

"Not your father?"

"They were very different."

Miriam noticed she winced as she said this, but then she laughed and added: "He loved to argue, and he and Isabel did that often. It's how she learned to be such a very good advocate for whatever she believed in." As she lifted her eyes to track the flashing light on the wall indicating the slow ascent of the elevator, she murmured: "I don't need to ask you if Isabel had changed in that regard."

The elevator finally arrived, and the two rode together down to the street level. Heavy clouds muted the November light, and a brisk wind signaled the arrival of a blue norther. Miriam placed the box she was holding into the backseat of Graciela's vintage Volvo.

"You drove here, from—?"

"From Fort Worth. This is a friend's car—I flew in from Atlanta."

Miriam had an urge to detain Graciela, the last vestige of Isabel. "May I ask you something about your family?"

Graciela nodded, but a subtle tightening of her posture telegraphed caution. She appeared skittish, and Miriam feared the smallest pressure—or one clumsy question—would cause her to bolt. If only she could blurt: *Who was Isabel? Please, tell me.*

"You'll think this odd, I suppose," Miriam trod carefully. "But your father, did he practice the Catholic faith?"

Graciela's handsome face looked amused. "Fanatically. He was a good Italian boy. Why?"

Miriam shook her head. She wasn't sure how to articulate what she wanted to know. "Just wondering. Isabel seemed to be . . . ah, critical, or, shall I say, not very interested in certain religions."

Graciela adjusted the collar of her ivory blouse. "It was a contentious subject in our family. My parents fought about it frequently."

Miriam said thoughtfully. "Perhaps that explains it. My family did too. My parents were both Jewish, but only my mother attended synagogue. My father was too interested in philosophy—of all religions—to focus exclusively on just one."

"We were evenly split. My mother and I were Jewish; Isabel and my father Catholic."

"What?" Miriam felt her conception of Isabel, in the past so firm, shape-shift once again. "Your mother was Jewish?"

"Oh, yes. Seriously committed to the faith."

"But if Isabel felt so close to her why would she make such a change . . ."

"I don't know. But after Mother died, Isabel converted. I'm not a psychologist," Graciela said, a faint flush in her pale cheeks. "I don't know what it was about, really. She refused to discuss it."

Miriam put a hand on Graciela's arm. "This is, well, extraordinary . . . Do you have time for a cup of coffee or tea?"

"I'm sorry." Graciela looked longingly at her car as if willing it to start on its own and take her away. "But I must go." Hastily, she said, "Perhaps our paths will cross again."

With a stirring of regret, Miriam watched her enfold her stately frame behind the wheel. Graciela exuded mystery, a certain untouchable quality. She represented to Miriam the essential unknowability of Isabel's life.

Graciela reached into a small box in the passenger seat. "I'd like you to have this," she said, passing a framed photograph to Miriam through the still-open door.

The picture was of a young Isabel, perhaps fifteen, seated on a thoroughbred. Dressed in a black coat, with gray gloves and a pearl pin set in gold at her collar, and wearing a helmet, she looked very grown-up, yet her broad smile proclaimed a childlike delight.

"She loved that bay," Graciela said with a wistful smile. "He was big, over fifteen hands. 'Horatio.'" She tilted her head upward and, for a moment, in the aggressive set of her chin, Miriam detected a strong likeness to her younger sister. "A big name for an even bigger spirit."

As Graciela closed her car door, Miriam felt a powerful longing to see Isabel and Horatio, those twin proud beings, bounding together in nature as they once had. But they had disappeared behind time's opaque window and could not be recalled. Graciela was now the only voice that could bring them back and, most likely, Miriam would not meet her again. Standing dumbly by the side of the car, Miriam struggled with the pain of her sudden nostalgia. She tucked the photo carefully under one arm. "This is lovely. Thank you very much. Someday, I hope I'll understand more about your sister," Miriam said shyly. "Such a complicated woman."

Unexpectedly, through the open window of the car, Graciela reached out a hand and gently touched the side of Miriam's face. "And difficult, yes? I've always thought if a woman isn't difficult, she really isn't worth knowing."

Exhibit D: Letter to the faculty from Richard Lester, November 7, 2002

Dear Colleagues,

As some of you know, I am stepping down as interim Chair of the Department of Literature and Rhetoric. I am also taking a leave from the University for an undetermined period of time. I will need all of my energies to combat a series of fraudulent charges leveled against me and to restore my reputation. I wish to take this opportunity to assert that I am innocent of any criminal involvement in the death of our colleague, Isabel Vittorio, a conclusion that anyone who knows me well no doubt has already reached.

However, I do feel that I owe the Department an apology. I allowed myself to become personally involved in the outcome of the recent search for a position jointly held in our department and the Department of Drama. Given my past association with the candidate, Paula Fabian, I should have recused myself as a member of the Executive Committee when her candidacy came under discussion. Instead, I used poor judgment and actively campaigned against Dr. Fabian. I'm afraid the allegation that I wrote a letter falsely accusing her is true. I did circulate a memo questioning Paula Fabian's qualifications, claiming that Dr. Fabian—aided by her ally, Professor Held—trumpeted her race rather than her expertise to advance her candidacy. Dr. Fabian, as most of you know, has never positioned herself as a token of race or gender. By making these false allegations, I tarnished the good names of both Dr. Held and Dr. Fabian.

I'm not sure I can forgive myself for such a self-serving act, but I beg the rest of you to find it in your hearts to excuse me. For years Paula Fabian and I have had in common particular research interests. Whenever two scholars mine the same patch, so to speak, rivalries can become troublesome. Indeed, it is possible for two researchers to arrive at similar conclusions. This is what happened in this case. Naturally, some people who had looked into the matter only superficially might think that one of us had relied overly on the other's work. I, for one, freely offer anything I have uncovered to Dr. Fabian; she may use my work whenever it serves her purposes. I can only hope she would afford me the same courtesy. You all remember the sentiment of the great T. S. Eliot that lesser writers are influenced by others, but that great writers steal boldly and openly. I would consider any use of my work by Dr. Fabian to be the greatest flattery I could receive.

I wish all of you well in the coming months. I want you to know that I regard my tenure in the Department of Literature and Rhetoric, and my association with you, its faculty, as the pride of my life. The last thing I would ever do would be to act in such a way as to taint the reputation of this great department. I can assure you that I will be cleared of all charges relating to the tragic death of Dr. Isabel Vittorio, one of my dearest friends, and a colleague, I think I can say, who was without peer. I hope to be back in your ranks very soon.

With humility and gratitude,
Richard Lester
Holder, The Shirley Divine
Endowed Professorship
in American Literature

A week later, on Monday, Bettina and Fiona met Miriam for breakfast in their usual coffee shop. Miriam showed her companions a headline on the front page of the *Austin Journal Observer* which trumpeted the hiring of Paula Fabian: "Ebony Power Assails (Ivory) Tower." A photo of the campus's most notorious building accompanied the story. "So, for now, Paula Fabian and the diversity initiative are being celebrated. As the wave of the future. And we are all heroes. Until the next time."

"Success breeds success," Bettina said, licking cruller crumbs from her fingers. "Nothing new there. Let them have their witticism du jour and make fun of the university. Who cares? We get Paula. Fiona, the expression 'ebony power' is a play on your expression, 'ivory power,' that you coined last year. Your term has legs—it's entered the lexicon! You should be flattered."

"Hardly. I doubt that anyone's memory is that long around here." Fiona shrugged off the reference to her moment of notoriety and instead turned to Miriam, who stared glumly at the newspaper. "You don't look happy, Miriam."

Miriam's face creased into a tired smile. "I couldn't be more pleased about Paula, my dear. I just can't stop thinking of Isabel. And the unfortunate Reggie Bradley. Really, the last three weeks . . . I have no words to describe them."

"You must be exhausted," Fiona said, pouring more green tea into her cup. "I know we've been over this before, but is there no way to tell whether Reggie Bradley or Richard Lester administered the fatal blow on that Saturday?"

"Richard has changed his story several times, I understand," Miriam said. "He's now claiming that he was under the influence of a prescription drug last Friday and that what he told me and Hannah was only fantasy and hallucination."

"Incredible," Bettina said. "I suppose he planted the diary in your office in his hallucinatory state, too. How nice for him."

Miriam continued: "Of the other three witnesses, only Hannah is still alive, and she cannot remember what happened. The grand jury will decide, but I would think that Richard will face charges of manslaughter, at least. He admits to being on the scene. And Hannah recalls him promising her that he would go for help. Yet he didn't try to resuscitate Isabel or call an ambulance. He wanted Isabel to die."

"I wonder what Sigmund thinks of his old friend Lester now," Bettina remarked. "Not only has Lester been exposed as a coward and a fraud. And as an absolute brute. But his actions toward Isabel . . . Sig loved her, I think. This will drive a wedge between them if anything could."

"Oh, that reminds me, I almost forgot to tell both of you the most extraordinary thing," Miriam began, fairly vibrating with energy. "Isabel's sister told me that their mother was Jewish."

"Holy cow!" Bettina blurted, sounding like the teenager she must have been in the late sixties.

"Why is that so important?" Fiona asked.

"We always thought she was so racist and anti-Semitic," Miriam said. "And yet she got involved with me and, more deeply, with Hannah. It seemed so contradictory. Until now, knowing of her mother's early death and Isabel's devastation at losing her . . ."

"She was abandoned by her mother, so she abandoned what her mother stood for? Maybe she exercised the only power available to her. A kind of psychic rejection?" Bettina asked.

"Possibly," Miriam said. "All this time, I thought she hated Jews. Yet, Hannah . . ."

"Looks so utterly Jewish?" Bettina countered.

"What do you mean?" Miriam felt a stab of annoyance. What was Bettina up to? "You know, you are the only person I would allow to talk like this. If I didn't know that you are not the bigot you sometimes pretend to be just to be contrary . . ."

"Oh, come," Bettina smiled. "Can't you just see the young Jewish-American Princess lurking in Hannah? You must admit she has a sense of entitlement." Bettina's green eyes took on a familiar wicked cast.

"You're a difficult woman, Bettina Graf," Miriam said. Remembering Graciela's comment about Isabel, she laughed in spite of herself. "And, for some reason, spoiling for an argument. I can see that. What happened—Marvin wouldn't play this morning?"

Bettina ignored this remark. "Just checking on your sense of humor. You've had to take yourself too seriously lately. It's not good for you."

"Bettina, I certainly wouldn't have chosen the last few weeks," Miriam began, looking slightly hurt.

"Oh, honey, I know." Bettina squeezed Miriam's fingers, abruptly contrite.

"Back to Hannah," Fiona said, wishing to move the conversation back to firmer ground. "I wonder if she'll ever recover her memory of the event."

"It might be a blessing for her if she never does," Bettina replied.

Fiona turned to Miriam. "Do you know what she plans to do?"

"She will keep her position at Maryland for now. But, she told me she is thinking of taking early retirement. She is feeling, she says, disillusioned about higher education."

Bettina and Fiona exchanged a sober look after this comment, but neither spoke.

After a pause, Miriam's face brightened. "She fell in love with Santa Fe when she was there with Isabel this fall, and she's thinking of moving there to open a gallery. Isabel left her some money, you know."

"Such strange turns life takes," Bettina murmured. "To think that out of Isabel's death some art might result." She shook her head. "I hardly know what to think of that."

"Oh, I think Isabel would approve," Miriam said stoutly. "She would want her money used for something beautiful."

Fiona looked pensive. "Isabel was beautiful in some ways. And brilliant. And terrible. I can't help but think of a nickname Henry James had for Edith Wharton: 'The Angel of Devastation.' In Wharton's case it was a joke, but for Isabel . . . well, she really was a fatal attractor."

"She inspired lust and envy," Miriam said. "And those two things are at the root of her death. No wonder they are called 'deadly sins.'" She poured more hot water into her teacup with a slightly unsteady hand.

"And what sense are we to make of Richard Lester?" Fiona asked. "It's hard to understand how such a successful man could have been so angry and envious of Isabel. Or Paula for that matter."

"But in his mind he wasn't successful," Bettina pointed out. "He fancied himself A Great Man, but people like Paula and Isabel punctured that fantasy: he plagiarized from one and coveted the power of the other. Think about it. None of his books was ever widely reviewed. The boys' club he was a member of wasn't *the* Boy's Club at this university: he didn't have the ear of the president, the provost, or even his own dean." She switched gears to ask Fiona: "And how is Darryl? I've heard he was injured."

"Just a minor tear. Calf muscle. He'll be fine." Fiona said.

"Good." Bettina returned smoothly to her prior subject. "Lester saw himself as a victim. The strides made by women and minorities, the student interest in multiculturalism, all left him, in his view, with less. In the end, he felt deserted by the tide."

"Of progress?" Miriam said, shifting her weight in her chair. "But the Richard Lesters of the world don't want progress. They look to the past for their days of glory. The days when they were the Young Turks, the wave of the future. Richard saw opportunity only by hoarding his share of the pie. Which, in his eyes, only grew smaller. He didn't see the opportunities in new ideas, new people."

Fiona folded the newspaper neatly and laid it to one side. "He's like the child who wants all the love of his parents. He thinks if he shares it with a sister or a brother, he won't get enough for himself."

"So he ended up entirely unloved." Miriam frowned. "How depressing." She thought, fleetingly, of Isabel; had she regarded Graciela merely as competition for her parents' love?

Bettina laughed. "Did you see that ridiculous letter he circulated? Painting himself as misunderstood and maligned. And to top it off, as the generous scholar—Paula is welcome to his work, indeed! As if she'd be caught dead with twenty-year-old material, which is probably the last time he did any research. What would Gertrude Stein say? 'There is no there there.'"

"Or we could paraphrase what she said of Ezra Pound," Miriam said with a smile: "Richard Lester is a village explainer. Amusing if you are a village. If not, not."

Bettina's face opened with pure pleasure as she lifted her coffee mug toward her friend in salute.

Fiona shook her head. "You two are tough. Poor Lester doesn't have a prayer."

"'Poor' Lester?" Miriam objected. "You weren't in the room with him when he went berserk." She sighed, her hands fluttering to the tabletop. She fingered her cup, the creamer, and sugar bowl, moving them into new positions like chess pieces. "As to feeling left on the shore when the tide has swept away, that happens to anyone who lives long enough. I'm beginning to feel like a barnacle myself."

"Nonsense," Bettina said. "You are reinstated as chair and the qualifier, 'acting,' has been removed. You are vital to the future of the department and the university. This is no time for pessimism or self-pity. We need you."

Miriam peered over her reading glasses to give Bettina a sour look. "I'm not sure that being named chair of this department is desirable. Look what has happened to two of the past three, Isabel and Richard."

Bettina arched her eyebrows. "That comment is, as they used to say, *infra dig.*"

"What does that mean?" Fiona asked.

Miriam patted Fiona's hand, "An expression in use before your time, my dear." She turned to answer Bettina: "Beneath my dignity? Not on your life. Or mine either."

Editor's Afterword

God! How I loathe haste and violence and all that ghastly, slippery cleverness. Unsound, unscholarly, insincere—nothing but propaganda and special pleading and 'what do we get out of this?' No time, no peace, no silence . . .

Lord Peter Wimsey, *Gaudy Night,* by Dorothy L. Sayers

And so, life goes on, but things do not stay the same. Now, from my desk in the chair's office, I cannot help but look over my shoulder often and anxiously. I have rearranged the office and replaced the furniture, but the ghost of Isabel stays with me. Sometimes I see her, the slim torso seated at a table, poring over a reference with that intense focus she was capable of, or touching one of her equestrian bookends with a long finger as if gently reminding herself of her own past and prowess.

Discussions of my personal life have died down, but skirmishes about sexuality and race continue in the corridors of Helmsley Hall. A new order and a new generation, led by Paula Fabian, Carlos Lambros, and Fiona Hardison, will hopefully carry the day. But the powers of reaction lurk beneath the surface, populating the waters of discourse in the manner of predators layering the ocean depths, prowling for someone smaller and weaker to devour.

Do I sound too dire? Too cynical? Remember that anything I could imagine pales in comparison to what has happened in real life.

I cannot begin to prepare you for the possibilities. The great Sherlock Holmes said it best, at the beginning of "A Case of Identity:"

> "My dear fellow, life is infinitely stranger than anything which the mind of man could invent. We would not dare to conceive the things which are really mere commonplaces of existence. If we could fly out of that window hand in hand, hover over this great city, gently remove the roofs, and peep in at the queer things which are going on, the strange coincidences, the plannings, the cross-purposes, the wonderful chains of events, working through generations, and leading to the most *outré* results, it would make all fiction with its conventionalities and foreseen conclusions most stale and unprofitable."

How astonishing! Holmes had never set foot on the grounds of Austin University, and yet, just the same, he knew the place well. He understood its peculiar witches' brew of ordinary outlandishness, bizarre correspondences, and happenstance. The banal moments of ordinary life set the stage for its dazzling bursts of unpredictability. No wonder we ricochet from boredom to terror and cower in between.

But Holmes is no longer here to explain life to those of us who soldier on in his wake, nor is Watson, nor my beloved duo of Peter Wimsey and Harriet Vane. And so, in consolation, I think I will retire to my armchair with a book until I am compelled to rouse myself once again in the service of . . . well, let's just be old-fashioned and call it truth.

RESPECTFULLY SUBMITTED,
MIRIAM HELD